Calling
the
Moon

Calling the Moon

16 PERIOD STORIES
FROM BIPOC AUTHORS

EDITED BY

Aida Salazar *and*
Yamile Saied Méndez

CANDLEWICK PRESS

Compilation copyright © 2023 by Aida Salazar and Yamile Saied Méndez
"The Rules of the Lake" copyright © 2023 by Christina Soontornvat
"Muñeca" copyright © 2023 by Aida Salazar
"Turning Point" copyright © 2023 by Leah Henderson
"Shiloh: The Gender Creamsicle" copyright © 2023 by Mason J.
"Holiday" copyright © 2023 by Saadia Faruqi
"Ofrendas" copyright © 2023 by Guadalupe Garcia McCall
"Mother Mary, Do You Bleed?" copyright © 2023 by Erin Entrada Kelly
"The Arrival" copyright © 2023 by Nikki Grimes
"Heavenly Water" copyright © 2023 by Veeda Bybee
"Sometimes You Just Need Your Prima" copyright © 2023 by Emma Otheguy
"Cannibal at the Door" copyright © 2023 by Elise McMullen-Ciotti
"Thicker than Water" copyright © 2023 by Hilda Eunice Burgos
"Shakthi Means Strength" copyright © 2023 by Padma Venkatraman
"Part of the Team" copyright © 2023 by Yamile Saied Méndez
"Bloodline" copyright © 2023 by Ibi Zoboi
"The Hadiyyeh" copyright © 2023 by Susan Muaddi Darraj
"From the Editors" copyright © 2023
by Aida Salazar and Yamile Saied Méndez

First edition 2023

Library of Congress Catalog Card Number 2022936744
ISBN 978-1-5362-1634-9

22 23 24 25 26 27 LBM 10 9 8 7 6 5 4 3 2 1

Printed in Melrose Park, IL, USA

This book was typeset in Minion Pro, Silver Script, and Prachar.

Candlewick Press
99 Dover Street
Somerville, Massachusetts 02144

www.candlewick.com

To my hijita hermosa, Avelina Claridad,
for allowing me to bloom alongside you.
To those who bleed and have yet
to bleed: your blood is beautiful.

AS

Para Magalí y Areli
And for every child, even that inside
the heart of every grown-up.

YSM

CONTENTS

The Rules of the Lake

CHRISTINA SOONTORNVAT

"This isn't a Burger King!" shouted Ms. McKinney over the rumble of the school bus. "You can't always get things your way."

This was Ms. McKinney's favorite saying, and she must have been shouting it at sixth graders since the '70s to shut down their complaining. Well, who wouldn't complain if they had to deal with the disappointment facing us out the window?

We were on our end-of-the-year class trip to Possum Hollow Lake. For a month, we'd stared at the promotional posters taped in the hallways that showed a glittering blue lake rimmed with waterslides, a tower crowned with super-soaking water guns, and the best part—the trapeze. For weeks, I'd daydreamed about gripping on to that metal bar, swinging out as far as I could go, doing the perfect backflip, and dropping into the cool, crystal paradise below.

But as our bus pulled into the gravel drive circling the property, all those dreams vanished. Possum Hollow Lake looked like—

"—where possums go to die!" shouted Eric Gunner. The kids around him burst into laughter.

Eleanor and Julie pressed up against me, and we stared out at the chalky brown water. "He's not wrong." Eleanor sighed, wrinkling her freckled nose.

"It's not so bad . . . It's natural," said Julie. "This will be like getting back to nature."

Sometimes I wondered if Julie's retinas ever got burned from looking on the bright side so much.

"Well, brown water or not, I'm going off that trapeze at least fifty times before we leave this place," I said.

"That's the spirit, Penny!" said Julie. "We're going to have fun no matter what."

The bus pulled up into a parking spot, and an older man with a shiny tanned face and a polo shirt embroidered with the logo of a swimming possum boarded with a clipboard in hand.

"Welcome to the lake, boys and girls!" he said in a Texas accent that put even Ms. McKinney's thick drawl to shame. "Let me assure you that despite the color you see out your window, the pH levels at PH Lake are just fine."

The joke fell flat, but he soldiered on. "We've had a lotta rain lately, which has stirred up the silt, but I promise that our lake water is continually refreshed from a spring-fed creek, and it's perfectly fine to swim in. Couple of rules here at the lake. Number one: Respect each other. No roughhousing, fighting, or chicken fighting. Number two: Respect our plumbing. We got two trailer facilities on the property, and that's it. You clog 'em up, you're gonna be doing your business in the woods."

Eleanor leaned over and whispered, "Do you think he planned his number-two rule to be about number two?"

Julie and I both snickered.

Our teacher's assistant, Ms. Gallegos, checked our names off her list as we filed off the bus. It was only ten in the morning, but already sticky and hot. I didn't care if the water was purple—I couldn't wait to swing off that trapeze and dive in.

And then, just as we were spreading our towels in the grass near the lake's edge, I felt it.

In books, they often describe dread as a sinking feeling "in the pit of your stomach." Totally wrong. Dread is a warm gushing feeling between your legs. It's the feeling of knowing you started your first period fifty-four miles away from your house.

I pulled Julie and Eleanor close and whispered to them what just happened.

Julie's mouth fell open. "Are you sure?"

I tugged down my jean shorts, trying to figure out if they were wet without making a scene. "I don't know . . . but I'm pretty sure."

"Okay, it's fine. Don't panic," said Eleanor. "Penny, you and Julie go to the bathroom, and I'll go ask Ms. McKinney where to get . . . you know. Products."

I grimaced at the thought of hard-hearted Ms. McKinney knowing I had started my period, but at least I wouldn't have to be the one to ask her. This was what made Eleanor a champion best friend.

Julie and I headed for the girls' toilet trailer. It was an air-conditioned version of a Porta Potty with beige plastic wallpaper, two stalls, and a tiny sink. I went into the smaller stall, pulled down my shorts and swimsuit, and assessed the damage. I pressed toilet paper into the bottom of my suit, and it came away dark red.

I could see the top of Julie's blond head over the stall door. "So did you really start? Is it bad?" she asked.

"Yeah, I did. And it's not too bad, but not great." I was grateful that I had worn the one-piece with a purple-and-black tie-dye pattern. The blood hadn't soaked through to my shorts yet, either.

"Does it hurt?" Julie whispered. She was taller than Eleanor and me by a foot, but her voice still sounded like it did in elementary school.

"I . . . don't really feel anything. My stomach kind of hurts a little—like crampy, but that's it."

The trailer door swung open, and I heard Eleanor call out, "Got it! Ms. McKinney had a pack of pads in her first-aid kit. Here, Penny. Sorry—it's kind of . . . on the big side."

She handed the blue plastic packet under the door. I unwrapped the pad, peeled off the plastic strip, and stuck it into the bottom of my suit. I flushed the toilet and stared at the stall door for a long time before opening it. Of all the days this could happen, did it really have to be today?

When I finally came out, Eleanor and Julie both gave me worried half smiles. "Are you okay?" asked Eleanor.

"Yeah, I'm okay." I walked to the sink—or should I say, I *waddled* to the sink. "But this pad is the size of a hot dog bun."

"Could you call your mom?" asked Julie. "Maybe she could bring you a smaller one."

I imagined Mom pulling up to the lake and getting out of the car to hug me tight, then handing me a pad that wasn't big enough to see from outer space and maybe a tub of coconut ice cream. But it was already ten thirty. Mom was the cashier at Sawasdee, our Thai restaurant on the square, and she wouldn't have time to get all the way out here and back before the Friday lunch rush. My dad couldn't do kitchen duty and work the counter at the same time, so he might have to turn customers away. There's no way I'd ask them to lose out on our best sales day of the week just to bring me a smaller pad.

"It's fine," I said as I washed my hands. "I'll just tell her after school."

As uncomfortable as the pad was, I was relieved to know I wouldn't leak through my swimsuit. But as soon as we swung open the bathroom door, and I saw all my classmates yelling and splashing and swinging out into the water, my relief turned to heartbreak.

"Looks like no PH Lake for me," I grumbled.

"What if you kept your shorts on?" offered Julie. "Maybe no one would notice."

"I just want to sit down for a minute if that's okay."

We went back to our towels, and I lay down on my side. I felt weird and my stomach gurgled and cramped.

A few yards away, Amber Daley and her friends lay sprawled in their bikinis on giant towels as thick as plush bathrobes. Right then I made a solemn vow that when I got older and became a millionaire, the first thing I'd buy would be a towel the size of a picnic blanket.

I looked up and saw Julie leaning toward me with a smile that I'm sure she meant to be sweet but was actually a little creepy. "What?" I said.

"You started your period!" she whispered. "The first one of us to do it—can you believe it?"

No, actually I was still in shock about the whole thing. I didn't think I'd have to worry about carrying pads with me until next year at least. I watched as Amber and her friends stood up and ran giggling toward the water's edge. Eleanor scowled at them with her death stare. I knew exactly what she was thinking.

It was Amber who had put the thought into my head that I wouldn't start my period so soon. She'd been one of the first girls in our grade who got hers. We went to the same gymnastics gym, and once when we were waiting for class to start, she'd said to me, "You're so lucky you're Asian, Penny."

She was always saying things like this. "Nice" things about me being Thai American that always made me feel weird, like "Boys like Asian girls because they're so exotic," or "Your mom's accent is *so* adorable." Was I really supposed to think those comments were complimentary?

That day at gymnastics, she'd said, "Asian girls don't get

their periods until they're way older. That's why they're so flat." She nodded to her own curvy chest and then to my barely- there breast buds, and quickly added, "That's totally a good thing in gymnastics, you know? They won't get in your way."

I knew immediately that it was pretty messed up and racist to say that to me. But as I watched Amber line up for the trapeze, I couldn't help being mad at myself. I had believed her. And when I told Julie and Eleanor what she said, they believed her, too. As much as I loved my best friends, sometimes I wished there were other Asian American girls in my grade to talk about this stuff with. Mom was always so busy working, and I never wanted to bother her. So I had just gone with it and let Amber fool me into getting caught off guard.

"Don't you want to get in?" Eleanor asked me.

Yes, more than anything. But I shook my head. "This pad is so huge that I'll probably bob on top of the water like a life preserver." I pulled my knees up to my (still-pretty-much-flat) chest. "But you two should go in. You don't have to sit here with me."

"No way," said Julie. "You've been waiting for this for weeks! We are not getting into that water without you."

Eleanor sat up with a determined look on her face.

"Julie's right. We're graduating sixth grade, and you are going off that trapeze. There's only one thing to do." She turned to look straight at me. "We're finding you a tampon."

Julie put her hand over her mouth and gasped.

"A tampon?" I said. "I just started my period and you want me to level up already?" I only had the vaguest notion of what a tampon even looked like. My mom didn't use them, and even though we had talked about periods, she only ever mentioned pads. It was sort of an unspoken understanding between us that tampons weren't something I needed to worry about.

From listening to the older girls at gymnastics, I had figured out that you wore a tampon inside your vagina, and that it was almost like magic. You could do nearly anything you normally did without worrying about bleeding on your clothes.

Eleanor stood up and held out her hand to me. "Come on. Before this day is over, we are getting in that disturbingly brown lake. *All* of us."

My eyes tracked Amber as she swung out on the trapeze and did a backflip—*my* backflip—over the chocolate milk water.

"All right," I said. "Let's do it."

★

Eleanor assured me that there had to be at least one other girl on the field trip who used tampons and had brought one with her. At first we tried to be discreet and just approached girls we thought might have started their periods already. But then I realized that was no better than what Amber had done, and we were stereotyping girls based on what they looked like. Now I understood first-hand that you couldn't tell just by looking at someone, and actually it was kind of rude to make that assumption.

So we straight-up asked around. Of course, we knew Amber had started, but there was no way I was going to ask her. Then Eleanor learned from one of her soccer friends that we should ask Margo Rainey.

"Oh, Margo is *so* super nice," said Julie. That was high praise coming from my nice bestie.

And it was true. In second grade, Margo had shared her glitter markers with me. If I could ask anyone for a tampon, it was her.

By then about half the kids had come out of the lake for lunch, and we found Margo sitting with her friends at one of the picnic tables.

"Oh, hi, Penny!" she said when I walked up. "How come you aren't swimming?" So nice, so concerned about my well-being.

"Well, actually . . ." I leaned closer and whispered my question to her.

She blushed a little and pointed to her backpack. "I do use tampons. But I'm sorry—I can't give you one because I only have one left."

Selfish, selfish Margo! Who only brings one tampon to a field trip?

"That's okay, no problem," I said, turning to walk away.

"Oh, but you should ask Alicia," Margo called out. "She usually has them with her."

Generous, sweet, giving Margo.

"Thank you!" I called back as I jogged away, the space-ship pad chafing my thighs.

The three of us found Alicia Flores waiting in line to fill up her water bottle. She carried a backpack covered with embroidered patches, and I said a silent prayer for it to be stuffed to the brim with tampons.

When we explained the situation, Alicia nodded knowingly as she reached into her backpack. "I got you covered, Penny." I expected her to pull out a discreet zipper pouch. Instead, she held out a Chapstick-sized paper packet and handed it to me as casually as if it were an actual Chapstick.

I took it from her and tucked it under my towel, then untucked it again. I wanted to be cool and unembarrassed, too. Then I tucked it back under my towel. Not quite there yet.

Alicia nodded down at the tampon. "I don't use the kind with an applicator because they end up in landfills. The wrapper on that one is biodegradable. You can flush it, no problem."

"Perfect, Alicia, thanks," I said, not having one clue about what she was talking about.

I ran for the bathroom trailer, Julie and Eleanor at my side. The three of us went into the big accessible stall on the end and latched the door behind us. I unwrapped the tampon and held it out. It was a tightly packed cotton nub about the size of my pinkie finger with a white string coming off the end of it.

"It's so small," said Julie.

"I think it expands as it absorbs . . . you know, the fluids," said Eleanor. "It looks pretty simple, right?"

"Well." I gulped. "Guess I'll find out."

Julie and Eleanor turned their backs, and I got down to business. Suddenly the simple cotton nub didn't seem so simple at all. How was this supposed to work? Should I tackle this from the front or reach around the back? What should my angle of attack be? How far up was it supposed to go?

We heard the bathroom door swing open, and light flooded the trailer. I froze.

Then Amber's voice: "Did you see Eric go off the trapeze? He's such a show-off!"

Eleanor and Julie had also frozen, and Julie clutched Eleanor's arm. Amber's friend giggled and chattered away as she went into the stall next to mine. I could hear Amber tapping her flip-flopped foot.

"Is anyone in there?" Amber called impatiently. "I have to go. Penny, is that you?"

I startled at my name. And then I dropped the tampon into the toilet.

"Shoot!" I hissed. I stood and yanked up my swimsuit and shorts.

Julie turned, saw my horrified face, and gasped.

"What are y'all *doing* in there?" said Amber.

I panicked. Julie panicked. Eleanor, who never panics, must have panicked, because she flushed the toilet. And then we all looked at each other and remembered the number-two rule of Possum Hollow Lake too late: Respect the plumbing.

"Come *on*, already!" said Amber. "I have to go and you're hogging the stall."

The toilet gurgled, made a loud *sluck!* sound, and then stopped filling up with water. We bolted out of the stall and nearly bowled Amber over.

"Finally," she said, going into the stall and latching the door.

We ran outside into the blazing heat and turned to watch the bathroom trailer.

"Oh gosh, oh gosh, oh gosh," said Julie. "Do you think we clogged the toilet?"

"Alicia told me the wrapper was biodegradable," I said. "Maybe the whole tampon will dissolve and it'll be okay?"

Eleanor stared at the trailer. "I think we're about to find out."

Five seconds later, we heard a scream. A flood of water gooshed out the door as Amber bolted out, shrieking, "MS. MCKINNEY!"

For the next hour, we lay in the grass, listening warily as the news spread.

"Did you hear?" called Eric. "Amber backed up the plumbing with her gigantic turd!"

"Shut *up*, Eric," shouted Amber. "I did not!"

Miraculously, Amber hadn't put it together that *I* had actually clogged up the toilet before she got in there. Poor Amber was a victim of circumstance, and I felt kind of bad about it.

Eleanor did not. "Serves her right," she said with a sly smile. "She shouldn't be such a jerk the next time."

I smiled back, but then frowned again when I looked out at the lake. The trapeze swung empty. No line. Everyone had gone off it so many times that they were sick of it already. Everyone but us. We probably only had an hour, maybe two, left before we'd have to get back on the bus.

Suddenly I felt Julie tug on my arm. "It's Ms. Gallegos," she whispered, pointing to our teacher's assistant, who was walking straight toward us.

"Hi, girls," Ms. Gallegos called out. "Can I talk to y'all in private for a minute?"

We looked at one another. Ms. Gallegos always picked up on things Ms. McKinney missed, and from the look on her face, she'd figured out what no one else had. I gulped and hoped they weren't going to call our parents—or worse, make them pay for the damages.

Ms. Gallegos tilted her head at me. "I noticed that you three haven't gotten in the water all day. I know you were so excited to come on this trip, so it made me think something was up."

"Well, we . . . um . . ."

"So I'm going to give you something," she said, reaching into her purse. "If you don't need it, that's okay."

She held out a zippered makeup bag. I took it from her and opened it. Inside was a variety of panty liners and pads that were a fraction of the size of the gigantic one I was currently wearing. And nestled in between: slim tampons of various sizes and brands.

I looked up at Ms. Gallegos. If there was only one pint of coconut ice cream left on the planet, I would have given it to this woman. "Thank you," I said.

She smiled. "You still have a little time before we have to get back on the bus. Not sure how many trapeze swings you'll get in, but it's worth a try." Before she walked away, she nodded at the line of boys and girls waiting for the remaining toilet trailer. "Oh, and now that this place is down to one bathroom, you might look for somewhere with a little more privacy." She pointed to the far side of the lake. "There's a hiking trail that winds along a little creek. I just walked the whole thing and no one's on it."

The three of us looked at one another. Then we gathered up our backpacks. It was time for a hike.

Ms. Gallegos was right. No one was on the trail. Still, we walked until the trees completely obscured our view of the lake. And just to be careful, Julie stood guard. "Nobody gets by me!" she said, holding up her palm and planting her long legs on either side of the path.

Eleanor and I walked a little farther into the trees. Inside Ms. Gallegos's zippered pouch there was a folded-up instruction sheet for how to use a tampon. Eleanor and I unfolded it and spread it out on the trail in front of us, like explorers reading a map.

Eleanor took one tampon out to use as a model. She muttered as she pointed to the diagrams. "Okay, this makes sense . . . This part's the applicator, and you just push this up here . . ."

After we'd studied everything in the pamphlet, I stood up. "Okay, well, here goes nothing." I took one of the smaller tampons with a plastic applicator, saying a silent apology to Alicia and the landfill.

I walked behind an enormous cypress tree near the creek's edge. I slipped off my shoes and made sure one more time that no one could see me. Then I pulled down my shorts and crouched down among the tree's knotted roots.

I didn't want to take my whole swimsuit off. Even though the tree trunk hid me from sight, it still felt weird to get naked out in the open. In fact, the whole thing felt weird. Was I really about to use a tampon for the first time? Here?

I looked behind me at the creek. The water was crystal clear—nothing like the muddy swill in the lake—and a cool breeze ruffled the leaves overhead. I inhaled, breathing in the scent of fresh moss and cypress needles. If I had to do something new and scary, at least it was in a place like this, with my friends close by.

"Just think of that backflip," I whispered to myself.

The whole thing was actually not nearly as complicated as I thought it would be. Instead of taking my swimsuit off, I pulled the bottom of it to the side. I peeled off the blood-soaked spaceship pad, rolled it up tightly, and wrapped it in a sheet of paper I had in my backpack. It was a little tricky to envision the tampon diagram upside down and backward. It took a couple of tries, but once I figured out the angle, everything slid into place. I tucked the applicator into the bottom of my backpack with the pad to throw away later. When I stood up, I could just barely feel something was different, but it wasn't uncomfortable.

"I'm done!" I shouted triumphantly. As I started back, I put my hand on the tree trunk and felt something. A rope.

My eyes followed the rope up and up to where it was tied to a thick branch overhead. A rope swing.

"Eleanor! Julie!" I called out. "Come here!"

They both ran up, wide-eyed.

"Well?" asked Eleanor.

"Are you traumatized?" asked Julie.

"What? No!" I laughed. "I did it, and it's in, and it's totally fine. *Look!*"

Their eyes followed mine up the rope swing and then back down into the cool, deep water below.

"Oh, you have got to be kidding!" said Julie.

"Like finding buried treasure," said Eleanor.

I held the rope out to her. "Should we do it?"

Eleanor nodded and grinned. "It's your day to go first."

Julie clapped her hands. "This is so awesome!"

Holding the rope in one hand, I climbed up the knobby tree trunk until I reached the lowest branch. I gripped the rope in both hands. It wasn't a trapeze—but, hey, life isn't a Burger King. You can't always get things your way.

I smiled as I swung out, out over the water and let go.

Muñeca

AIDA SALAZAR

I am not Amá's first-choice daughter, not even by a long shot. Yet I am the one who agreed to work in a factory with her for the summer. I am not the oldest, who *should* have the most duty but has to prepare "for college." I'm not one of the youngest, who are too busy playing outside. I'm not the two older boys, who don't do anything because they are basically macho royalty in our house for no good reason. And I'm for sure not the second oldest, who cleans the house like an abuela on steroids.

I'm the middle child of seven who happened to finish her last day of the year with no need for summer school, the one who technically qualifies for a work permit but who doesn't have a job, the one who doesn't care about cleaning the house until it sparkles. My entire thirteen-year-old life is filled with one obsession—to get my period before summer's over and I start eighth grade. Other than that, my life is pretty much nada. Zip. Zilch. Zero. I have no excuse to say no to go work with Amá.

The morning is just peeking through the horizon as I climb into our old orange-brown van with Amá at the wheel.

"¿Lista?" Amá says, and smiles.

"Ready." I answer, not entirely awake despite the machaca burrito I wolfed down with milk.

Suddenly I realize how strange it is to be alone with Amá this early in the morning, earlier than when I get up for school even. But more than anything, it's weird because I am *actually* alone with her! This never happens with seven kids swarming around her every day, fighting for her attention, but also because our house is always filled with people asking things of her, too. See, Amá is a sobadora, a bonesetter who was taught by my grandmother and her grandmother before her in the art of adjusting sprained joints, crooked backs, wobbly hips, stiff necks, and a whole bunch of things that I don't even know about. People in Maywood call her "the bone mechanic" in Spanish because she is so good at fixing achy bodies, though she doesn't charge folks like a real mechanic should. People pay her what they can, which isn't much and the real reason we've got to take these jobs at the factory. Anyway, my point is that there's always someone around, and Amá knows a whole bunch of stuff about how bodies work and *now*, we are alone.

So, I figure, here's my chance. I'm going to get her to tell me all the things she knows about periods. I want to hear everything she knows about blood, wombs, moods— without leaving out any of the gory details. I mean, everything that I haven't already learned by reading all of those "menstruation" books I checked out from the library or by spying on my two older sisters. What I really want, though, is for her to tell me when my period is coming because literally everyone else in seventh grade claims they've started. It feels like I'm the last one to be picked for kickball or something. It totally isn't fair.

Just as I begin to ask, "Amá, when do you think . . . ?" she revs up the engine, and the sound of the loud muffler plus the radio blaring ranchera music drown me out.

"Vamos, Lali," she says to the van.

Amá named the van Lali because after she'd had it for a gazillion years, it started to make a noise with its spinning tires that, to Amá, sounded like *lali, lali, lali*. She loves the old heap, even though it's painted in a glimmering orange brown and still has the wood platform that once held a waterbed but now holds a thin spring mattress with a mess of blankets. Lali is everything to her, even though to us kids, it is beyond embarrassing. We beg her to drop us off a block away from school so that other kids don't see us coming in the dingy orange-brown booger of a van. Once a year, she and Papi pile us into it and take us on an eighteen-hour drive to Mexico for las fiestas in our pueblo in December. Amá usually whistles or sings the whole way there. She packs all sorts of secondhand clothes, shoes, and personal supplies underneath the bed frame.

In Mexico, she is like Santa Claus because she makes sure she has a gift, pulled out from under Lali's bedframe, to give every single person in our family. Amá is all generous like that. Even with things she doesn't have. Maybe because she grew up poorer than we are now, sleeping on dirt floors and everything, and knows what it's like to go without. I don't know. But as long as Lali works, it is going to be in our family.

As the van whistles *lali, lali, lali* and bounces along the potholed streets over the Fourth Street bridge into downtown LA, I shout, "Amá!"

She turns down the music and says, "Tell me, muñeca."

It surprises me that she calls me a doll right then because she never—I mean never—calls anyone that. Well, maybe except when we are sick or when she wants to be extra sweet to someone else. Maybe she senses I am about to get super personal with her. Or maybe she is happy that

at least one of her kids came to work with her. Whatever
the reason, I'll take Amá's little bit of sugar because it
makes me feel . . . I don't know, special, I guess.

"When do you think I'm going to get my period?" I
accidentally continue to shout even though the radio has
gone quiet.

Amá's face looks surprised, but then relaxes when she
answers, "Your luna? Pues, I don't know, mi'ja. Everyone's
timing is different. Some get it early like your sister Nena,
who got hers at nine and a half. Otras get it later, like I did
when I was fifteen. It depends on your naturaleza. Just like
the moon's cycle, nobody can rush it."

"You mean I might have to wait until I'm fifteen?" My
heart races as if I've done a bunch of jumping jacks.

"Claro, everything will come in due time. But what's
the rush, eh?"

"Can't you do one of your sobadora moves on me so
that it comes faster?" I ask.

"Ay, mi'ja. I only fix what's hurt or broken, not what's
natural. Every body is unique. Todo a su tiempo. No need
to stress over it."

This is highly discouraging. I can't believe I might
actually have to show up to eighth grade with this same
no-period and, might I add, curveless body because "every
body is unique." Just my luck.

We pull up to a parking lot of a huge brick-and-cement building, where dozens of Lalis are parked—all different shapes and colors but beat-up and crotchety just like ours.

A woman keeps the door open for us as we walk in. "¿Son madre e hija?" she asks.

Well, duh, lady, I want to say. We *are* mother and daughter. I mean, it is *so* obvious. Same larger-than-life forehead. Same big brown eyes. Same moist sand color in our skin. Same big knobs for cheeks when we smile. I'm just a scrawnier and much flatter-chested version of her. And I have tons of zits sprawled across my forehead that literally appeared out of nowhere just a couple of weeks ago.

"The office is through there, amigas." The lady points, and we walk into a gathering of about ten people at what I can only guess is an orientation.

A balding rail of a man stands in front of us. His teeth are movie-star white except for a couple of missing molars I notice when he introduces himself as Mr. Chen. "After you fill out this paperwork, we will walk through the site and I will show you what you need to do."

I whisper my Spanish translation of what he says to Amá. She doesn't know a speck of English, though she's lived in the United States so long. How could she? Amá only went up to third grade in Mexico. She was never able to do much more here. We live in Southeast LA, and almost everything she needs can be found in Spanish because everyone speaks it here. Other things like school notes, DMV papers, and important stuff, Papi or one of us translates for her. Amá says she went to "la universidad de la vida." The university of life is how she has learned to survive el norte.

A couple of women lean in. They look at me with bug eyes as if to ask me to translate for them, too.

Amá nudges me and says, "Sí, mi'ja. Translate."

So not only am I supposed to spend my whole thirteenth summer quite possibly not getting my period and stuck inside this muggy building working on Lord knows what, *but* I am also going to have to translate for every Spanish speaker here. Great.

Mr. Chen walks us into a huge warehouse that's stacked to the rafters with cardboard boxes and reeks of overly perfumed hairspray. The Spanish-language radio is playing my mom's favorite station—KLUV—which makes Amá's grin real bright. In the center are four long lines of tables linked together. People stand side by side as they face the tables and work. Some are assembling thin hot-pink cardboard boxes with plastic windows. The people in the next row over are taking out blond-haired, pale-skinned plastic dolls, about the size of my torso, from sky-high stacks of big cardboard boxes. People working at the third table are dressing the dolls in little outfits, combing their hair, spraying them with that stinky hairspray. The fourth line of people is tying their arms and legs down with twist ties into hot-pink cardboard linings and loading the perfectly made-up packaged dolls back into big empty cardboard boxes.

Okay, so dolls. We are supposed to dress and box up dolls. I was so busy obsessing about when I'm getting my period that I didn't even bother to ask Amá on our ride over what the job was about. Just great. The truth is, it doesn't even matter because all I can think about is how I'm going to have to fake my period all through eighth grade and probably ninth grade, too. Fifteen is a ridiculously long time to wait. Like, really long.

"These are our assembly lines," Mr. Chen continues. "You will be working on one of these, but *I* will select which one." Mr. Chen notices me translating and pulls me by the arm to stand beside him as he continues to explain. My face feels so hot and red, I bet even my zits aren't noticeable. I feel a sharp tugging in my guts like maybe I need to poop. When I look at Amá, she gives me several quick little nods and shoots me some eyes that say, *That's right. That's why I send you to school in el norte, so you can help our gente when it is needed.* Ugh. Amá with her always-helping ways is so extra.

"Just look at what your neighbor is doing and follow along," he says, not to the group anymore but to me. I clear my throat and begin to translate, but then Mr. Chen scolds me: "Speak up. They need to hear you."

I nod and try again, fighting the urge to double over because my guts are starting to ripple with sharp pains. Uh-oh, maybe these torzones are because of the machaca burrito I had this morning. It feels like my guts are twisting and getting ready to push out a big poop.

When I look over at Amá, her head is completely turned and focused on the doll-dressing row. She is almost googly-eyed with adoration. It is the melty-faced look she only gets when she sees a baby.

"All right, let's begin." He counts the first three people on the left and sends them to the first row.

"These people will work on assembling the doll packages," I repeat in Spanish.

When Amá sees this, she slowly inches away from them. She can tell how this is going down, and I can see her trying to get in on the third row. Mr. Chen picks the second set of people, which doesn't include her. Then Amá quickly moves in front to make sure she is picked next. Mr. Chen doesn't even see Amá making moves, and so he picks her for what I know she wants—the doll-dressing row.

I get stuck with the last row, putting the finished

packages back into new cardboard boxes, which I guess I don't mind since I am so over playing with dolls anyway.

The place suddenly gets loud with Spanish as the workers on the line show us, step-by-step, how we are supposed to do things. I hope it means that I don't have to translate anymore.

A man next to me works lightning fast. "Watch closely, chaparrita. Ours is the easiest job." Chaparrita? Sure, I am shorter than everyone else because I am basically the only kid here, but who does he think he is, my tío or something? Anyway, he's right: our job is to tie down the dolls and slide them into the hot-pink boxes so their faces look out the plastic windows, then close the top lid, secure it with tape, and put it back in the bigger box. Super easy, right?

But then why do I feel queasy, like my guts are folding in on themselves? I take big gulping breaths and begin to work. I try not to think about how creepy these dolls look with their plastic white skin and plastic hair and mechanically blinking eyes that look dead when they open and close.

Though her back is to me, I hear Amá getting all excited about playing with the dolls.

"Ay, these muñecas are so precious. Look at their little outfits! They are so well made. And they fit! Mira, just look at their eyes, light blue like the sky. And their hair looks like it is made of gold." Amá turns to me, cradling a doll in her arms like a baby. She looks like she is about to fly away with happiness.

I suddenly remember that once Amá told me about how she and her sisters made dolls from scraps of old clothes and burlap sacks. She got married to Papi at nineteen and started having babies right away. She never got a lily-white girl doll like these, not of her own, at least. She got all of us brown babies, cuter than these dolls, I think. But honestly, we *did* get zits on our faces, and hopefully not for too long. It makes me happy for Amá to be able to play dolls, even though they are creepy and not brown, and even though she is all grown up and is really supposed to be working. She seems too in love to notice my face pruning up in pain. I wish she would at least come over to see if I'm okay.

My lower panza pain does leave once I start moving. I get to thinking about my never-coming period again and scan my mind to remember anything Amá told my sisters about their lunas. I remember when my oldest sister had just gotten some fancy "NoWet" underwear, which are basically like super-absorbent underwear you wash so you don't need a pad. They're kinda genius. Anyway, Amá was shocked at how well they worked. She said that in her rancho, women made pads using the same scraps of old clothes and burlap sacks they used for dolls, and sometimes they made them of soft leaves and grass. Then, once the homemade pads had soaked up their luna blood, the women would bury them in the ground and they would just turn into compost. She said everything was connected—us, our blood, the earth, and la luna. But of course, it's probably nothing I have to worry about now that I am basically going to be a child until I am fifteen.

After a few hours of hustling at the factory, the pain in my gut returns strong like a tug-of-war.

"Amá, my stomach hurts," I finally yell over the song blasting on KLUV. "I think I have torzones."

"¿Qué, mi'ja?" She turns to me. At least her mom sonar hasn't been affected by the dolls.

"I feel like throwing up," I say, feeling a warm dizziness buzzing in my head.

"Go get some water, mi'ja. Lunch is going to come soon," she says, first frowning at me like she doesn't believe me, then throwing her eyes over toward the water fountain near the office.

I walk slowly over to the fountain and drink about six small paper cups full of water. I figure this feeling is either from that darn machaca burrito this morning or the fact that Amá is showing more joy at being with dolls than she ever does with us.

I try to walk back to my station, but I can't take it anymore as barf inches its way up my throat. I'm not throwing up here! So I book it to the bathroom.

Mr. Chen shouts at me, "Hey, girl, where are you going?"

I ignore him and burst into the stall and bend over the toilet. Nothing comes but drool. I seriously don't know what is happening. So I sit down to see if something will squish out of me another way. When I look down at my panties, I notice there is a small, round, bright brownish-red dot right in the center of the crotch.

Could it be? Oh snap! It's here, it's here, my luna is finally here! Hey, Period! Where the heck have you been, anyway? Don't you know I am literally the last girl in seventh grade to get it?

I am sooo glad I don't have to show up to eighth grade a total fraud! Oh, wait, is *this* what it feels like to get your period? You get too many zits, knots in your panza, and want to throw up and poop or both? That's when I realize, *OMG, I'm in a doll factory bathroom getting my very first period! Where the heck is my mom?*

I start hacking a maxi pad by wrapping half the roll of toilet paper around my hand and trying to figure out how to put it on my panties so it stays when I hear someone come in.

"Mi'ja, are you okay?"

"Amá!" My avalanche of questions, my wooziness, my panza achiness, my relief that she's here—it all tumbles together into that one word. Amá. She never let a scrape go by without her saying, "Sana, sana, colita de rana." And we would use this baby rhyme on each other, too. But this isn't a scrape on the knee. I am thirteen and too old for a silly kiddie rhyming healing spell to work on me. The pain feels like it's deep inside. My unique body. I don't think Amá's bone-mechanic skills can help me with this.

"Do you think it was the machaca?"

"No, Amá. I started my luna. But it hurts my panza real bad."

"¡Válgame, María Purísima!" she prays. "Mira, just when you were asking, it comes. Let me see . . . No. There isn't a machine in here. Mi'ja, why don't you make a pad with toilet paper?"

"I already did."

"Good! That's the best part of having older sisters. You're probably more prepared than most."

"Pero, Amá, why does it hurt so much?" My whimper turns into a full-on cry.

"Now, that's not a good sign. That didn't happen to your sisters on their first time. Hmm? I know, let's go ask Mr. Chen if we can take an early lunch."

"No, no, no! I don't want to tell Mr. Chen!" I say. Just

thinking about it feels like an explosion of embarrassment detonating in my head.

"Well, *I* can't tell him. He doesn't understand me, mi'jita," she says. "It's just a half hour before noon, anyway."

"Can't I just sit here until lunch?" I let out some gas and feel a slight relief.

"What, and suffer unnecessarily? Mira, we only need to get you to Lali so I can lay you down."

"But do *I* really have to tell him?"

"No, no. Don't worry about it, mi'ja. I'll see if one of our new friends out there will help me explain to Mr. Chen."

"Please, Amá. Don't tell him!"

"No, amor. A little white lie is all I'll have to tell. God forgives those easily."

As I wait for Amá to come back, I break into a sweat, and the pain is like a growing orb in my lower body. I groan and hug myself. I feel nothing but anger at her, for not speaking English, for paying more attention to the dolls than me, for bringing me to work in this factory, for not knowing when my period was coming and saying stupid things like "all in due time." I feel a few drops of blood fall into the toilet, and when I look down, the bright-red liquid surprises me with the way it spreads in pretty ripples in the clear water. I am legit bleeding.

Just then, Amá walks in and says, "Lista. We got the okay."

I unlock the stall, and she comes in to help me up and checks to see if my hacked pad is in the right place. Luckily, we don't have to walk through the workspace to get back out to the parking lot.

When Amá opens up Lali, I feel happier than ever to climb into that beat-up old van and its flimsy old mattress to lie down. Amá revs her up to get the AC going because the LA heat makes it volcano-hot inside Lali. Now the pain comes in crashing waves. It grows strong and then relaxes, grows strong then relaxes. Back and forth. *Lali, lali, lali* and the whir of the AC are a soothing song in my mind, though I feel like a wounded animal.

"Come here, pobre muñequita," Amá says as she lays her hands on my lower belly, takes a deep breath, closes her eyes, and stays still. Amá's given me sobadas a bunch of times before, but somehow this massage feels so different. "What's happening is that your uterus is out of place."

"What? Why?" I begin to ask and then add, "None of the period books ever said anything about an out-of-place uterus." She sees my face loaded with confusion and responds, "Your grandmother and many sobadoras like me believe that sometimes, when we take a fall one too many times, our matriz will shift out of position. It causes us to cramp when our lunas come and needs to be realigned with your body. It's our way of healing. It's older than the stars. And probably not going to be in those gringo menstruation books of yours."

"Amá, it hurts," I almost growl.

"I'm going to give you a special sobada, a womb massage, to set it back into its place."

"Me duele." I can't take it and shake my head from side to side.

"Quieta." She hushes me and starts to bend me like a rag doll. She pulls and pushes at my skin, my joints, and my back. With every position she puts me in, I wince with pain but then feel the tiniest bit better as my body sounds off dull firecrackers under my skin. *Crackle, crackle, crackle.*

I hear her praying quietly. Then finally, she pulls some hand cream from Lali's glove compartment and rubs her hands briskly as if to get them hot. Amá moves her hands in big, smooth circles right where it hurts, which she ends with a quick move up to my belly button.

Amá looks down at me with the same sweetness she gave those dolls, and I feel guilty for having been mean to her in my mind. She grabs my hands then and moves them across my belly in the same big circles. My hands slide with the secrets and knowledge my mother, my grandmother, and her mother kept—our own kind of medicine. Together, we pull an imaginary string out of my belly button with our fingertips, and Amá blows it into the air. Maybe I am too distracted by what we are doing to notice, but suddenly the pain is almost gone.

"Do you feel any better, muñeca?" Amá's eyebrows lift with the question.

"Sí. I can hardly feel the pain anymore."

"Well, let's see if Lali can get us to a café to get you a manzanilla tea to finish the healing."

I close my eyes, not sure how to say it, but the words "Gracias, Amá," squeak out with tears of relief. But then a little sharp pain comes haunting back for a second. Amá places her hands over my panza again. They are warm with all that she knows beyond period books. She doesn't have to say, "Sana, sana, colita de rana," because her hands hold the magic of that childhood spell, and her touch, her mamá's muñeca touch, only for me, is more than enough to make it all the way better.

Turning Point

LEAH HENDERSON

Mica and Nica walk behind Mom in a perfect line, chins up, shoulders back. Hair in perfect topknots—her mirror. While here I am in the back. Hitting the pavement hard, leaving a trail of mud behind.

"Must you, Imari?" Mom asks as we make our way into the mudroom. But it really isn't a mudroom at all, except where I stand, with a muddy soccer ball under my arm. My sisters hang the ribbons of their pointe shoes on wooden pegs, and I knot the laces of my cleats and loop them around the last one. As the shoes smack together, dirt hits the floor. I go right for the closet and grab the miniature broom Mom bought just for me. "Come over here and let me do something with that hair. Does it have to stick out every which way? Why don't you let me make it into a smoothed-out bun?"

I dodge her hands the way I fake out players on the field. A perfect bun is not for me. I like my curls free. Besides, can I help it if after a header or two, a couple of them really want freedom from my ponytail elastic?

"Mom, it's fine," I say. "We're home. No one's going to see."

"I see." She looks at me like *How did I get this child?*

My heart burns a little, but I shake it away. It doesn't matter.

Nica runs her hand over her hair as if my popping curls might be contagious, and then she and Mica prance off. Yes, prance, like they're still on some stage.

"I like Mari's curls," Mica whispers, but zips her lips fast when Nica throws her a classic Mom stare—right eye narrowed, left brow reaching for the sky. They're three minutes and forty-eight seconds apart in age, and Nica will never let Mica forget it, and even though I have three years and nine months on both of them at twelve, sometimes Nica feels like my second mom, too.

I grab my soccer bag as the side door opens and Dad strolls in. My face splits into a smile. Then his briefcase and two shopping bags are down on the floor and he's loosening his tie, like he's ready for some freedom, too.

"Hey, how's my Rocket? How was your game?" he asks as he leans in and kisses Mom. "Hey, beautiful," he says to her. She's already trying to straighten his tie again.

"I scored two goals and had an assist," I say, cheesing wider than the distance between goalposts. We played the only team that has a better record than we do, so that's saying something.

"Ah, so you showed 'em a thing or two." He nods. "That's my girl."

"Your girl needs to bring that smelly bag to the laundry room and go take a shower. You'd think she likes walking around caked in dirt."

"She was working, Viv. That's what happens when you're doing your thing on the field. You get dirty sometimes. But go get cleaned up." He nods toward the stairs. "I need my sous-chef to help me throw down in the kitchen. We're making my world-class stuffed peppers tonight."

Mom is about to protest about the need to get "that dirty" like she does *every* time, but Dad kisses her again. He puts his suit jacket over his arm and grabs the groceries. "Get to it, Rocket. So we can make our masterpiece!"

"And get those shin pads out of that bag. They need air!" Mom says between kisses with Dad. "I don't want them stinking up the whole house. And spray that bag with disinfectant!"

"Yes, ma'am."

I rush to do everything Mom expects so I can be Dad's sous-chef.

Midnight black, Othello lays on the steps, wagging his tail as I greet him. "Hey, Thello. I scored two more today— that makes eleven for the season." He nudges me to pet him, and as soon as I do, he rolls on his back so I can get to the good spots.

"Shower. Now. Imari," Mom calls.

She can't even see me. But she knows everything happening in this house even when you think you're invisible.

"Sorry, little man, gotta go." I jump up and grab my bag.

Thello grumbles but rolls onto his stomach and hops up to follow me.

In the upstairs study nook by the wall of windows and bookshelves, Mica is standing on the couch. She leaps off, lands wobbly in fifth, and stumbles backward as Thello and I come up the stairs.

"Buuuusted," I sing as Nica eyes me, feet perched on the edge of the couch, ready to take flight.

"Get a run in those new tights, or let Mom see you standing on the couch, and I'm not saving you," I warn, coming closer.

I run my finger across my neck, and Mica's eyes go a little wide while Nica's narrow. Then Nica arches that one brow again. She's scared of nothing. I like that little bit of rebel in her.

"Your funeral," I say as I come to my door.

In my room, I kick my bag into the corner and race to get in the shower. I don't want Dad starting without me.

I finish showering and wipe off, dropping my towel over the side of the tub. As I'm reaching for my clothes, I feel more water running down my thigh. I guess I missed a spot. But, yikes, it looks like I missed . . . "What the heck?" I pull the towel away and freak. Blood! I grab at my leg, searching for a cut, before I realize how far up the blood's coming from. I race to the toilet and sit, grabbing wipes and cleaning myself off. Small droplets of red hit the toilet water and spread wide. This doesn't seem good. Did I get kicked somewhere I can't see? I wipe again and again. And realize exactly what's happening. Ms. Claiborne's mentioned it in class before. Not much, but she has. I need to relax. I'm not dying. Or at least, I hope not.

I think I just got my period.

Dad whistles in the hall as he knocks on my bedroom door.

"I'm coming," I shout from the bathroom and then quickly add, "Dad . . . um?"

"Yeah, baby girl?"

"Never mind."

"You sure?"

"Mm-hmm, I'm okay. I'll be down in a minute."

"All right, hurry so we can light things up."

I shake my head and roll my eyes. Dad can't help but be corny. I smile. Then it slips, because even though I need his help—and I know he would totally try—he's clueless when it comes to stuff like this. Though he'd read *everything* he could to figure it out. But instead of asking the person I know could help me, I stubbornly wad up a handful of toilet paper and push it into my underwear. That should work for now. I'll google what to do after dinner. And I'll probably need to figure out how to get to a store.

After flushing the toilet, I try to scrub the blood out of the towel with soapy water until the evidence fades into the yellow and white stripes. It's stubborn, though, not totally disappearing. So I bury it at the bottom of my hamper and add a couple clean towels, just in case. I know it sounds bizarre, but as I straighten, I feel my reflection staring back at me in the mirror over the sink. I mean like really staring.

Just talk to her, it says.

Nope. I pull on an old Juventus jersey and black shorts and switch off the bathroom light and my reflection. When I open the door, Thello is on the other side waiting for me on my bed, tail wagging.

"Come on, boy. Let's go help Dad."

He looks past me into the bathroom as if he knows something big just happened there, but he doesn't say a thing.

When I get to the kitchen, Dad has Donny Hathaway blasting from the speakers. I can already tell it's going to be a good cooking night. I grab the black apron he bought me last year that says BEAUTIFUL BLACK MAGIC IN THE KITCHEN, while his reads CULINARY WIZARD FROM THE MOTHERLAND.

Dad's put all the ingredients on the counter, and I know my first jobs—washing, cutting, and deseeding. As he dances around the kitchen singing, he leans a wooden spoon toward me. I'm backup vocals on this one and that's cool. When it's Chaka Khan or Beyoncé, it's all me.

But when Mom walks in the kitchen and turns off the music, everything stops, including the water for a second, like it's not sure it's safe to come out of the faucet anymore.

"Ba—" Dad starts, but Mom shakes her head, looking at me with a smile, as if I just did a pirouette.

"Mom?" I ask, the green pepper still in my hand.

"Imari, is there anything you want to tell me?" she asks.

I look between her and Dad. There is no way she could know. How could she know? My eyes zip down then back up.

Phew.

Nothing. Good thing I have on black, though.

"Um, no," I say. I want to turn back to the sink, but it's not wise to turn my back on Mom when she's speaking. So I just stare. Her eyes roam over my face. What's she looking for?

"You'd make the perfect Clara!" she says. Her face is shining, like *I need sunglasses* kind of shining.

"A perfect who?" I've absolutely no idea what she's talking about.

"I just got off the phone with Katlynn's mother. Katlynn told her . . ."

I try not to roll my eyes for the third time today. Mom hates when I roll my eyes, but whenever she mentions Katlynn—the last person you'd ever want to sit next to in class, because you might lose an eye with the way she waves her whole body when she raises her hand for *every* question—and her mother in the same sentence, things are never good.

"Clara from *The Nutcracker*. Marlene said they'd thought about doing *Coppélia*, but decided on *The Nutcracker* in the end."

They? Who?

"Why didn't you tell me?" she asks. "It's being cosponsored by your French Club and the theater department. Auditions are Friday."

That's what she's on about? I almost drop the pepper

in relief and shrug. Why would I have told her about that? No way I'm trying out for any part. Nope . . . uh-uh. There's nothing to tell. Katlynn and her mom can have all that. And as my sisters burst into the kitchen, I'm just glad I don't have to blast my business to the whole family that, yes, I just got my period.

"That's why you're turning off Donny Hathaway? Come on, beautiful," Dad says, wrapping his arms around Mom, dancing and humming in her ear.

That's it, Dad. Keep her busy so I can get back to cooking.

Mica and Nica twirl around them, hopping up and down as Dad sneakily pushes the play button on the music.

All through dinner, Mom talks about how wonderful it will be for me to play Clara. But somehow she's forgotten: *I don't do ballet.* Besides, I need to figure out what to do about my situation and how I'm going to get to the store. I could call Nasha—she's my best friend, after all. Her mom is always sending her to the store around their way. So maybe she can grab me something, but I know she'll squeal to her mom without thinking, and Nasha comes by her squealing honestly. Mom would definitely find out.

I'll think of something. I know I can. That's what the internet's for.

When I get to my room, I race to the bathroom and

wad up another roll of toilet paper. Then I flop on my bed and slide my finger across my iPad screen. Toilet paper isn't a long-term solution. But what do I type? I try: *my first period.*

Yikes!

A ton of stuff comes up—tampons, pads, period underwear, discs, cups. Cups? What am I going to do with a cup? There are videos about period horror stories. Most embarrassing period moments. And videos about what moms said, or didn't say. I pick a link for *first period.*

"What to expect and how to get prepared."

Too late. I'm already past the *preparing phase.* The next site is all about talking to a mom, a big sister, a dad, or the school nurse. But none of those options are going to work right now, either. Mom and I never get on the same roadway, as Dad says. So, I don't even want to think what talking to her about this would be like.

I skip to another video that is a *huge* mistake. It's all about what happens after this girl wads up a bunch of toilet paper like I did, but at school. Why didn't they label this most embarrassing period story? I'd die if someone thought I sat in chocolate sauce, like the girl in the video, and then, to make it worse, her teacher and school nurse didn't help her. Clearly, TP is not the safest bet.

There is a light knock on my door. "Come in, Mom," I

say, knowing it's her before she even has a chance to speak. I clear my screen and turn toward the opening door.

"Listen, I know you don't think of yourself as a ballerina. But you used to go to every class I taught before you started soccer, remember?" She comes in and sits next to me on the edge of my bed. "You liked it."

No, *you* liked it. I had no choice. "Not really," I say instead.

"Well, I don't remember it that way." Mom reaches out and tries to smooth back my curls again. She can't help it. But they can't help springing out of place, either. "I think the role of Clara would be a fabulous opportunity for you to get back into it."

It's like she doesn't even hear me. Or see who I am— a soccer player, not a ballerina.

"It's a small production, Imari. You could come back and take classes with me to prepare. I know your grandmother would love to help. It'd be wonderful."

I push my hands deep into my lap, trying not to ball them into fists.

She squeezes my knee, looking around my room. Soccer posters of Pelé, Kylian Mbappé, Paulo Dybala, Crystal Dunn, and Maria Alves are spread across my walls; trophies, certificates, and medals sit on my shelves, along with pics Dad took at some of my games and tournaments. I have a few jerseys that never made it to the hamper hanging over the back of my chair, and I know what Mom is about to do before she does it. I spring off the bed, knocking over my iPad, and rush to grab them up to drop them in my hamper. The hamper with the telltale evidence.

"Imari Camille, what on earth has gotten into you? Slow down." Mom stands with her hand on her chest. "We might as well pull everything out of there." My collapsible laundry basket is out before I know it. "I don't understand how one little girl can fill a hamper so quickly."

Pushing out the basket, she starts toward the hamper.

"I'll do it," I shout. "I mean, I'll bring it to the laundry room and, um, load the wash . . ."

"Okay?" Mom's face scrunches up. "You sure you're all right?"

"Yes, ma'am." I shove the jerseys in the hamper and close my bathroom door. Then I take the basket and my iPad, which Mom picked up off my floor. "Just been thinking about the tournament this Friday—that's all."

"It's just a game. You'll be fine."

I want to explain that it's not *just a game*. The way a dance recital for her isn't *just a recital*. But what's the point? I know she wishes I was anybody but me sometimes.

"Well, if that's all, I'll leave you to it." She steps toward me again, running her hand over my curls. "But think about Clara. It would be wonderful."

"Yes, ma'am." There's no point arguing. But there's also no point in thinking about an audition that's the same day as the first tournament game, not that she's even noticed.

When Mom reaches my door, I can feel the toilet paper bunching up, and I panic a little, thinking of chocolate sauce. I open my mouth, then snap it closed. Then blurt out, "Can we go to the store real quick?"

"What store? Why? What do you need? Poster board? A notebook? I can send your father out now. That'd be easier."

Of course, this isn't going to be easy. "Um, never mind. Don't worry about it."

"No, really. Imari, what do you need?" The question just hangs there. Then I think about all the embarrassing stories on the internet and don't want them to be me. "I . . . um . . . just need some cups. Or maybe pads—I'm not really sure."

At first she looks a little confused. "Cups?" Then her face lights up, and she steps back into my room. "Aww, Imari. Precious." Suddenly my face is smashed against her dress, and she is rocking me back and forth. "You got your period. Why didn't you tell me? We have so much to do!"

So much? Like what? "I just need some cups or pads. Honestly, that's it."

"Nonsense." She cradles my face in her hands. "This calls for more than that."

"That's not what the websites said. They said it's no big deal."

"Of course it's a big deal!" She holds me at arm's length for a moment, smiling. "It is the biggest deal. It is for all young ladies. I'll be right back." She bounces up and rushes toward my door, then looks back again. "Oh, Imari, I've waited for this day."

Then she's gone, and I drop onto my bed and bury my head under my pillow just as Thello comes into my room.

"I told you she was going to make a big deal out of this." Thello ignores me and walks in a circle in his favorite spot while I yank the pillow back, dreading whatever Mom's doing.

She comes back with a box almost bigger than her. It's wrapped in cream-colored paper with thin dotted black lines. And of course, it's tied with a pink bow. "Here," she says, laying it on the bed like it's a trophy. But it isn't one I've earned.

"What is it?"

"Open it and see."

I just stare.

"Go on."

I scooch forward and pull at the ribbon. The bow unravels. I carefully peel back the taped edges because Mom hates ripped-open gifts she's carefully wrapped.

There's a hot-pink box inside. Hot pink! In my experience, nothing good for me ever started with hot pink.

Inside isn't what I expect. I don't know what I expected, but it wasn't this. I look up at Mom and then back down again. That site that said *what you need to prepare* has nothing on her. I don't know if every girl-stuff brand is in this box, but it looks like it.

"We can still go to the store to pick out what you want. These are just a few things I thought you might need," she says quickly as if I'm disappointed by the selection. She reaches into the box and pulls out three containers of tampons, but there are more. "They're all different, sweetheart. Some with applicators. Some without. Some for a heavy flow. Some for a light. Here's a scented box." When she hands it to me, I sniff. Nothing. "But I also got you two that aren't." She looks back into the box that now seems never-ending. "There are also pads with wings and pads without."

"Wings?" What in the world?

"Don't make that face, Imari. This is just a box of options. Once you know what you like, you can ignore the rest," Mom says. Then she claps her hands. "Tonight is a celebration of you. Your Turning Point Celebration."

"My *what*?"

"Your Turning Point Celebration. The day that begins your journey into womanhood."

I didn't see anything anywhere on the internet about any "turning point," which sounds like a made-up ballet term. I think she still has Clara on the brain. And "journey into womanhood"? I'd never call Mom a liar, but she's definitely making this up. Isn't she? I eye her suspiciously as she continues to pull stuff out of the box. When did she do all this?

She hands me a flappy purple thing. "It's a hot-water bottle. You may thank me for it down the line, but I hope you won't need it, or these. She takes out a bottle of Advil. Then one of Aleve, and then a box of something called Pamprin.

"Oh, wait." She takes the box back. "What's the expiration on these?" she says more to herself than me. "We can get you some more tomorrow. I've had this box ready and waiting for you for a while."

What's a while? Don't pills last years? Has Mom really been thinking about me? About this? Of course, she has.

It's not about me slide-tackling in the mud; it's about me being "a girl."

"For tonight, why don't you try the overnight pads." She nearly sticks her whole head in the box. "They're somewhere at the bottom of all this."

"There's a bottom?" I say peeking back inside.

"I heard that," she says, eyeing me from inside the box. Then she sits back, a dark-blue package in her hands. "It's okay if you prefer trying tampons and a panty liner in the morning. I can talk you through that, too. I know as a dancer, I prefer that over a pad, so maybe you would, too. But you can try what you like. Okay?"

"Okay," I say, ready for her to go. Why can't she just be normal and hand me one box? Not fifty with wings and scents and things!

Mom holds out the dark-blue package with stars and gets off the bed when I take it. "I need to call your school."

My head pops up in horror. "Wait! Why?" Oh. My. Goodness. She can't tell my school about this. And she definitely can't leave it on a voice mail in the middle of the night. Who knows who'll hear that message!

"I told you, it's your Turning Point Celebration, and it needs to be celebrated. No school for you tomorrow. We have to acknowledge this new part of your journey."

I stare. Mouth open.

A huge sigh that starts in my belly escapes when Mom finally leaves. Oh my goodness, how ridiculous can she be?

"I know there's no such thing as a Turning Point Celebration, Thello." He gives a wide yawn, teeth showing, not caring a bit about my situation.

I drag the box off my bed and barely make it to my desk without stumbling. Standing on my chair, I take everything else out of it. Pads, tampons, wipes. Then I stop.

At the very bottom is an envelope with my name in Mom's perfect penmanship.

I pull it out and sit on my desk, my feet in the chair (even though Mom would have a fit).

Dear Imari,

I have created step-by-step instructions for all you will find in this box. Sometimes package instructions just don't do.

Love, Mom

Is she serious?

I open the piece of folded paper and nearly drop it. Mom has drawn girl parts and underwear all over it! I'm used to her diagrams for beginners' ballet class, but this is something else. However, the longer I stare, stuff starts making sense. I grab the overnight pads, her directions, and head to the bathroom. At least this one part might be easy.

In the morning, a bunch of pink, red, and white balloons walk into my room with Mom's and Dad's legs attached. Whose idea was this? Mica and Nica poke their heads in, too.

"Stop pushing." Nica nudges Mica's shoulder.

Mom strolls to the bed, holding a tray till I sit up.

"Breakfast in bed," she says. "Your favorite. Strawberry and Nutella crepes with lots and lots of whipped cream."

And she didn't even forget the rainbow sprinkles. She can't stand those sprinkles. There's also orange juice and a champagne glass. I look at it, then over at Mom, as Dad ties the balloons to my bedpost.

"Don't get too excited," he says. "It's sparkling cider. But don't drink it yet." He hurries back out the doorway.

"She doesn't look any different to me," Mica whispers. "Why is she getting a turnover celebration?"

"It's not a *turnover* celebration," Nica huffs. "It's a turn-it-up celebration. You know, a *real* party."

Mom and Dad look at each other when Dad comes back, not bothering to correct them. Then Dad stares at me for a long time.

"My baby girl isn't a baby anymore. You're becoming a beautiful Black young woman." He shakes his head and pulls a bouquet of flowers from behind his back. He usually sends flowers to me at school for my birthday— been doing it since kindergarten—but this is different. He's giving them to me the way he gives them to Mom, and he says, "For the beautiful Black Queen that you are." I take them and smell them, just like she does, hiding the bigness of my smile. Maybe this whole period thing isn't so bad after all—no school, breakfast in bed, special flowers. But it still feels a little off, being celebrated for something I didn't actually have control over. I wish Mom would be this excited when I score a hat trick.

"Go get the other glasses, hon." She squeezes Dad's shoulder. And if I didn't know any better, I'd think Dad just wiped his eyes.

In two seconds, he's back with two more champagne glasses and two plastic pink ones for Mica and Nica. Everyone has an equal amount of sparkling cider. But actually, I have a little more. We clink glasses and drink. The bubbles tickle and our fake champagne is the perfect kind of sweet.

"Okay, everyone out." Mom claps, taking Mica's and Nica's glasses before they find their way to my floor. "Let her enjoy her celebration in peace."

Dad gives me one more forehead kiss, and they all turn for the door. Mom slows.

"Be ready at nine thirty, all right? Our first appointment is at ten."

"Appointment?" I ask, a mash-up of crepe and strawberries puffing out my cheek.

"Yes. And you have a day full of them. So be ready. And, Imari, just for today can you wear something . . ." She looks up at the ceiling as if the right words might be up there. But I already know what she wants to say, but won't.

"Pretty?" I add for her.

She smiles. "Let's just say something nice. Whatever that might be."

Her hand rests on my door. "You all set with everything for now?" She nods toward the "Period Survival" box on my desk. Half the stuff from inside is now spilling over in piles I don't think I could get through in a lifetime. Or I hope not. I don't think I have that much blood in my body. "Need me to explain anything?"

"No, I think I got it." I don't know why, but I don't admit to her that her diagrams really helped this morning.

Othello pushes past her leg into the room and plops on his bed as she closes the door.

"Where've you been?" I say to him. "A lot's been happening around here."

His tongue hangs as he pants, and I know just where he's been. Soaking up rays in the sunroom after having his breakfast.

"Well, don't think you're getting any of this." I shovel up another mouthful of crepe, whipped cream, and sprinkles.

"Ready?" Mom asks as my seat belt clicks into place.

"I guess."

"Come on." She nudges my knee and pulls out of the garage. "This'll be fun."

Cucumbers on her eyes and polish on her toes is fun to her. I'd rather eat the cucumbers and skip the polish.

A sportscaster's voice blasts through the speakers.

"Oh, my word, turn that down for me, will you?" Mom always gets flustered in Dad's car, as though every button is in the wrong place. But since it's her day for carpool, she didn't have much choice since Dad's doing it instead. No way five eight-year-old ballerinas are fitting in here safely. She takes a breath, then speaks like she was never ruffled. "Turn it to whatever you like. This is your celebration."

"It's fine." Kind of like everything else has to be fine.

"What's the matter, Imari?" She glances at me while turning out of our neighborhood.

"Nothing."

"Well, show a little excitement. This is a big day. You're a young woman now."

I give a half smile. Yippee!

"Okay, fine, sulk, but you aren't going to ruin this celebration with an attitude, young lady. So I'll give you a few to get it together. Got me?" Her eyebrow raises. Yep, exactly where Nica gets it. "I'm trying to do something nice for you, Imari."

My eyes lock on hers, annoyed. "But it's what *you* want, not me." The words slip out before I can snatch them back in.

I stare forward, biting my lip, feeling her watching me. She starts to respond, but stops.

Then starts again. "That's exactly what I said to my mother a long time ago." Her voice is even quieter than the sportscaster's, whose voice barely comes through the speakers now.

I want to ask when? Why? But I know she'll probably only say "Oh, never mind" like she always does. So, instead, I stare out the window, wondering. The houses, trees, and fresh-cut lawns change to sidewalks, cafés, and shops. At the red light, I look over at the soccer fields at the side of my school grounds. I should be headed to gym class right about now with Nasha, not a stupid spa!

A car behind us honks.

"Mom? The light."

"Oh, right." She holds her hand up and peers into the rearview mirror. "Sorry." She waves even though the other driver can't see her as he speeds around us. She glances at me as I watch the fields move past the window. Then suddenly I'm sliding across the seat, grabbing for the door handle.

"Mom!" I shout as she makes a U-turn. "Did you forget something important?"

She doesn't answer at first. "Yes, I have." She looks over at me and smiles the kind of smile people make when they're a little sad.

"What?" I ask softly.

She's quiet as the left blinker clicks in the silence.

Soon the nose of the car turns into the school's back parking lot. I'm so confused. Maybe she's changed her mind? I shouldn't have said what I said. She is trying to be nice.

"Sorry, Mom." I'm not sure if I should get out of the car or wait. When she doesn't move, I say, "Um . . . the doors back here are locked."

"You're not going to school," she says in her ballet-teacher determined voice, the sad gone.

"I'm not?" Now I'm really confused.

"No." She climbs out of Dad's low-to-the-ground car. "You coming?"

I look around again and then take off my seat belt and follow her to the back of Dad's car. She's already bent over in the trunk, pulling a duffel bag closer to her.

"I'd be careful if I were you," I say before she pulls back the zipper. "Stuff probably stinks in there." I eye the bag suspiciously. Even though I like dirt, I'm not a fan of funk, and surprise funk is the worst funk. Ew!

But when Mom opens the bag, I don't even have to pinch my nose. Nothing's stinking. I wouldn't be surprised if she goes to the garage at night and sprays it with disinfectant.

"Perfect," she says, yanking it out of the trunk. "Let's go, you."

"Where?"

"To practice."

"Practice what?"

"PKs," she says.

I stop. Does she really want to do piqué turns on the soccer field?

Then I watch, eyes wide, as she stalks across the parking lot into the grass, blush-colored high heels sinking into dirt, duffel bag slung over her shoulder, wrinkling her cardigan.

What in the world?

I search the deserted parking lot. Have aliens taken my mom?

"Put some smoke under those Converse, Rocket!" Mom yells. She called me Rocket. She never calls me Rocket. "Come on. Get a move on."

I sprint across the baseball outfield, catching up to her. When we reach a goalpost on the soccer field, she dumps the duffel in the grass.

"Why the long face?" she asks, studying me.

Ugh, is she kidding? I don't know what's worse: possibly getting mani-pedis or practicing piqué turns for Clara where everyone near a classroom window can see.

"Mom?" I start as she reaches to unzip the bag again.

"What?" She looks at me like I'm the one who's lost it.

She peels off her cardigan, then folds it neatly and lays it in the grass.

Okay, she's not totally gone. Or is she?

She tosses a soccer ball to me from the duffel bag, kicks off her high heels, then hikes up her skirt a little and crouches a bit. "Okay, let's go."

"Huh?"

"Am I speaking a different language or something? What's wrong?"

Or something. Mom's standing between goalposts,

basically barefoot. Bugs probably coming for her toes. And she's asking me what's wrong?

"Kick it, child." She widens her stance, palms up. "Let me see your best penalty kick."

"A penalty kick?" She's not talking about a ballet move? My mom knows what a PK really is?

I glance down at the ball and then back up at her. What is going on? She must hear my thoughts because she gives me an unsure smile, dusting off her hands.

"You were right," she says. "This is your day, not mine. It should be about what you want, not me."

I look down at her stockinged feet in the grass, not believing this. Reading my thoughts again, she says, "I used to play softball, you know. I was pretty good, too."

"Softball?" My mom?

"I was a little older than you and loved it."

"Why'd you stop?"

"Your grandmother wanted it that way. Wanted me to be a ballerina. So I was." Mom looks off, then back at me. "Luckily I love ballet, too. It wasn't a tough choice. I did both for a while. But I know the same isn't true for you. I shouldn't have pushed so hard to reshape you."

I hear the words she says, but I don't quite believe 'em. And besides, I can't imagine Mom getting sweaty, let alone willingly playing in the dirt. A giggle slips out of me.

"What's so funny?"

Does she really need to ask? "It's just cool—that's all," I finally say.

"Well, there are a lot of cool things about me you don't know. And I realize there are lots of cool things about you I haven't gotten to know, either, but I want to."

I still hear her speaking, but I'm not sure I hear her right this time, either.

"Moms make mistakes sometimes, Imari. But like everyone else, we can learn. And I think you'd be a pretty cool teacher." She claps her hands together again, crouching and eyeing the ball. "And I could teach you a couple things, too. That is, if you'd like to learn 'em?"

And right there on an empty soccer field, me and Mom in the dirt, I realize a Turning Point Celebration, my period, and what comes out of a hot-pink box might not be so bad after all.

Shiloh: The Gender Creamsicle

MASON J.

SUNRISE

Today at soccer, I'm not playing like much of a winner.
Usually my feet strike bright as gold lightning;
whenever I'm on the field, I dash quicker than a cheetah.

My teammates are all chasing each other
making jokes and jumping around
as if they're horses in a corral.
Which only makes it more obvious
that I'm moving slower than a turtle.
My legs are more wet noodles than anything else.

Coach Crystal's whistle blows;
she motions for me to bring it in.

She can see I need a break; I'm not doing my best.
Although I'm a little embarrassed, she's right.

I peel off my practice jersey and walk over to the bag area
     to rest.
With each step, the grass under my cleats turns into
     magnets.
I have to sit down, drink water, get something to eat.

Uh-oh, I feel a headache coming on.
I look up at the sky before staring at the ground.
Even though I don't feel like eating,
I grab a few handfuls of Goldfish crackers,
then the Ziploc goes back in my lunch bag.

It is as if my belly is a whole hive of bees.
They are making me dizzy from all their honey.
I close my eyes and try to count to ten.
Keep trying to steady myself.
By seven, butterflies fly around my shin guards.
At ten, something even stranger happens:
Mr. Sun tap-dances past a parade of fluffy clouds.
Once his performance is over, he takes a bow,
gently fist-bumps my head,
transforms into an orange slice,
and moves slowly into the ocean.

I close my eyes to sense all his warmth
but my body still feels funny
so it's back to a low battery, almost on empty.

My skin feels hot, like a sunburn.
The air around me goes from dry and crisp to wet and
        soft.
It reminds me of the sidewalk smell after heavy rain.

Brand-new sensations drop like a Slinky
through
my
body.

My knees become acorns hitting the ground
when I realize something is crawling
down my leg.
I quickly stand up,
begin swatting at the air,
only to realize I am bleeding.
But it doesn't hurt. It kind of feels nice,
as if I were putting aloe vera on a sunburn.
What is going on?!
My heart becomes a drum while I search in the grass
for whatever I sat on.

Two brown hands look like I've been picking
    blackberries.

Coach sees me quietly freaking out and shouts,
"That's okay, Sheila . . . I mean, Shiloh—
human bodies are similar to soccer: fun, surprising,
    and confusing!"
I try to yell back but I can't,
and the fact even after the whole season,
Coach Crystal still can't remember my new name
makes it so much harder to ask for help.

My throat is too dry even to talk.

Sensing trouble, my best friend on the team, Theresa,
    runs over.
She stops in her tracks and gasps as she gets closer to me,
"OMG! You're a mess. You gotta go home."

Too mad to even make sense, I clap back,
"LISTEN, 'RESA . . . IF YOU'RE . . . NOT . . .
    GOING TO HEL—"
Then Coach Crystal runs up
before the *p* in "help me" comes out.
"Hey, now! No cursing!" Then she swiftly switches
    her tone:

"Oh, sweetie, you've gotta call your mom to come and
get you.
Hannah K. used the last pad at our game on Saturday."

Then it all makes sense:
it's not a bug.
I'm not going to find any glass
because there is none.
My monthly moon has come.
Right here in front of everyone.

I want to scream and maybe even cry.
I've never been sent home.
And I don't even have a phone yet.
So I have to be extra nice when I don't want
to use Theresa's phone to make the call.

Waiting for Mom to answer is a game show.
Ring
Riiing
Riiiiing
"Hello! This is Donna." Finally! Mom's voice on the line.
"Mom, my monthly moon came at soccer, and you need
to come to get me."

Mom squeals while saying, "Don't move. I'll be there as
    soon as I can."
I wish I could be as happy as her.
But I feel like a wart-covered frog on a log,
ready for my chance to hop away as quickly as I can.

During the ride home, Mom screams,
squawks louder than a parrot.
She dials number after number,
tells anyone who will listen,
"Sheila got her period! My daughter is a woman!"
She tells:
a man inside the booth where we pay our bridge toll,
two older people trying to cross the street.
Even the birds who pooped on our van get the news.

I can't be a part of this, so I hide under my hoodie.
Wishing I could be anywhere else but in the back seat.
Peering out with one eye to see a purple sky turning
    dark blue.

All my favorite stars—Capella, Andromeda, Hercules—
    start to outline San Francisco.
I imagine I'm a bat in a cave, thirsty for blood
    (and candy),

soaring around the beach with my friends the crows
and seagulls.

SUNSET

We get out of our van and hurry inside.
Mom throws open the door and runs into the kitchen,
yelling, "We're home! We're home! We're home!"

My nana doesn't have her hearing aids on, though.
With Mom's uproar, she can't hear a thing.
Somehow it seems she's been waiting.
Nana pours three cups of tea from a silver pot with heat
coming out.
I watch it as it swirls around her face,
the white steam doing somersaults in a hazy grin.

When she finally notices me
she giggles and hands me my favorite mug.
"You have to stop growing, babygirl."

I take one look at the red stuff and gulp loudly.
Waaaait . . . Are they going to make me drink blood?
Then my thoughts are stopped.
Nana starts scolding me: "Shiloh, don't you go thinking
about them vampires."

Like a fortune-teller
Nana often knows what I'm thinking.

"No need to be scared.
It's tea . . . red raspberry leaf.
It's right for your body."

I love raspberries, so I take a big sip.
Wow! Was that a mistake.
This does *not* taste like raspberries.

It tastes worse than a dirt-and-coffee mixture.
I want to spit it out, but Mom promises it'll make me
        feel better.
I take tiny sips and think hard about
how to secretly pour it into the sink.

Then I realize Mom was right:
the bees in my stomach have stopped swarming.
Also, my legs don't feel weird anymore.

Nana smiles and speaks in her creaky slow voice:
"Humans and animals have bled for over a hundred
        thousand years.
Today is a happy day for you because it means a new life
        can happen."

But I'm not happy. I feel this isn't right.
People do not grow from eggs, and if they do, I want no
         part in it!
Nana sees my face, laughs, and rolls her eyes.
"Right now, you don't have a choice. Maybe someday,
         you will."

As I sip more of the bloody-looking tea,
our house tablet rings.
Yay! It's my aunt Carmen
with a pic of her dog, Rocky, at the beach in her
         FaceTime square.
She is a punk rocker who moved to a farm in Ohio
because the rent in the city is too expensive.
I start to say hi when Rocky begins howling
and Carmen breaks into a rock song she's made up,
playing her broken electric guitar with stickers all over it.
We can't see her, but we sure can hear her.
Somehow Rocky is even barking along in tune.

"Congratulations on menstruation, you're a woman now,
we're going to scream and shout . . ."
I leave the meeting quickly, hoping she didn't notice that
         we answered.
Whoops—
Ugh, she did hear and calls right back.

Mom, Nana, and Carmen go on and on
talking about how good it is
to have another woman
and I can't even stand to hear it.
I've told my family over and over,
I am a gender Creamsicle: orange and white.
Not a Popsicle or ice cream. I am in between.

It's been two years, and mostly they understand
but sometimes they forget and treat me like a girl.
To that, I say, "No, thank you."

I turn the camera off, and Carmen apologizes.
Says her webcam isn't working too well, either,
but Rocky wants to say sorry.
"Sorry, sorry, sorry." They both say it three times to make
          sure I hear.
"It's okay, Carmen—we miss you in California," I reply.

She clears her throat and reminds me that because I am
          eleven and a half,
I am nearly old enough to fly alone and visit her.
Now I feel bad for hanging up.
Mom suggests Carmen can finish her song later,
maybe during my moon party since she'll be watching
          on Zoom.

SUNRISE

For several days, people text, call, and send video messages.
Everyone laughs loudly and talks about my party.
But Aunt Carmen is nowhere to be seen or heard on any
    of the video calls.

I try to speak up about what I want
but as usual, the adults ignore me.
Nobody hears me say they don't have to give me a party
or not to call it a period.

Instead of listening, they debate: If I'll wear a short or
    long dress.
What Nana will cook or will food be delivered.
How we can't invite my uncles and boy cousins except for
    the babies.

But what about my fave cousin, Manuel Jr.?
He's a gender Creamsicle, too, with hair to his elbows and
    rainbow nails.
Surely he can sneak in.
"No Boys . . . Not Even MJ!" Mom and Nana shout at the
    same time.
Geez, I wish I could be a kid again.
Not a girl, not a boy, a kid.

SUNSET

Finally, it's my party!

As much as I didn't want to have it, I am excited now.
After days of arguing with my family,
not one, but two miracles happen.

First, I get to wear formal "boys'" clothes:
My suit is bright pink.
The bow tie is sparkly.
But I don't care:
At least it is not the dress or skirt Mom wanted.

The other miracle came this morning.
Aunt Carmen texted my uncle.
She flew in from Ohio for my party
and needed someone to get her
from shopping at our favorite bookstore,
Dog Eared Books in the Mission District.
I can hardly wait to see her.

Before we can get to the venue,
everything moves in slow motion.
Nana spills coffee on her sweat suit.
We have to drive her home to change.

Aunty Gabby's puppy ate half of a shoe.
So she isn't able to DJ after all.
It seems like hours pass, but we finally get there.

The Scottish Hall we rented looks like a castle,
with dark-green velvet curtains
from the ceiling to the floor,
crisp black-and-gold carpets,
a giant sparkling dance floor.
I pair my light-up Bluetooth speaker with the sound system.
One by one, the women and girls file in,
aunties with girl cousins,
my soccer teammates and their moms,
friends from the Genders & Sexualities Alliance,
        and Outdoor Explorers Club.
Even without the men and boys,
this party is better than I could've ever imagined.
I forget all about Manuel Jr. and my uncles.
Mostly because everyone brought my favorite foods
and without all the greedy guys here, I can eat as much
        as I want.

Gosh, do I love food. I don't know how I can choose
        where to start:
cacao drinks, fresh watermelon, cherries, mango,
        blueberries, grapes

fried alligator, red beans & rice, catfish, corn bread
seaweed, inari sushi, chicken teriyaki, shrimp tempura
wings, brisket, sweet potatoes, mac 'n' cheese
tamales, flautas, elote
and, of course, a massive platter of carne asada tacos
(with extra radishes and no cilantro, just how I like them).

I got a lot of really cool presents:
a period planner
a star map
so many temporary tattoos
coloring books about birds,
and finally, my first cell phone!
We all dance till my suit has smiley face–shaped armpit
        stains.
It turns out, Mom was right; this is super fun.
I smile so much my face hurts.

The night has been almost perfect,
except I haven't seen Aunt Carmen yet and the party is
        almost over.
I'm taking a break on the comfy chairs, picking at my
        third or fourth taco,
when a bright light shines from across the room.

A handsome gentleman in a light-purple linen suit walks in.
He's with a beautiful woman, and her dress matches
        his suit.
I don't recognize them, but they seem very important.
And all my aunties are swarming them.
I finish my taco and walk over to see this mystery man.
As I get closer, I realize they aren't a man at all.
It's Aunt Carmen!

Her hair has been cut short, but her smile is just as wide
        as ever.
I run over to tackle her with hugs!
She laughs and apologizes for being late.
The woman in purple hands me a big box
before walking off to grab a plate.
I don't even know what to say.
Aunt Carmen is a gender Creamsicle like me and MJ!
We are also the only two in suits here tonight.
It could be weird, but it isn't.
Instead, we look like royalty,
a pink prince and lavender king.

She leans into me, then whispers,
"Not too shabby for an old punk, eh?"
"Not bad at all," I say, looking her up and down.
We crack up, and she puts her hand on my shoulder.

"You know, Shiloh, our bodies were made from mud and
        salt water
then sprinkled with bits of family history; scientists call
        the sprinkles DNA.
They connect us to our ancestors through
the heart, muscles, bones, and blood."

Mom walks by, sipping her coffee.
"You two cannot hide over here gossiping. Come rejoin
        the party."
So we follow the fun; Aunt Carmen, Mom, even Nana
        are all clapping and dancing.
It's the best night of all my life.

Although this seemed like a bad idea at first
I'm glad we were able to find a way
to make sure there was room for everyone.

SUNRISE

I have had nine cycles now.
They can be both challenging and relaxing.
My moon party seems so long ago.
I almost wish I could do it again.
I try my best to keep away mean thoughts about
        my body.

I've learned my cycle and use my period planner to
keep me healthy.
I don't push myself at practice anymore.

I talk to my friends or grown-ups whenever I am
struggling to understand myself.
Things are more comfortable,
I can drink the raspberry leaf tea without gagging.
Nana even convinced Mom to let me have cacao for
breakfast.
My cycles don't surprise me anymore;
I open my door when they are ready to come in.
When my bleeding ends, I have more energy and focus
than ever.
I catch up on homework and finish my chores in no time
at all.
Dreaming colorfully, and more often, I write down each
dream as I wake up.

Although I am used to it, there are still times I want to
drift away.
I try not to think that way, though.
Instead, I imagine myself soaring above seas,
thanking my body for staying in tune with itself.
I do not get embarrassed or sad.

I use the moon as my guide
and the sun as a power boost.
Though annoying people try to tell me
the in-between is wrong,
I know I look the way nature wants me to.
I braid new maps into my hair.
Draw star maps on my hands.
Earth teaches me all life grows from roots,
contains seeds
full of beautiful smells and extraordinary magic.

Although I am not a girl
like many people with moontimes, this body is mine.
And I will let it rest every time it needs to,
the same way the sun sets at Ocean Beach every evening.

To my teachers, storytellers, and sheroes: P. Smith, Rulan Tangen,
Kumu Hina, Storme DeLarverie, Gladys Bentley, Dolores Huerta,
Cheryl Dunye, Carmen Piteo, Lenore Chinn, Pam Peniston,
Jewelle Gomez, Mickalene Thomas, Hulleah Tsinhnahjinnie,
and my grandmothers—Kameyo, Marie, and Pauline.

Holiday

SAADIA FARUQI

Ramadan is the best month of the year, no matter what anyone thinks. "No food or drink from dawn to dusk," I say, waving my arms toward the sky.

I'm walking home from the bus stop with my next-door neighbor Jenny. "I don't get what's so amazing about being hungry," she says, frowning.

I give her a pitying glance. "It's not about hunger or thirst," I inform her. "It's about sacrifice. About giving up something to improve yourself."

Jenny's face clears. "Like dieting!"

It's my turn to frown. "Not exactly . . ." I begin, but we're at her house and she runs up the driveway without saying goodbye.

That's typical Jenny. We're not exactly friends, but Mama insists I walk with someone because the school bus drops us off at our neighborhood entrance two blocks away. I watch her go inside her house: tall, blond Jenny, who started wearing a bra in fifth grade. Okay, training bra, but even that's a big deal. Mama says nice Muslim girls don't think about undergarments until they're in middle school. She says she never spoke about this stuff when she was growing up in Pakistan. Well, this is America, and I'm in sixth grade now. Right after Ramadan is over, I'm dragging Mama to the Target in the mall to try on some you-know-whats.

"Watch out!" Someone pokes my back from behind, and I whirl around. Bilal. My fourteen-year-old brother thinks it's his duty to be as annoying as possible, especially in public. "What were you girls talking about?"

I shrug. "Nothing. Just Ramadan."

He laughs. "Why do you care so much about it, anyway?"

I glare at him, then turn away to stomp home. "For your information, it's going to be an epic year," I shout as I half walk, half run. Our house is just ahead, a big brown two-story with a towering oak in the front yard, slightly bent as if it's bowing in greeting.

"Oh, because you, Layla Ahmad, are finally big enough

to keep a full fast?" he scoffs, right at my heels. Unlike me, his high school bus drops him off right at the end of the street. Lucky.

I grit my teeth. He's been fasting for a couple of years now, and he thinks he's all grown up or something. I, on the other hand, have only been allowed half-fasts until now. "What's your problem?" I argue. "Mama agreed I could fast on the weekends this year. I'm almost twelve. I can do it!"

He brushes past me without saying anything and goes inside. I manage to slip in before he bangs the heavy glass front door shut in my face. Ugh, he's so infuriating!

"Is that you, Layla?" comes a gruff voice from the kitchen. My grandmother is standing in the doorway, hands on hips, our cat, Bowtie, rubbing against her leg. "I need help cooking the iftar. We have guests coming."

I sniff. I can smell cinnamon and spices, and a hint of something tart. Cilantro? Breaking the fast is always a scrumptious affair in the Ahmad household. Dadi may look like a grumpy old Pakistani lady with her long white hair tied in a braid, but she can make all sorts of delicious foods appear like magic on the iftar table.

And I'm her sous-chef. Always helping. Never in charge, of course. "Coming, Dadi," I call, sighing, throwing my backpack on the ground in the hallway. Bilal's already galloped up the stairs to his room, probably to play video games. He spends hours up there, recording himself playing *Fortnite* with commentary in a fake British accent. Why are older brothers so weird?

"Sucker!" he shouts from upstairs. Bowtie meows.

"You better come down and help, or I'm telling Mama when she gets home!" I shout back.

No reply.

Mama's late coming home because she had to swing by the airport first to pick up her baby sister. Aisha Khala enters the house with her signature dramatic shrieks. "Oh, this Texas weather is really terrible!" she complains, fanning herself.

I hug her tightly, closing my eyes at the jasmine perfume she always wears. "Salaam alaikum, khala!"

Her eyes crinkle. She's wearing a brightly patterned tunic over black jeans, and her hair is long and flowing, just like those shampoo ads on TV. She just graduated from college and is so much fun to hang out with. "Layla, look at you. You're even prettier than last time! And Bilal, you got so tall! What are you eating these days?"

Bilal shrugs and looks down at his phone. To

compensate for his rudeness, I hug her again, grinning wide. "I'm so glad you're here," I say. "You should live here instead of New Jersey."

"Somebody's in a good mood," she whispers back. "Finally convinced your mom to let you fast, eh?"

Aisha Khala always knows exactly what I'm thinking. "Just for the weekend, but it's a start," I tell her. "All my Muslim friends started fasting in elementary school."

"Every family has their own rules—you know that! Stop comparing yourself to others." She lets me go and picks up Bowtie from the floor. "And you, mister!" she croons. "Have you been a good kitty?"

I roll my eyes. "He's always stealing food off the table."

Aisha Khala laughs. "I bet that makes your grandma really angry!"

Mama takes off her hijab and smooths her hair. She's in what I call her professor outfit: gray trousers, white blouse, and of course the ever-present hijab, which is purple with white flowers today. "Speaking of grandmas," she says, "it's almost iftar time, and I need to help her in the kitchen."

"I'll come with you," Aisha Khala says. "Any special request I can whip up, kiddos? Rooh Afza in cold milk, perhaps? Or my famous fruit salad?"

The sisters link arms and head to the kitchen, talking loudly. I trail behind. Dadi's already at the stove, stirring a pot of rice pudding. "Welcome, my dear," she tells Aisha Khala with a smile. "I hope you're not too hungry. It's still an hour to iftar."

Aisha Khala shakes her head, inspecting the floor as if it's the most fascinating thing she's ever seen. "Um, I'm on holiday this week, Aunty," she mutters.

I blink. Holiday? What does that mean?

"Lucky you," Dadi replies with a knowing glance, turning back to the stove.

Mama clears her throat loudly. "Layla, please take your khala's suitcase to your room. She's going to bunk with you."

"You never ask Bilal to do anything," I whine.

"He's fasting, and you're not!" Mama replies.

I decide it's not the right time to talk about equal rights in the Ahmad household. "I *want* to fast . . ." I grumble under my breath as I stalk off.

At iftar that evening, I can't stop talking about the upcoming weekend. "My friend Sarah had a big party to celebrate her first full fast," I hint. "It's a big deal in her family, you know."

"Didn't I tell you not to compare yourself to your friends?" Aisha Khala chides in a low voice. I stare at her. She's looking a little green as she surveys all the food on the table: beef samosas and potato cutlets, tangy fruit chaat and spicy French fries. And of course, biryani in her honor. Dadi always makes her signature biryani for out-of-town guests.

Bilal kicks me under the table. "Just pray you can last the whole day," he tells me. "It will be so sad if you have to break your fast because you couldn't stand it, you big baby."

"Shut up!" I stab a spoon into my rice pudding, wishing it was his face.

Mama frowns at us. "Quiet, both of you. Your fighting gives me headaches!"

Dadi pushes a samosa at me. "Where's your baba?" she asks, obviously trying to change the subject. "I made his favorite foods."

"Working as usual," I mutter.

"He's got an extra shift at the hospital," Mama adds. "He won't be back until late."

Dadi grunts. "They should at least let doctors get some rest in Ramadan."

Mama sighs. "He's trying to put in some extra hours so he can take the day off for Eid next week."

I turn to Aisha Khala. "I'm going to have a sleepover with my best friend, Sarah, the night before Eid," I tell her.

She's not even listening. Her face is pale. I'm just about to ask her what's wrong when she stands up so quickly, the table shakes. She's looking like she's about to vomit.

"Carry on—I'm fine. Just cramps," she chokes out, and rushes away.

I watch her go. Is she okay? What's wrong with her? What's even the point of visiting your favorite niece if you're not feeling well? At the last minute, she turns and winks at me weakly. "I'm sure we can do a little celebration for you this weekend, Layla," she says.

The next morning, I wake up early. Friday is free-dress day at Hanks Elementary, and I need to pick the perfect outfit to signal my upcoming entry into the big-kid crowd. Ramadan-ready, as Baba would say.

I step over Aisha Khala sleeping on an air mattress by the windows, and search through my closet for something that screams "mature." Everything I own is Pakistani-inspired "modest wear," as Mama calls it. Doesn't matter that Mama and Baba left Pakistan when they were both kids, and nobody's even visited since 2007, when Dadi's only daughter—Baba's sister—got married to some landowner there.

There's a sharp tug in my lower stomach, and I pause. Since Mama's agreed to let me fast on the weekend, maybe we can take a trip to Target for a training bra today after school. The tug intensifies, and I take a breath. *Baby steps, Layla. Get the weekend out of the way first.*

I'm reaching for a long denim shirt Baba brought me from a medical conference trip to LA when I feel a wetness in my pajama bottoms and think, *Oh nuts, did I need to pee this bad?* I rush to the bathroom before a real accident occurs and my babyhood is established forever.

In the bathroom, I quickly pull down my pajamas and get the shock of my life. The wetness isn't pee, at least not any normal pee. It's bright red and soaking into the cotton of my pajamas, and it's . . . Ow, my stomach tugs again as if somebody's grabbed my insides with an iron fist and is using them as a stress ball. What on earth is going on? I look around wildly, pull up my pajamas, and run to my parents' room across the hallway, half shouting, half whispering, "Wake up, I think I'm dying, I need a doctor." Then I remember Baba and stop for a second, a hand over the iron fist in my stomach, thanking God that an actual doctor lives in the house.

Ten minutes later, Mama stands with me in the bathroom, hands on hips. I'd also like to hold my hands on my hips because it's cool, but instead I'm hunched over, pressing both hands to my stomach. The worst thing is Mama seems happy more than anything else.

Wait, happy? I wish I'd woken up Baba instead. He'd know better than to smile in such a teary-eyed, weird way when confronted with a medical emergency.

"My baby's all grown up," Mama whispers.

"Mama!" I whisper back furiously. "What are you talking about? I'm bleeding. Call an ambulance or something."

Mama's smile grows bigger. "It's okay, sweetie. This is normal. I can't even believe this is happening! Wow, my big girl! And by the way, this makes me feel really old, you know!"

I wish it wasn't against the rules to smack your mother. "What. Are. You. Talking. About?" I repeat through clenched teeth. Yeah, I definitely should have woken up Baba instead.

Mama stops. "Sorry. This is new to me, too. I can't believe I'm having this conversation. Aaah, I'm not prepared." She takes a deep breath, and finally the smile is gone. "Okay, you got your period. It's this thing that happens to girls when they hit puberty. Once a month, they bleed from . . . there. For about a week or so. Usually. And you have to put a pad to soak up the blood . . . Wait a minute. Do I even have pads your size? You're so thin . . ."

She whirls away to search through the drawers under the sink. I stand very still, trying to get my brain thinking again. I've heard about periods, of course. Mama and Baba refused to sign the permission slip for sex ed last semester, but Jenny had whispered about it afterward, laughing slyly.

She'd been more focused on boy body parts than anything else. She'd made periods sound like just a few spots of blood, not this . . . red, achy mess.

Maybe this is all a nightmare. Maybe Bilal has played a prank on me. Last year, I woke up one morning with red dots all over my face and was sure I'd gotten some terrible skin disease. Turns out Bilal had sneaked into my room at night with a red marker. I didn't speak to him for a week.

No, Bilal wouldn't do this. This is too real. Too scary. The blood trickles down my left leg slowly, making me itch. Should I wipe it? Should I scratch my thigh? Why is everything so gross?

Mama turns back, waving a little violet square package in the air like a trophy. The smile is back. "I got it. I think this will fit."

By the time I get cleaned up and back in my room, my stomach is on fire. Aisha Khala's gone, probably having breakfast downstairs by now. "You'll get cramps from the periods," Mama announces. "You better get back into bed. I'll bring you some Tylenol. No need to go to school today."

I crawl into bed. "But it's free-dress day," I protest. "And I have to tell everyone about my first fast tomorrow . . ."

Mama's on her way out the door, but she stops like a car braking abruptly on the highway. "Oh . . . jaan . . . I'm so sorry. No fasting for you. We don't pray or fast when we get our periods. Think of it as your holiday. For being a big, big girl."

All I can manage is a whimper. I close my eyes, hoping I'll go back to sleep and get a do-over on this awful, awful day. Jenny made getting your period sound so glamorous. "It means you're a woman," she said with a knowing look that confused me.

Jenny didn't mention all the blood and stomach cramping. I groan. How can this be a holiday? From what, a normal life? A pain-free existence?

Bowtie wanders into the room. "You're so lucky you're a boy," I tell him. He jumps onto the bed and curls up on my legs as if he knows just what I need. I doze off, then jerk awake at the sound of a knock on my door. If Mama's come back to smile about me being a big girl one more time . . .

"Hello, jaan." It's Aisha Khala, looking as glum as I feel. "Heard you're not feeling too good."

I burrow into my comforter. "I got a holiday," I mumble, half sarcastically. It's a little bit true, though. I'm not at school, at least. Imagine having to deal with this stomach pain and Mama's little violet pads in the nasty bathrooms at Hanks Elementary. Ugh.

Aisha Khala crawls into bed with me, gently pushing Bowtie aside. "Same here. And it's the kind of holiday that actually sucks. I'd rather go to Paris, to be honest."

A little chuckle escapes my lips. "Me too."

"So . . . do you have any questions?"

I shake my head no. Not right now, at least. I can't stop thinking about Aisha Khala's thighs streaked with blood, which is gross because I shouldn't be thinking of anybody's thighs, really. Still, her body is warm and comforting next to mine, and I snuggle and sigh until I fall asleep.

Sarah calls after school, when I'm sitting at the kitchen island chopping beans for Dadi. "So, what will you eat at your first suhoor?" she asks. "I recommend oatmeal or something, with lots of nuts. Nothing spicy, or you'll get a mean heartburn by the afternoon."

I blink rapidly. My stomach still feels like pulsating hot iron, despite the Tylenol Mama gave me. "I'm not fasting," I reply flatly.

"What? Why not?"

I look at Dadi, but she's rummaging in the fridge for something. "I got my period," I whisper.

Sarah's squeal is so loud, I pull my phone away from my ear. "OMG. I'm so jealous! I can't believe you got your period before me!"

I put the phone back to my ear. "It's not that great, to be honest."

"Are you kidding? Of course it is! It's like . . . a big deal. It means . . ."

"Yes, I know. It means you're a woman. With blood coming out of your . . . whatever. Does that even make sense? Like, why am I bleeding? Where is the blood coming from? Why does my tummy hurt like I got punched by the meanest bully in Houston?"

There's a long pause. Then Sarah says quietly, "I don't know."

"Me neither."

Sarah sighs. "Sorry it hurts, though. I didn't realize."

"Yeah."

Mama walks into the kitchen with a laundry basket full of clothes, Bowtie following her like a faithful attendant.

"Listen, I gotta go. I'll talk to you when I'm feeling better." I jab a finger on the screen to disconnect the call and hurl the phone onto the counter.

Mama sets the basket on the floor and sinks onto a stool next to me. "Bad mood?" she asks, placing a hand over my forehead.

I push her hand away. "What else do you expect? All my dreams are dashed."

Mama smiles. "Don't be so dramatic, jaan. It's not the end of the world."

I stare at her in disgust. "Maybe not to you."

Mama waves a hand at me. "I told you. It's your holiday. You get a free pass on these days. Stay in bed; don't do anything; just relax."

I can feel my face heating up. "But I don't want to relax . . . I wanted to fast tomorrow! It's not fair."

Bowtie meows loudly at me.

"See? Even the cat is telling you to stop stressing." Mama leans forward and kisses me on the top of my head. "Want me to heat up some chicken noodle soup for you?"

I shudder. "No, thanks."

Aisha Khala shuffles in, looking tired. She sits down and sighs loudly.

Mama shakes her head. "Great, now I have two big babies on my hands."

"Shut up, Mina."

I stare at Aisha Khala like she's grown horns. She-devil horns. "Do periods make you cranky?" I guess. I'd googled periods—correct name: menstruation—earlier and then wished I hadn't. Who knew I had an organ called a uterus and that it shed its lining each month in a gross display of trash takeout? Who approved this mess of biology? And why are boys exempt?

Mama is still looking at us with pursed-up lips and a disappointed face. I feel a sudden flash of anger at her for not explaining any of this to me before. She's my mom. Isn't she supposed to prepare me for stuff?

But she's already turning and walking away. "Cranky, moody, emotional . . . it's all part of the package!"

"Perfect," I groan.

This time, Baba comes home in time for iftar. Dadi stands at the head of the table like a warden, eyeing him with her arms crossed over her chest. "Eat some samosas," she prompts. "You look exhausted."

Baba takes one and passes the plate to Aisha Khala. "How was your fast, Aisha?" he asks politely.

She almost drops the samosas on the floor. "It went fine, thank you."

I stare at her throughout dinner. When everyone else leaves the table, I turn to her with arms folded across my chest. "Why did you lie to Baba?" I demand. "You weren't even fasting today."

She shrugs. "What? It's not really a lie. We just can't tell the menfolk about this period business. It's embarrassing."

"But . . . he's a doctor. He literally studied the human body for years."

She stands up and starts to stack dirty dishes into a pile. "I know. It's just . . . not done. South Asian people are very hush-hush about personal things."

"But . . . why? Isn't this natural?"

The stack of dishes is now so high it's teetering like a dirty Tower of Pisa. "Layla, jaan. That's the way it's been for centuries. I'm not going to mess with tradition. What would people say?"

I don't get it. Aisha Khala's always been my hero, the cool aunt I can tell anything to. But right now, she just seems . . . exhausted. I watch as she balances her load on both arms and walks away to the kitchen.

Since it's the weekend, Mama allows a late-night movie after Baba's gone to bed. Bilal wants to watch *The Mummy* again. "We've seen it a hundred times already," I whine.

"I don't care. It's the best movie!"

I pick up Bowtie, then sink into the couch between Aisha Khala and Dadi. "No matter how many times you watch that movie, you're not going to be as cool as Brendan Fraser," I tell Bilal.

He throws a pillow at me. "I already am," he says in a very bad British accent.

I'm not in the mood to laugh. I rub a cheek against Bowtie's fur, trying not to give in to the anger inside me. Tomorrow was going to be my first fast. Mama would have hugged me, and Baba would have taken a dozen pictures as I ate my first real iftar. Dadi would have smiled one of her rare smiles and murmured a dozen prayers of thanks.

Instead, there's nothing except stomach pains—sorry, uterine cramps—and an older brother who insists on watching a dumb movie about fake Egyptian gods. I close my eyes and lean against Aisha Khala. The injustice of this entire situation is just too painful to think about.

"What's the matter with you?" Bilal asks, staring.

I open my mouth, then remember how Aisha Khala had acted with Baba earlier. "Nothing," I mutter.

Dadi holds up her hand. "Let Layla decide today," she commands.

Bilal's mouth falls open. "What? Why?"

I sit up a little. Things rarely go my way in this house. "How about *Avatar*? Aisha Khala probably hasn't seen it."

"The one with the blue people?" Dadi says. "Perfect."

Bilal sinks on the carpet. "*Avatar* is okay, I guess," he concedes.

The movie is a blur. I can't concentrate because I keep wondering how many days this blood extravaganza will last. Google said a week but that some bodies take longer. *Being a woman sucks*, I tell myself. Especially a woman on holiday.

Bilal gets bored halfway through and leaves, Bowtie in his arms. The rest of us sit around, munching on peanuts and sipping chai as the movie continues on low volume. The warm chai soothes my cramps just a tiny bit, and I start to relax for the first time since the morning.

"They should have Urdu subtitles," Dadi grumbles. "I can't understand these American accents at all."

I put my head on Dadi's shoulder. Sometimes I can't imagine my tiny grandmother giving birth to Baba, who's so tall he can touch the ceiling if he stands on tippy-toes. Then I realize that this means Dadi also used to have periods, and I cringe, because it's not a good idea to imagine your seventy-year-old grandmother spewing blood from her lady parts. Ew. Ew. Ew.

"I heard you started your menses today," Dadi says gruffly, not looking directly at me.

I blink at her. "Periods," she explains. "We used to call it menses in my day." Ugh. Did a newsletter go out or something? How does everyone know? I try not to roll my eyes. "Now you're going to congratulate me on becoming a woman, right?"

Dadi sighs. "I remember when I started bleeding. I was in school when it happened. The girls started laughing, and I turned around and saw that the back of my uniform was all red."

I'm totally horrified. "What did you do?"

"What could I do? I ran out of the class, and all the way home." Dadi is looking at the TV screen as if her memories are a movie. "I locked myself in my room and cried and cried."

I hug her sideways. Suddenly my own story this morning doesn't seem so awful. "Sorry, Dadi."

Aisha Khala pats my arm. "Welcome to the club, Layla," she tells me. "We all have our horror stories, you know."

Mama nods, as if she's thinking of something very unpleasant. "Mm-hmm."

Dadi waves at them. "We shouldn't scare the girl." She turns to me with a sigh. "Layla, periods are a part of nature. It's not something you can control. And in time you will learn to live with it, my Layla jaan!"

I'm not ready to be placated. "By lying to people about it?" I look pointedly at Aisha Khala.

Dadi scoffs. "That's a cultural thing. In Pakistan we never, ever talked about it. Not even among friends. I never understood that. Pretending it doesn't happen? How dumb do you think people are?"

Mama claps her hands. "I know what will make you feel better! How about tomorrow morning we go to the mall and buy a training bra?" she asks, smiling.

Wait a minute. Are boobs and periods both signs that I'm growing up? I'll need to check on Google again. "That would be great," I reply, smiling slightly.

But something is still bothering me. "It's not fair, though. Why do I get to lose my fasts because of this . . . thing? Bilal doesn't. Baba doesn't."

Dadi gives me a stern look. "You don't lose them at all. Who told you that?"

Mama swallows a big gulp of chai. "I don't think I explained everything yet. This whole situation has come as a surprise to me, too!"

Dadi shakes her head. "You have to make up your missed fasts after your period ends. You have until the beginning of Ramadan next year, so you can take your time. But the fasting doesn't go away just because it's your holiday."

I groan. "I'm starting to hate that word."

"Holiday?" Mama asks. "It's such a lovely word, jaan. It means God has given you a few days of rest while your body goes through a difficult phase."

"Yes, it's a good thing." Dadi searches for the right word. "A . . . concession from the Almighty. A time to relax and heal and take care of yourself."

I think about this. If nature—or God—has given me these terrible periods, I also get time to rest and recover from them. "That makes sense," I finally say. Then I pause. "Do you think I could talk to Baba about this? I don't want to go around pretending with him."

Mama and Aisha both look alarmed. "No!" they say together, very loudly.

Dadi rolls her eyes at them. I have to grin because I've never seen her do that before. "You can do whatever you want. That's what I like about young people. You can throw away the useless traditions about periods that have bound us for so long." Dadi pats my head and stands up. "Now, *you* may be on holiday, but I have to pray before I go to sleep."

I help Mama pick up the teacups and take them into the kitchen. "I'm sorry you're not getting to be a part of Ramadan the way you wanted, my love," she begins. "I'm sorry you're not getting your party yet, but just be patient. We can do that later."

I'm hardly listening. The pots and pans on the counter have given me an idea. "I know how I can still be a part of Ramadan," I whisper.

The next evening, with plenty of Tylenol in my system, I shoo everyone out of the kitchen. Dadi grumbles like an angry bear, but I gently push her out. "It's my turn to make iftar," I tell her. "There's no reason we can't have a party even though I'm not fasting."

"Don't touch the oven without gloves!" Mama calls out anxiously.

Ignoring her, I take out flour and sugar and cinnamon and get to work. Google isn't just good for menstruation talk, you know. I got a bunch of easy baking recipes from a Muslim cooking blog the night before, complete with step-by-step videos. Bilal peeks in as I'm putting a straw-berry cake in the oven, gloves on, and asks, "Need any help?"

Bilal offering to help? I try to keep my eyes from bulg-ing and point to the half-done spicy chaat. "Mix that," I order.

"Who's going to taste this?" he asks when he's done. "We're both fasting, right?"

I hesitate, thinking of Aisha Khala and Mama and all the generations of women before me who've been lying to spare men the embarrassment of biology. I decide I don't want to be like them. "I . . . er, I'm not fasting." I square my shoulders and tell him in a low voice.

He frowns. "How come?"

I take a look at his face, wondering if he's going to call me a baby. But for once, he's not teasing me. I turn away and shrug like it's no big deal. "I got my period. Mama says we don't fast during these days."

There's a silence in the kitchen that screams at me. I don't want to turn back to look at him. Then I hear him say, "Okay, then you get to taste this chaat, I guess."

And my face breaks into the widest smile.

Ofrendas

GUADALUPE GARCIA MCCALL

In loving memory of my papi,
el Señor Onésimo García (1940–2020)
because your memory is a blessing.

If they could be compared to anything, the days after their mother died, the three little sisters were most like hummingbirds. Their little bodies fluttered around each other in a swirl of vibrant, psychedelic emotions that blurred their eyes and tightened and fastened around their tiny hearts.

Because La Santa Muerte—that feminine personification of death—had walked by in her elegant flowered dress and scooped up their mother's soul in one fell swoop while she drove home from the grocery store days ago, Lucia, Marta, and Paola were in a frazzled, flustered state of unrest. Nothing could make things better. Nothing could bring reason to their circumstance. And they dared anyone to try.

Because of the high funeral costs, the family was destitute. Lucia, the eldest daughter, knew her father was having to make sacrifices. And despite all her begging not to, her papi had quit his nice out-of-town job, saying that at thirteen, Lucia wasn't old enough to take care of her twelve- and ten-year-old sisters.

To Lucia's surprise, the women in the neighborhood had taken care of everything. Doña Luz had sewn gray funeral dresses for her and her sisters. She'd put yellow bows on them to make them look pretty, because she said they were nice girls and nice girls deserve pretty dresses. Doña Estela and Doña Pepita had cooked tamales and taquitos and gorditas to feed the guests at the wake. Doña Sofia baked empanadas and rolled out her special buñuelos, which became the centerpiece at the buffet table.

After the funeral, the family and friends went back to the house to have one final meal together, something Lucia wasn't expecting. But she took it in stride, moving about the living room, picking up discarded plates and cups, because she had to do something to keep busy.

She didn't want to cry until everyone left.

On the other side of the kitchen door, she heard a woman laughing softly. The sound stopped her. Were people allowed to laugh so soon? She certainly didn't feel like laughing.

Prying open the door just a fraction of the way, enough to peer into the kitchen, Lucia saw something she wasn't expecting. The younger women of the neighborhood—Doñas Lola, Mirna, Carlota, and Juanita—were all clustered together around her papi, who appeared to be penned into the corner between the cabinets and the stove.

"Ay, pero don't worry about the girls," Doña Lola said. "We'll check up on them."

Mirna nodded. "I know it's hard to imagine, but they'll be all right, Sonny."

"So much to think about, when raising girls." Carlota sighed. "Pimples and periods and hormones. You must be overwhelmed just thinking about what's coming."

Appalled by the women's tone, Lucia looked at her papi's face. Was he overwhelmed? Was taking care of three young daughters, with pimples and periods and hormones, going to be too much for him? She hoped not, but, then again, her mother had always taken care of their "hygiene" needs. As far as Lucia could remember, her papi had never been aware of that part of their lives. How would he handle it when she asked him for feminine products?

"You don't have to do this alone, Sonny," Mirna whispered, leaning a little too close, Lucia thought, to her papi's face. "Remember. I'm right next door."

Juanita put down her plate and placed her hand on Papi's arm. "You can count on me, too. Just call me, anytime, day or night, and I'll come right over."

"I can talk to the girls when the time comes," Mirna suggested. "About their cycles and all."

Lucia's face burned. Something about the way the women touched Papi made her uncomfortable. And she and Marta already knew everything they needed to know about menstruation. But Lucia didn't know how she felt about having someone like Mirna talk to Paola when she got her first period. It just didn't feel right.

"Anything you need—food, advice," Doña Lola said. "A little company."

Suddenly something startled her papi.

"I have to go," he said. Then he shifted on his feet, grabbed his keys off the counter, and pushed his way through the wall of women around him.

"What is it?" Mirna asked, reaching out to stop it. "What's wrong?"

"Nothing. Everything," Lucia's papi said, looking around the kitchen as if he couldn't find the way out. Then, finding the door, he pushed it open.

Lucia scooted back and watched her papi rush by her in a hurry. "Papi?" she asked when she saw his red face.

"I have to go," Lucia's papi said, as he looked back at the women in the kitchen. "I didn't sign up for this."

Because the girls' grief kept them inside the house, like hummingbirds trapped in a netted cage, Lucia didn't think about the scene in the kitchen again until days after the funeral, when she and her sisters noticed a strange phenomenon. The neighborhood women started stopping by their house daily to leave ofrendas—little offerings— tiny treats piled high on pale ceramic plates they bought at the dollar store. They baked these little ofrendas them- selves—miniature lemon meringue pies, fudge brownies, empanadas, cookies—an assortment of desserts they left on their kitchen countertops with kind little notes.

Lucia and her sisters ate them. Their papi, on the other hand, only smiled and mumbled his thanks.

"Have you noticed how Papi's face turns bright red every time these ladies come around?" Paola whispered, lying between Lucia and Marta in bed. "It's like he's embar- rassed to take food from them."

"He's not embarrassed," Lucia said, but she didn't elaborate because she knew Paola would figure it out sooner or later.

"What do you mean?" Paola asked, shifting in bed, so that she was looking straight at Lucia. Her big brown eyes were luminous, reflecting the full moon coming in through the open window, where their mami's red camellias swayed and sang their sweet jasmine-like song for them every night.

"Nothing," Lucia said, covering her eyes with her forearm. She was exhausted from trying to keep her mami's house nice and tidy, in case she could see it from Heaven.

"You're too young to know," Marta said. "Besides, it's none of your business."

"Papi's none of my business?" Paola asked. "Why not?"

"It just isn't! Now, go to sleep," Lucia said, pounding her stout pillow with her fist.

"Are you on your period?" Paola asked. "'Cause you're being kinda mean right now."

"That's not nice," Marta said, from her side of the bed. "Besides, it's not true that women act up when they're on their period."

Paola huffed and yanked the blanket up and away from Marta. "It is so true."

"It is not," Marta insisted. "Hormones affect everyone

differently. What's true for one person is not true for another."

"How do you know?" Paola demanded, sitting up in bed. "Where's your medical degree? Huh?"

"I don't need a medical degree," Marta whispered.

Paola crossed her arms in front of her. "Then how can you be so sure?"

Marta sighed. "Because I've been on my period for two days and you didn't even know it," she admitted.

Lucia rolled onto her side, to look at the glowing moon outside. "Go to sleep. Both of you. Or you're going back to your room."

Lucia's threat silenced the girls. She didn't hear a word out of them until Doña Lola walked over to the house early the next morning.

"Who wears red heels with a tangerine dress?" Paola frowned as she peeked out the large living room window.

"Who wears heels to deliver a plate of homemade tamales?" Marta asked as they clustered together on the couch, their bare knees buried into the faux-leather cushions, while they stared at the loudest woman in their neighborhood leaving after making her delivery.

Doña Lola turned around and waved at them, and the girls waved back, because they really did appreciate the food. She was the first one to bring over something savory, a real meal, instead of a bunch of sugar-loaded treats.

"Tamales," Lucia mumbled, musing to herself out loud.

"She's trying to set herself apart." Marta pushed the curtain closed.

Lucia considered her sister's words. "She's got no chance."

"You don't think so?" Marta asked, turning away from the sight of Doña Lola strutting down the street to her house on the corner.

"I just don't think tamales are going to do the trick," Lucia said, following Marta into the hallway. "Not when you consider Mirna's empanadas."

Marta nodded. "Or Juanita's homemade buñuelos."

Their papi was leaving the kitchen and headed their way, so Lucia and Marta hushed and stepped aside. He was holding his metal lunch box in one hand and his keys in the other.

"What's up?" he asked. His eyes glistened as he smiled warmly down at his three daughters.

"Nothing." Lucia looked at Marta.

Their papi gazed from one to the other to the other, a frown on his face.

"You sure?" their papi asked, reaching over to caress

each of his daughters' faces. Lucia's cheek. Marta's chin. Paola's nose. They all got some love. "'Cause it looks like you've all got something brewing behind those pretty smiles."

Lucia raised her eyebrows. "We've got tamales in the kitchen. And I'm sure more treats are on the way."

Their papi stared at Lucia for an awkward moment. He fiddled with the little side handle on his lunch box. "I, uh . . . I have a chambita I have to do this morning. It's nothing big, just putting in a toilet for a friend out in Quemado, so I'll be back this afternoon, okay?" He looked up at Lucia directly. "You got this?"

Lucia rolled her eyes. "Don't I always?" she asked.

"You do," her papi admitted, and he leaned over and kissed his daughter's forehead. "You're a good eldest daughter—the best hija mayor in Texas."

Lucia nodded and buckled down on her emotions. She didn't want him to know how tired she was of having the neighborhood women coming in and out of her mami's house. It had been two weeks since the funeral, and they wouldn't stop dropping off their little ofrendas.

The whole thing made Lucia sick to her stomach. Or was that her period showing up early? she wondered.

"Did you take some tamales?" Paola asked him.

Their papi nodded.

"Of course you did," Lucia said, sounding more sarcastic than she would have liked.

Their papi cocked his head and frowned as he considered Lucia's tone. "What?" he asked.

"Nothing," Marta said.

Lucia shrugged and said, "Just go. Do what you gotta do." Their papi shook his head and walked off.

Lucia was sure her papi knew she was aware of what those tamales were all about. He was just pretending they didn't understand how the grown-up world works.

Marta, Paola, and Lucia ran back to the living room and curled up on the couch to look out the window again. Lucia and her sisters clung to the windowsill like abandoned house cats, looking longingly at their father. Their papi owned their hearts, and they weren't ready to share him with anyone else.

As their papi drove away, Lucia turned to Marta. "Well?"

Marta pushed herself away from the window and jumped off the couch. "My money's on Carlota's extra-gooey chocolate chip cookies."

"Really?" Lucia asked.

Back in the kitchen again, Paola took a plate from the rack on the counter behind them and started piling tamales onto it while Marta picked a red, wet corn husk off the counter and showed it to Lucia. "He ate three of them."

Lucia gasped. "And he took more for lunch!"

Marta put her fist over her lips and squeezed her eyes tight. "I'm not saying I hate him," she finally said. "But he's not my favorite person right now."

Lucia could tell Marta was trying hard not to cry, but then something broke inside her, and her sister hung her head and started sobbing—a low, sad sob that escaped from her lips like an hilo, a long, loose thread full of lament, and Lucia knew her sister was coming undone.

Lucia reached out and hugged Marta.

"It'll be okay," Lucia whispered. "I'll talk to him."

"What's wrong?" Paola asked. "What happened?"

"Don't eat that," Marta screamed at Paola. "Why is she eating them?"

"Why shouldn't I?" Paola asked, biting into a tamal before putting her plate on the table. "They're good. I think it's nice that Doña Lola brought them over."

"And what about the rest of her stuff, huh?" Marta pushed away from Lucia. She grabbed the plate of tamales off the counter and tossed them in the garbage can. Then she turned around and stared at Paola, who sat wide-eyed at the kitchen table. "How are you going to feel when Doña Lola puts her dresses in Mami's armoire? What are you going to do when she takes down these curtains and rips off this tablecloth to make room for her junk?"

Paola put down her tamal and frowned. "What are you talking about?"

"Wake up!" Marta yelled, flailing her arms up and then bringing them down to hit her thighs. "They're trying to get with Papi, you moron!"

"What? Who?"

"All of them! Doñas Lola, Mirna, Carlota, Juanita! They're all trying to take Mom's job!" Marta screamed, her eyes bulging and her face red with agitation.

Paola pushed her plate away and started to cry.

Anguished, Lucia tried to hug her little sister, but Paola rushed out of the room in a hurry. Her chanclas slapped against the linoleum as she ran to her room and slammed her door shut.

"Don't say anything," Marta said, and she left the room, too.

Lucia sighed.

She tried checking on Paola, but her baby sister hid under her covers and told Lucia she needed to be alone. Instead, Lucia stepped out into the garden and started weeding the area around the tomato cages, so nothing could interfere with the growth of the vines. When she was done, she sat back and looked all around.

Beyond the vegetable garden, she saw her mami's man-zanito. Its small, oblong fruit had begun to ripen, blushing a dark reddish brown. Lucia collected the tiny apple-like jujubes in her apron and took them inside to rinse.

From her place at the sink, Lucia saw Paola leave her room and quietly step into the restroom. Her hair was disheveled, and Lucia could tell from her sister's pout that she'd fallen asleep after all that crying.

Lucia gave the manzanitas one last rinse, dried them, and put them in Mami's favorite summertime container. She set the yellow bowl in the center of the table as a healthy counteroffer to Doña Lola's greasy tamales and went back out to select some roses for the centerpiece vase.

And in all that time, Paola didn't leave the restroom.

Marta came out of her room and headed for the bath-room. She tried the door, knocked, and listened. She did that several times and didn't receive an answer for a while. But when Paola finally yelled, "Leave me alone," Lucia went over to check on her.

"Paola?" Lucia jiggled the doorknob. "Are you all right?"

When there was no answer, Marta and Lucia stared at each other.

"Are you still mad at me?" Marta asked, putting her ear to the door.

When they heard a soft sobbing, Lucia and Marta begged Paola to open the door.

"What is it?" Lucia kept asking. "What's wrong? Did the tamales make you sick?"

"Honey, whatever it is, you can tell us," Lucia insisted. "We're your sisters."

After a while, Marta went to the kitchen and came back with a thin steak knife. She picked the lock and opened the door, and they went in to see what was going on. The first thing Lucia saw when they got in the room was the box of feminine pads sitting on the counter beside the sink.

Paola was sitting on the rim of the bathtub, staring at it. "I think . . . but I'm not sure . . . it's my period," Paola cried, and she covered her face with her hands. "I don't know what to do with those stupid things."

"¡Ay, manita!" Lucia said, using the Spanish word for "little sister" because she felt so close to her in that moment. *This is it*, she told herself. *This is what's missing. This is what mamis are for. If she were here, if the Santa Muerte hadn't taken her, mami would be hugging Paola. She would be comforting her, making it all better.*

So, Lucia did the only thing she could do. She put her arms around her baby sister, kissed her forehead, and pushed the wisps of hair away from her forehead. "There's nothing to it," Lucia said. "Marta and I are here; we'll show you what to do."

Marta took out a pad and started showing Paola how to use it. Because Marta had it all under control, Lucia took the box of pads and started to put it away, but it felt light, so she shook it and looked inside.

Horrified, Lucia counted the contents twice. There were only five more feminine pads left in the box.

Marta checked the box and said, "That's not enough for two."

"Three," Lucia said. "I am three or four days away from getting mine, too."

Paola started to cry. "What are we going to do?" she wailed.

Lucia was cradling Paola and Marta was rubbing her back gently when there was a soft knock at the door. Because it was broken now, the door opened, and the sisters screamed.

But it was only their papi, checking up on them.

"What is it?" their papi asked, concerned. "What happened?"

"We're busy!" Lucia pushed the box of feminine pads behind the toilet with her foot, hoping her father wouldn't see it.

But their papi's eyes widened, and the color washed off his face so quickly—he looked like he'd just seen La Santa Muerte herself.

Lucia was sure she was too late.

"Oh!" he said. "I'm sorry. I didn't mean to . . . Um."

When the girls all said, "We're fine," and "Dad!" and "Can you shut the door, please?" their papi reached for the handle.

"I'll fix the door . . . later . . ." he said as he pulled it shut.

"Can you take care of this?" Lucia asked Marta, and her sister nodded.

When she left the bathroom, Lucia found her papi standing at the end of the hall, by the living room, with his hands stuck deep into his pockets.

"What are you doing home so early?" Lucia asked, shuffling her feet as she looked at the floor.

"I finished the chambita," her papi explained.

"Oh, okay," Lucia said. But then, because her papi didn't say anything else, Lucia raised her eyebrow and asked, "Did you need something? Want me to fix you lunch?"

"No, no." Her papi shook his head. "I'm okay. I ate those tamales."

"Oh, yeah, I forgot," Lucia said, and she forced herself not to think about that.

She wanted to mention the pads to him, to tell her papi they were out of supplies, but he looked so uncomfortable that Lucia stayed silent.

"Okay, then," her papi said, and he turned around and walked away.

Lucia went back to the bathroom, but Marta and Paola were done in there, so they went off to their room. Because it was almost dinnertime, Lucia went into the garden and picked a lovely calabacita off the vine. Zucchini casserole was Paola's favorite, and Lucia wanted to make the dish for dinner. However, when she came back in, Lucia's papi was waiting for her in the kitchen.

"Listen," her papi said. "I got paid on the spot for that little chambita. Want to go to the grocery store?"

The store? Yes. Yes. They have pads there, Lucia thought, because that's where her mami used to get them. Aisle thirty-three. Lucia knew exactly where they were on the shelf.

That's when it hit her. How was she going to get pads for her and her sisters? Papi didn't know anything about that sort of thing. But Lucia didn't know if she should explain it to him. What is it he had said that day in the kitchen, right after the funeral: *I didn't sign up for this!*

There must be a way, Lucia told herself, because she had to figure out how she was going to tell him that she needed a box of "supplies." If her mami were still alive, Lucia wouldn't even have had to tell him anything. Her mami would have just gone to the store, put them in her cart, and paid for them herself. Her papi wouldn't even have been there for the transaction. But in that moment, Lucia knew that was all on her. It was her turn to be a "mother"—to make sure the monthly supplies for herself and her sisters made it home every month.

In the truck, Lucia looked over at her papi.

He was absorbed in his "man's world," just driving around town without a care in the world. *How should I do this?* Lucia wondered as they pulled into the grocery store parking lot and her papi got out of the truck.

Should I wait until his back is turned and just grab them and drop them in the basket and hope he doesn't notice? Lucia wondered as her papi grabbed a cart and started rolling it down the first aisle.

What if he skips that aisle, just walks right past it, and heads out to the register because he thinks we're done? What then? Because he doesn't know what we need; he's not psychic, Lucia told herself as her papi put four boxes of fideo—the thin vermicelli her family loved to eat like a soup—into the cart and moved on to inspect a huge bag of elbow macaroni on aisle fifteen.

Just be brave. Just be casual. It's no big deal, Lucia

kept telling herself aisle after aisle after aisle. The words pounded in her ears, throbbed at her temples, and ended up giving her a headache the size of Texas.

Lucia rolled the thoughts around in her mind until she and her papi were two aisles away from the feminine products, and then she knew for sure nothing was going to happen. It had become very clear to her—it was definite—she couldn't ask him to get feminine pads for them!

She just couldn't!

It wasn't his job. He said it himself, that very first day, after their mother's funeral. *I didn't sign up for this!*

By the time they were on aisle thirty-one, in the health and beauty section, Lucia's knees were as weak as over-cooked fideo and her stomach hurt. Her armpits were sweat factories. Her cheeks were ripe manzanitas, and her eyes burned because she was trying hard not to burst into tears.

Her papi, however, had piled the cart full of groceries and was happily pushing it around the store, oblivious to Lucia's dilemma. As he read a bottle of dandruff shampoo, Lucia decided that it would be best to wait until they were out there—in the parking lot—before she said anything. She had it all figured out in her mind. She'd wait until her papi was busy putting groceries in the truck, and then she'd tell him she'd forgotten to get *their* shampoo and ask him for money.

It was the perfect solution. But would it work? What if he decided they didn't need extra shampoo? What if he said they could use Mami's shampoo?

"What's on your mind?" Her papi's voice startled Lucia, and she jumped back and almost knocked down a display of hair mousse.

"Nothing," Lucia said, straightening the slim bottles on the display case behind her.

Her papi pushed the cart forward, following Lucia as she moved down the aisle.

"Well, that's not what it looks like," her papi said. "Pareces colibrí, all flutter and no song. You haven't said a word the whole time we've been here."

"Well, that's what not having anything on your mind looks like, doesn't it?" It was more of a sassy statement than a question.

Her papi turned the corner and parked their cart in front of the endcap, so that he and Lucia were standing between aisles.

"What is it?" her papi asked. His voice was soft, low, and Lucia could tell he was really concerned. And he should have been, because Lucia figured with Paola getting her first period, it was official—they weren't kids anymore. The pimples and periods and hormones were all happening. Right now.

Lucia thought about how she and her sisters all reacted differently to Doña Lola's tamales, and suddenly she was angry. Angry at Doña Lola. Angry at their situation. And angry at Papi for not putting a stop to it.

Her papi didn't know it yet, but his world was about to get a whole lot more complicated. They were all señoritas now, which meant more responsibilities. More growing pains. More opinions. The way Lucia saw it, her papi didn't need to be adding anything to his plate.

Not yet, anyway.

"Well?" her papi asked, still waiting for an answer.

"Did you really like the tamales?" Lucia asked, looking at her papi directly for the first time since she'd started making the rounds of the store.

Her papi frowned. "I did, yes," he admitted. "Didn't you?"

"No," Lucia said. "In fact, I didn't like them at all. And Marta hated them. She really, really hated them!"

Her papi put his hands on Lucia's shoulders because a sudden rush of emotion had come over her and she was crying now.

"Hey, it's okay," he said.

Then he looked at Lucia as if he were waiting for her to connect the dots for him.

Lucia didn't want to embarrass her papi, not at the

grocery store, in front of a bunch of strangers, but she couldn't stop crying.

"Would you say you liked the tamales more than the chocolate chip cookies?" Lucia finally asked, keeping her eyes averted, looking down at the worn linoleum tiles on the floor as she hiccupped, because she just didn't know how to tell him what she was thinking—what she was feeling deep down inside. "Because you don't have to choose, you know. You don't even have to eat any of it. Not the lemon meringue or the brownies or the empanadas. Nobody would blame you if you did . . . but you don't have to. It's not . . . I know we're a lot of trouble . . . And I know . . . I know you didn't . . . you didn't sign up for this. But we can do without any of that."

Her papi pulled Lucia into an embrace. He took a deep breath, sighed, and said, "We're not talking about tamales anymore, are we?"

Lucia wiped the tears out of her eyes and shook her head.

"No, we're not," she whispered, because something was caught in her throat and she just couldn't get the words out. "I'm sorry we're so much trouble."

Her papi reached down and caressed Lucia's cheek. "Oh, baby, I wasn't talking about you when I said that I didn't sign up for this."

"You weren't?" Lucia asked, looking up at her papi's soft hazel eyes.

Lucia's papi smoothed back her hair and stopped at her earlobe, giving it a little tug. "No. I was talking about those awful women," he said. "I didn't sign up for any of that. Hey, you know who made the best tamales?" he asked.

Lucia shook her head. "No."

"Your mother," her papi said, leaning over to kiss the crown of Lucia's head.

Before she could stop them, a second bout of tears started rolling down Lucia's face. Her papi took her in his arms and pressed her against his chest.

"It's okay," her papi said. "We'll get through this."

Lucia wiped away her tears and gazed up at the aisle numbers hanging from the ceiling. Thirty-two. Thirty-three. They'd almost made it. Two more aisles and they would have been there.

Lucia knew she could still tell him, but she also knew she couldn't go through with it. She couldn't put her papi through one more ordeal that day. It was enough that he'd had to stop and calm his hija mayor down in front of all the people who went quietly around them so as not to disturb them.

"Are we done?" Lucia asked her papi because, except

for that box of pads, there was nothing else they needed from the health and beauty section.

"Just one more thing," her papi said. "Come on."

But instead of turning back and heading toward the food aisles, Lucia's papi pushed the cart forward and turned into aisle thirty-three.

He stood in the middle of it with his hands on his hips. "Small. Medium. Unfragranced." He read the words on the boxes aloud to himself. "Ah, here we go. Assorted sizes. What do you think?"

Lucia grinned and nodded—relieved.

Her papi offered Lucia the big box of pads. She took it and found a space for it between the chocolate cookie cereal and the giant package of toilet paper in the cart. In that moment, when her papi smiled and pushed their grocery cart out of aisle thirty-three, Lucia knew she and her sisters had nothing to worry about. Their mami's love lived in their papi's heart.

Mother Mary, Do You Bleed?

ERIN ENTRADA KELLY

Eleven-year-old Jessa Ramos regretted the question as soon as it left her mouth. Her mother, Rosalita, narrowed her dark eyes at her from across the square table.

"How can you ask such a question, anak?" she said.

Her mother gathered a pinch of tuna and white rice with her delicate fingers and popped it into her mouth. Once upon a time, Jessa believed all mothers ate rice with their hands. Now she knows differently, so she uses a fork like her white friends at school.

Jessa shrugged and stared at her plate. "I was just wondering," she mumbled.

It didn't *seem* like a terrible question, but it hovered in the air like a dark cloud, nonetheless.

Did the Virgin Mary get her period?

It didn't seem like a terrible question at all.

"Mother Mary is clean and pure," her mother continued after she swallowed her food. "She would never bleed like that."

Jessa was on the second day of her period.

She bled and bled.

When Jessa had seen the drops of blood in her underwear the day before, she hadn't called for her mother first. She called for her sister, Reyna.

Reyna was fourteen years old. Reyna was beautiful. Reyna was popular. Reyna knew how to do things, like apply lip liner and curl her hair, and Jessa never knew *how* or *when* or *from whom* Reyna learned them. Reyna was born into the world with all the answers. Jessa was born with nothing but questions.

"Reyna!" Jessa called from the bathroom. "Reyna!"

Reyna's bedroom was adjacent to the hallway bathroom, so Jessa assumed her sister would hear her and come to the rescue, even if she'd be annoyed about it.

Reyna rarely needed rescuing of her own. It was another way she and Jessa were different.

Unfortunately Reyna had recently become obsessed

with the *Dreamgirls* Broadway soundtrack and when Effie White sang "And I Am Telling You," Reyna turned it up at full volume.

Their mother came to the bathroom instead. She knocked twice and opened the door. Jessa would have preferred her sister, but at least it wasn't her dad. He wasn't home, anyway.

Jessa showed her the stained underwear. The undies had little cartoon pandas all over them, which seemed strange with the blood.

"What should I do?" she asked.

Jessa wasn't scared or joyful or disgusted. She knew it would come someday, after all. And here it was.

Her mother reached under the sink and took out a maxi pad.

"Use these," her mom said. "Never tampons."

"Why can't I use tampons?" Jessa asked.

"Because you're a good girl," her mother replied. Before Jessa could ask anything else, her mother hurried on, showing her the sanitary napkin. "These are the wings."

"Wings?" Jessa said. She imagined the generic Kotex flying like a bird. She couldn't help it—she giggled.

"Why you laughing?" her mother asked.

Jessa shrugged. She didn't know how to explain it.

Things were just funny sometimes. She didn't know why.
They just were.

Her mother never really understood her jokes, anyway.

Ten minutes later, Jessa had a clean pair of underwear with
a pad stuck to the crotch. She sat on the bed and helped
her mother fold the laundry.

"How old were you when you first got your period?"
Jessa asked.

"Twelve."

"Will I get cramps?" She had thought it would hurt,
but she didn't feel anything. She wished she felt crampy—
it would make it more real. Right now she just felt like a
girl with something bulky in her underwear.

"Probably," her mother said.

"How long will I have it?"

"For decades and decades."

"No, I mean—how long until it goes away again? A
week?"

"It depends."

"Do you still get your period?"

"Of course. I'm only thirty-eight, anak."

Thirty-eight sounded ancient to Jessa.

"Did Lola show you how to put on your pad, like you
showed me?"

Lola was Jessa's grandmother. Lola lived in the Philippines. That's where Jessa's father was now. He'd lost his job a few years ago and it had been difficult for him to find a new one in the States, so he spent months in the Philippines sometimes, helping with his family's grocery store in Cebu. Jessa didn't mind too much—he called as much as he could, and he always referred to her as his "little parsnip," for no reason at all—but she wished she could visit the Philippines, too, one day. She wondered if she would be just as popular as Reyna if she lived in a place where everyone looked like her.

And she wanted to try halo-halo, a sweet Filipino dessert her father had told her about.

"She did," her mother said, as she matched pairs of socks and folded them over. Jessa preferred to bunch hers together in a ball, but her mother always made her un-ball them.

"Does Lola still get her period?"

"I don't know, anak," her mother said, her voice laced with irritation. "You ask too many questions."

"What's wrong with asking questions?"

"You don't need to know everything on this earth," she replied. "You'll get all your answers in Heaven."

That night, Jessa snuggled in bed with Whiskers, her stuffed animal. Whiskers was a cat with bells in her tail.

Whiskers jingled every time she moved. The only person who knew she still slept with a stuffed animal was her best friend, Madison Blakely. Madison didn't sleep with a stuffed animal, but she once admitted that she kept a blankie under her pillow.

Jessa wondered if they were the only eleven-year-olds in the world who still cuddled with stuffed animals and blankies.

Jessa closed her eyes.

Time for prayers.

Technically she should have been kneeling. But some-times—most of the time, truth be told—she felt too lazy to kneel. Plus she didn't like the way the carpet dug into her knees.

When Jessa was younger, she asked for individual blessings. *God bless Mama, God bless Papa, God bless Lola, God bless Reyna, God bless Madison, God bless my teachers,* on and on. Back then, she was worried about forgetting someone, so she'd name almost everyone she knew, with a few notable exceptions, like Emily Bolger, who called her names, and Martin Piper, who spit in her Coke once. It became exhausting, so she'd decided on a shortcut: *God bless all the people I love.* God was all-knowing; He'd know whom she meant.

"God bless all the people I love," she whispered now.

It was intimidating, talking to God. When Jessa imagined Him, she saw a long, white beard, a wrinkled face, and furrowed eyebrows, as though He was watching her and didn't like what He saw. God seemed like an angry grandfather.

That's why she preferred talking to Mother Mary.

And tonight she had questions.

"Mother Mary," Jessa whispered, "do you bleed, too?"

She had the sense that this was a bad question. Her mother's reaction only confirmed that. But Mother Mary never judged. You could ask her anything. There were no images of an angry Mary or a vengeful Mary. She was perpetually peaceful.

"Is it bad to have a period?" She paused. "I started mine. But it doesn't feel like anything. Do you think it should feel like something?"

Mother Mary didn't answer, of course. But Jessa felt better having her questions out there, traveling up to Heaven.

"Are you wearing a tampon?" Madison asked. She was cross-legged on Jessa's bed. Jessa sat across from her, leaning against the headboard with Whiskers in her lap.

"No," Jessa replied. She was on day three of her period. Her underwear still felt bunchy. This morning, she'd slipped on a pair of plain blue underwear. She had others, of course, but the prints and colors seemed too babyish now. "My mom says I can't wear tampons because I'm a 'good girl.'"

Madison's blond eyebrows furrowed. "What does that mean?"

Jessa shrugged.

"My mom wears tampons," Madison said. "She says they're more comfortable."

Jessa's chest warmed, the way it did when she was embarrassed. She didn't want Madison to think she was saying anything bad about Madison's mom. She loved Mrs. Blakely. Mrs. Blakely had long hair, which she pinned on top of her head with a pencil. And she let them eat fast food anytime Jessa spent the night.

"I think it's because she doesn't want me to . . . you know . . . stick anything in there," Jessa said.

"Carmen says that when you put a tampon in, you lose your virginity," Madison whispered, as if the room was full of eavesdroppers. She said it matter-of-factly, as if she didn't know if it was true or not.

Carmen Lynch was like Reyna—she was a girl at school who seemed to know everything.

One of the reasons Madison and Jessa got along so well was because neither of them knew anything about anything.

"Do you think that's true?" Jessa said.

Madison shrugged and pulled out her phone. "Let's google it."

Jessa didn't have a phone yet. Her mother said she would get one on her twelfth birthday. Everyone had a phone but her. That's how it seemed, anyway. Madison got her phone years ago. On days when Jessa was feeling particularly sorry for herself, she'd think about all the things Madison had that she didn't—an iPhone; round, blue eyes; thick blond hair that people always complimented; good grades; a mother who answered all her questions.

Madison scrolled and scrolled. "There's nothing wrong with using tampons. It doesn't make you lose your virginity." She put the phone down and looked at Jessa. "I guess your mom just doesn't want you to, you know . . . stick things in there."

There was a moment of silence before they both erupted into laughter. They laughed until their sides hurt. They weren't sure what was funny. They just knew something was.

Reyna's popularity seemed effortless. At school, Jessa's brown skin and slanted eyes were a liability. The kids said things like *Are you Mexican or something?* or *What are you, Chinese?* and it was clear that they thought both of those things were bad. And when Jessa mumbled that she was Filipina, their expressions didn't change, so that wasn't the right answer, either. But somehow Reyna had managed to turn her Filipino-ness into an asset. The kids thought she was "exotic."

According to their mother, there were two reasons being Filipina worked for Reyna and not Jessa. First of all, Reyna had a pointed nose, which she inherited from a mysterious Spanish ancestor buried deep in their family tree. Jessa had a "Filipino nose," as her mother called it, which meant it was too flat.

Second of all, Reyna had a better personality. Their mother had never said those exact words, but Jessa could read between the lines. *Your sister is always happy, not asking questions*, her mother would say. *That's why she is popular.*

Being popular took up a lot of Reyna's time, so she didn't have much to offer Jessa. Any time Jessa knocked on her door, Reyna released a loud sigh, which is what she did on the fourth day of Jessa's period.

"What do you want?" Reyna said when Jessa poked her head in.

Reyna was laying bathing suits on her bed. Summer had just begun, and she was going swimming with friends the next day. Reyna had hordes and hordes of friends.

Jessa only had Madison.

Dreamgirls played from Reyna's phone, which was perched on her dresser. Reyna swayed to the music as Jessa closed the door behind her.

"I have a question," Jessa said.

Reyna usually answered Jessa's questions, even though they irritated her. Probably because Reyna knew that there were certain questions their mother couldn't—or wouldn't—answer. All of Rosalita Ramos's answers came from the Bible.

"Surprise, surprise," said Reyna.

"I was just wondering," Jessa began. She sat on Reyna's bed and looked at the bathing suits. She hoped her sister chose the red one. It was the prettiest, in Jessa's opinion. "Why do we get periods?"

Reyna lifted the yellow bathing suit from the bed, laid it across her body, and stared at herself in the mirror.

"Every month, our uterus gets ready to carry a baby. So the lining gets thicker," Reyna said, turning this way and that. "What do you think of this one?"

"I like the red," Jessa said. "So, what does the thick lining have to do with having a period?"

Reyna tossed away the yellow. Picked up the red.

"If we don't get pregnant, then our body has to get rid of all the extra lining," Reyna said. She tilted her head at her reflection. "It comes out as menstrual blood."

"Oh," Jessa said. "How do you know all this stuff?"

"I took a sex ed class last year." Reyna looked at Jessa's reflection in the mirror, her eyes round. "Don't tell Mom." She whispered: "I had to forge her signature."

"I won't," Jessa said, and she meant it.

Maybe Reyna wasn't so perfect after all.

Every month, our uterus gets ready to carry a baby.

That meant Mother Mary probably had a period—right?

The thought calmed Jessa as she lay in bed that night after her prayers.

Jessa tried to imagine the Virgin Mary getting her period and calling for her mother. But what would she have worn? There weren't any tampons or pads back then, were there?

How did she stop the bleeding?

It was difficult to imagine this woman—with her milky skin, submissive smile, and flowing robes—having a period. Every image Jessa had ever seen of the Virgin Mary was the same, as though she was only capable of one emotion. But Jessa wasn't sure what that single emotion was. Kindness? Acceptance? Love? Understanding? Empathy? Sorrow?

Jessa couldn't comprehend feeling one way all the time. She was a whirlwind of emotions on any given day.

When school was in session, she would wake up annoyed because she didn't like mornings. When she got answers wrong in math, she was frustrated and disappointed. When the kids at school made fun of her by pulling their eyes and making them slant, she felt sad and sorry for herself. When she was around Madison, she felt happy and loved, but she also felt jealous and guilty. When she was around her mother, she felt confused and frustrated, and sometimes happy.

Jessa could feel many different things all in one day, sometimes all at the same time. There were nights when she cried for no reason at all, and days when she laughed just because.

But Mother Mary was always the same.

Jessa nestled deeper into her pillow.

"I wish I was more like you," she whispered.

The spots in Jessa's sanitary pad had faded to a dull pink by the end of the fifth day. That night, she sat on the couch and watched television with her mother.

There was an image of the Virgin Mary on the wall next to the television. There were images of Mary everywhere, but this was the one Jessa examined the most—not just because it was near the TV (although that was part of it), but because it disturbed and scared her. She'd never tell her mother so, but the image—*The Immaculate Heart of Mary*, it was called—showed the Virgin pointing to her heart, which was bright red and shining in a pool of light. The heart was pierced straight through with a dagger, and it wore a crown of thorns.

Despite all these things—the dagger, the open heart, the thorns—Mary still looked peaceful and complacent. Her face resembled that of a creamy porcelain doll.

Jessa laid her head on her mother's shoulder and stared and stared at the image as the show moved into a commercial break. Her mother kissed her on the head. For all of Reyna's perfection, Jessa knew one thing for certain: Reyna did not share a reverence for Mary like Jessa and her mother did. Their mother often called Jessa her *good, good girl*. She never used those words for Reyna.

This was their private time together, watching their favorite program on Sunday nights while Reyna danced around in her room. In moments like this, Jessa's heart swelled with so much love for her mother that she didn't know what to make of it. There were times when her mother pinched Jessa's nose and said it was too flat. There were times when her mother said she asked too many questions. There were times when she said she should be more like Reyna. In those moments, Jessa thought she actually hated her mother, which felt like the cruelest thing a daughter could ever feel.

But right now, she loved her mother so much, she could stay on the couch forever.

Jessa wondered how she could feel so many different things about one person.

"Mom?" Jessa said, her eyes still on Mary.

"Yes, anak?"

"How do you think the Virgin Mary feels in that picture?"

Her mother lifted her head.

She didn't have to ask which picture Jessa was referring to.

"Love," her mother said after a brief pause.

"Love?"

"Yes. See how she is showing us her heart? Even though her heart is hurting, she still loves us. All of us. Even when she is suffering, she feels love. That's what she is telling us in the picture."

Jessa wondered how she would feel if she suffered like Mary. If she was turned away from every inn. If she had to watch her son get beaten and crucified. If she had a dagger in her heart and a crown of thorns.

She decided she would not feel love.

She would be angry.

I wish I was more like Mary, she thought.

"You know, anak, when I was a little girl, there was a woman in my barangay who said her rosary every night in front of her statue of the Blessed Virgin. She was a very devout woman. One morning, she ran out into the streets, yelling, 'Umiiyak ang Birhen! Umiiyak ang Birhen!'"

Jessa sat up so she could look at her mother's face. She loved her mother's stories from back home. She'd heard most of them already, but she'd never heard this one.

"What is 'umiiyak . . . ang . . . Burr . . ?'?" asked Jessa. She didn't know how to speak Tagalog; the words were strange on her tongue. She liked to try it sometimes just to see how it felt in her mouth, but no matter what, the words were heavy and garbled and didn't know how to shape themselves.

"It means 'The Virgin is crying! The Virgin is crying!'" her mother replied.

Their show came back from the commercial break. Jessa reached for the remote and muted it.

"Mother Mary was crying?" Jessa said.

Her mother nodded solemnly. "Yes, anak. We all went

to see. The Virgin was crying blood. She was crying for the sins of the world. She was crying for us because she loves us. We all prayed. For days and days, we prayed. *'Blessed Mother, forgive us.'"*

Jessa imagined people crowded around the statue, clamoring and praying.

"What did she look like? The statue, I mean. Did she look like a doll?"

Her mother paused. "Mother Mary is whatever we need her to be."

When her mother turned the volume back on, Jessa laid her head on her mother's shoulder again.

But Jessa wasn't watching the television.

Her eyes were on the Blessed Mother.

Mother Mary is whatever we need her to be.

Jessa imagined the Virgin's nose. The more she imagined it, the wider and flatter it became. No more narrow angles.

Her skin deepened from snowy white to chestnut brown.

Her eyes changed shape and color, too. No more sparkling, Western blue.

And her hair was thick, black, and slightly coarse.

She was on the other side of the world, standing in a

faraway house, watching a woman pray. So full of love and sorrow that it made her cry.

But not regular tears.

Tears of blood.

Because Mother Mary bleeds, too.

Just like me.

The Arrival

NIKKI GRIMES

KEEPING TRACK

I hit the school track
for my morning sprint,
running full out,
head held high enough
to sniff victory,
ready as ever
to break my own record,
feet fleeting as any guy,
strong thighs pumping,
arms swinging free
till I see a boy
on the sidelines

licking his lips,
staring at my breasts
bouncing wild
against my chest.
Resisting the temptation
to fling my arms
across my body,
I slow to a jog, instead,
pretend like I planned to
all along.

ARRIVAL

A sticky wetness
between my legs
sends me running
to the girls' room.
In the safety of the stall,
I discover a horror
down *there*,
in my underwear:
a smudge, a smear,
a trickle of red.
I'm hemorrhaging life!
Will I soon be dead?

QUESTIONS

Deep breaths, deep breaths,
I tell myself
while wadding up toilet paper
to staunch the wound.
But. The. Blood. Won't. Stop!
What's happening to me?
Do I have a disease?
Did I eat something bad?
What did I have for breakfast?
What did I have for lunch?
Maybe I cut myself down there.
That's possible, right?
But if so, when? How? Where?
Calm down. Calm down,
I tell myself.
Still my heartbeat drums
like the seconds before
a qualifying meet.
Only this time,
when the gun goes off,
I'm standing still
while a jillion questions

race around
the track of my mind,
but no answers are waiting,
and there's no finish line.

IN SEARCH OF ANSWERS

I pad my pants with tissue,
leave the stall,
scrub my hands,
then make the hundred-yard dash
to the nurse's office.

SCHOOL NURSE

"No need to worry,"
says the nurse. "It's just your first
menstruation, dear."
My blank stare makes her reach out
and take my hands in her own.

"It's your period.
It's all perfectly natural.
Your body's changing.
You're becoming a woman.
Periods are part of that."

I look at my breasts,
proof of unwanted changes.
Now here's another.
And track? What about that?
I don't even dare to ask.

HOME

I go home wearing
a sanitary pad. So
why don't I feel clean?

CRAMPS

Stabbing pain that night.
Mom lets me skip school
the next day.
Slowly, the awfulness subsides.
Slowly, I realize I'll survive.

MIRROR, MIRROR

Months pass,
and my changing body
becomes more familiar.
And, like Nurse said,
my period is just
part of the package.

The new curves
aren't half bad,
I suppose.
This woman-me
definitely looks different,
but I'm strong still,
my bronze legs
as muscular and capable
as ever.

TRACK MEET

This morning,
I do a few lunges
to limber up
before I hit the track.
I cut my eyes at the boy
who likes to
lick his lips at me.
I square my shoulders,
press my chest out,
and give him a stare that says,
"You ain't even
got a chance."
Message received,
he looks away.

I smile and brace myself
at the starting line,
ready to take off
and carve my initials
on the wind.

Heavenly Water

VEEDA BYBEE

I feel like I've been walking for weeks. In reality, it's only been two hours since we left the car at some remote gravel parking lot in the middle of Yosemite National Park. For the next three days in this California forest, my own two legs are the only source of transportation. A backpack the weight and size of a very large dog is strapped to my shoulders. To keep from tipping over, I turn slowly to face Dad. "How much longer?"

Dad peers up at the bright-blue sky. The wind sweeps across his face, sending a few strands of black hair across his forehead. He wipes his brow. "I'm not sure, Callie," he says. "I think we're close."

Dad points to the stream of water flowing next to us. "We follow this river. Our campsite is next to a waterfall."

I try to peer down the narrow trail, where my friend Vanessa and her dad are somewhere up ahead. All I see is more trees. More mountain. More water. More misery.

I groan. "I hate the wilderness."

Benny turns around. My ten-year-old brother has been ahead of me this entire hike. He's rubbed it in, too. Knowing that he is better than me at something has given him energy. I'm two years older than Benny. He likes to remind me that despite our age difference, he's almost as tall.

My brother leans on his walking stick and waits for Dad and me to catch up. "I bet the Greens are already at the campsite," he says. "The Shumans, too."

Our family, the Yangs, trail far behind. Mostly because of me.

Stopping next to my brother, I take a swig of water from the Nalgene water bottle attached to my pack. "So what?" I say, letting the water flow down my throat. Even warm, it's refreshing.

"It just means we are last." Benny sighs. "I hate being at the end."

He ticks off a list with his fingers. "Our last name is at the end of the alphabet. My birthday is in December. I'm the youngest in the family and now look. Last family to arrive at our campsite." He frowns at me. "I bet Vanessa's family has already set up their tent."

I glare at Benny. "You know my pack is heavier than yours. Nei Nei packed a ton of things in my bag."

Since we've been at Dad's all weekend, our grandmother has insisted on helping us get ready for this big backpacking trip. She helped me pick out clothing that would dry fast. My pack holds clothes, toiletries, and our inflatable sleeping pads. Dad's bag has the tent, the camp stove, and heavier items. Benny is mostly carrying food.

Dad places a hand on my shoulder. "Your grandmother was very kind to help pack. You know she just wanted to make sure you had everything for the trip. It's not her fault."

I adjust the shoulder straps on my pack. I can't start hiking again. I'm so tired. I just want to put this backpack down for a while. I need to distract Dad from getting us back on the trail. "Do you know she slipped me a note along with my pads?"

Dad blinks. He seems stunned. "A note for . . . *what*?"

I hold a hand out. "Don't make this strange," I say. "I'm on my period right now. Nei Nei included a note about it in my backpack."

Dad swallows. "There's nothing strange about being on your, um. Period."

His voice drifts off into uncertainty. Dad is trying to show he is totally cool talking to his twelve-year-old daughter about menstruation. I got my first period last year. I think he knew this, but it was around the time he was moving out. A lot has changed since then.

"I got a note, too!" Benny says. "What does yours say?"

I use this moment to shrug the pack off my shoulders. Benny takes his bag off, too. Dad doesn't object. Talking about my period seems to be distracting him. The extra weight is gone, and for the moment, I feel lighter.

"When I was getting ready for the trip," I say, "Nei Nei got excited when I told her I needed pads. She said this is a time for my Heavenly Water."

Benny looks disappointed. "She didn't say anything cool like that in my note. What's Heavenly Water?"

I can't believe I'm having a conversation about my period with my ten-year-old brother and single dad. It's keeping the backpack off, so I'll take the chance.

"Some sort of Chinese water-power connection to my period," I say. "Nei Nei was shocked I didn't already know about this. I had to remind her that Mom is white. She doesn't have things like water or moon cycles to explain menstruation."

Benny digs into his front pockets and pulls out a meat stick. He takes it out of the plastic wrap and starts to chew.

"Wait," he says, pausing in mid-bite. "Is this heavenly thing something that's going to happen to me?"

Dad kicks a small rock in our path. He runs his hands through his hair. I wonder if he knew the great outdoors would pull out such great conversations. "Everyone goes through puberty," Dad says with a little laugh.

It sounds forced, and he is talking fast, like he's trying to remain calm. "Women, um, experience something different."

I reach into the side pocket of my backpack and pull out a piece of paper. "Different is right," I say. "I'll read what she wrote."

Dear Callie,

You've reached an important moment in your life. How wonderful to experience Tian Gui, Heavenly Water. This is a life force that will give you strength. How fitting for you to receive such a gift when you are close to nature.

You are made of pure Qi, or heavenly energy. Gui is water that gives life, the essence of energy needed to give life. Like the clouds above, this is a gift showered upon you. Your time of menstruation is renewing.

Life giving. Think of this during your weekend as you
begin this time of replenishment.

Love,
Your Nei Nei

I put the note back into my pack. "Supposedly I'm
going to get some water-energy mojo from my period this
week."

I can't believe I'm talking so openly with my brother
like this. Maybe this crisp mountain air is doing something
to my brain. I'm either braver or just care less.

Benny looks a little jealous. "My note from Nei Nei just
said to not eat all the M&M's in one day. Also to stay away
from bears."

Dad laughs. For real this time. I think he welcomes a
pause from talking about menstruation. "Your grandma is
right," he says. "We have three days out here. Ration out
the chocolate."

He looks at Benny and me. "We've had a long-enough
break. Let's get going."

I sigh. The break wasn't as long as I'd hoped. "Is it really
a vacation if you have to be thoughtful with chocolate?"
In jest, I shake a finger at Dad. "Why can't you be like

other divorced fathers on their weekends and take us to Disneyland or buy us each a Nintendo Switch?"

Dad smiles. It's contagious. I smile back at him. Just like that, we are joking again. It's almost as if we haven't spent the last few months apart.

"Being in nature will work wonders for us this weekend," he says. Dad tips his head to the side, as if he's concentrating. "Do you hear that? The rushing water?"

All I can hear is the dread in my heart, knowing I need to pick up my pack again. "No."

Benny stops in mid-chew. "Nope, I don't hear anything."

"It's there." Dad looks a little happier, as if he's the one drawing energy from the Tian Gui. "This means we are close. Come on. Let's follow the water."

He gives me a wink. "The Heavenly Water."

I put a hand to my face. Maybe the air is too thin up in the mountains. Why in the world did I tell Dad about my period?

We set back on the path. The closer we get to the campsite, the harder the hike gets. The trail is no longer straight but goes uphill in a zigzag pattern. As we huff and puff up the incline, Dad tells us this is something called a switchback. He says switchbacks supposedly make climbing hills easier, but I think he's wrong. I don't think anything but a car or pulley with wheels will make this hike more bearable.

I stab my walking stick into the dirt with each step. "We keep going and going, and it feels like we aren't getting anywhere."

I hear the whine in my voice, but I don't care. I'm sweating so much, I feel damp everywhere, even in my shorts. This backpacking thing is hard.

"Just a few more bends, Callie!" Dad says, also out of breath. Even Benny has slowed, hiking right next to me now.

After a few minutes of walking in silence, Benny quickly raises his head. "I can hear the water!" he says. "It sounds fast. I bet the waterfall is just ahead."

His steps quicken and he disappears around the corner.

His words are like an open curtain, parting the way for me to listen to what he could pick out. I can hear the water, too. It's a quiet sound at first. Like a distant rumble. Then the water comes more clearly. The white noise flows around me, as though it's calling me in.

The promise of rushing water down a mountain gives me strength. I push myself to keep going. One foot in front of the other until suddenly I'm at the top of the trail.

The trees part around a small campsite with two tents already set up. There's a bathroom close by and just beyond the site is a stream of water, flowing from the edge of a small cliff.

Benny is already at the river, splashing around. "We made it!" he whoops.

I look over at Dad. He's grinning. I smile, too. I take my pack off and dip my hand into the river. I take in the rushing water and the majestic outline of trees against rocky mountains. The water is cool and seems to flow all around me. Maybe Nei Nei was right. This Heavenly Water has given me strength.

Months ago, Mom said we would be spending our first summer after the divorce with Dad. I didn't know if I could even be in the same room with him. Now here we are. At the same waterfall together. Dad and Benny splash around. When Benny manages to jump on Dad's back, I giggle. We are all so happy to be together.

I hear a squeal of excitement. Vanessa is running over. She's tall and white. Blond hair flies around her face. "You made it!" she yells, wrapping me in a hug.

Dad gives her dad a fist bump, and the fathers chat about the hike. They walk over to the campsite, and Dad starts to set up our tent.

Vanessa is jumping up and down in her pink sneakers. "I'm so proud of you, Callie," she says. "Look, you didn't even die on the first day like you thought you would."

I laugh. "Well, the first day isn't over yet."

I watch Benny try to skip rocks in the water. I think of Mom, and how even though this trip is just a bunch of dads and their kids, she would like to see us here. I dig into my pack and pull out my phone. "Will you take a photo of me and Benny?" I ask Vanessa.

"Sure!" she says.

I hand her my phone. I put my arm around Benny. It's really not fair how tall he is already. I get on my tiptoes, but he does the same. We are trying to out-height each other and just end up giggling. We smile at Vanessa and the phone.

"Hey, Yangs!" Vanessa laughs. "This is a happy moment. Open your eyes for the picture!"

Her words hit like cold water, snapping me out of this happy moment. All the feelings of triumph and accomplishment over making this hike disappear as my friend turns the shape of our eyes into a joke. My smile is frozen on my face.

Benny looks up at me with shock in his eyes. I don't know what to do.

Neither of us say anything to Vanessa when she hands me back my phone. She runs ahead to her tent while Benny and I trail behind. Last, as always.

I look over at Benny. "She didn't mean that," I say.

Benny meets my eyes. The very ones that were just shamed. "Nei Nei says our Asian eyes are beautiful," he says. "She says they are like shining half-moons when we smile."

I hold my breath. This sounds familiar. Nei Nei's loving words warm me. They take over Vanessa's numbing joke.

I think of my grandmother, and how she knew I would need extra strength this weekend. Maybe not just from the hike, but from hurtful words from a friend.

I look over to the water. It's like I can feel its energy flowing through me. "Nei Nei is right. Our eyes are beautiful."

The rest of the afternoon, I'm polite to Vanessa and the others. When we explore around our campsite, I try to brush off the sting of her comments. I can't help it. It doesn't go away. Her words replay in my head, over and over again. *Open up your eyes. Open up your eyes.*

This evening, I finally do. I'm outside the tent when I look up to the sky. Above, stars shine like bright flecks of salt on dark paper. Its vastness is overwhelming, but in a comforting way. All those tiny stars giving off light. Next to them hangs the white glow of a half-moon smiling.

"You okay, Callie?" Dad says. I look over to see him standing next to me.

I'm quiet for a moment. "I don't know," I say. It's the truth.

Dad is thoughtful. "You've done some really hard things today. I think your grandma was right about the Heavenly Water."

I try to study his face to see if he's joking, but it's too dark for me to tell. "What do you mean?"

"Didn't she say something about your pure Qi? The heavenly energy? I've felt it from you," he says. His voice is even and still. I can tell he's not laughing.

The rushing river is all around us. I can hear the Gui, the water that gives life.

"Really?" I answer.

"Really."

The light of the moon shines bright on the water. Inside me, there is a feeling of renewal. This time of menstruation is giving me new strength. Dad places a hand on my shoulders, and we walk over to the rest of our friends.

We sit in the dark, next to the waterfall. With flashlights and camp lights flickering, our little group takes turns alternating between chatter about our day or bursting into random songs. When Dad belts out a haunting and powerful version of Dolly Parton's "Jolene," the other dads join in. There's something hilarious and spectacular watching a bunch of grown men singing a woman's country song.

When it's time to end the night, I walk over to Vanessa.

"Hey, can I talk to you?" I say.

"Sure!" She links her arms in mine. "You've been really quiet today. Are you really tired?"

"Something you said earlier today has been bothering me, and I wanted to talk to you about it."

It's Vanessa's turn to freeze. "Oh?"

I pause and listen to the sound of the running river. Its life force seems to flow through me, giving courage. I've never talked to a friend like this before, but something about today made me feel like I could. Maybe it was conquering the hike, breathing in the fresh air, or the Heavenly Water from my period giving me renewed life. Whatever it was, I knew that I could stand up for myself. "When we were taking a photo by the river, you said Benny and I needed to open up our eyes. It made me feel really sad that you joked about my appearance. Especially because mocking Asian eyes is something that is very racist."

Vanessa drops her arm from mine. "I am so sorry. I just meant—" She stops herself. In the dark, I can see her shake her head. "No. I don't need to make excuses. Whatever I meant it to be, that was a terrible thing for me to say."

Silence hangs between us, like the large glowing moon above.

I clasp my hands in front, like a twisted knot. "This was really hard for me to say. I know you care about me and wouldn't want to say anything to hurt my feelings. But it did."

Vanessa steps closer. In the darkness, I can see her trying to meet my eyes. "I'm a total jerk," she says. "I'm really sorry. I was wrong."

Her words are kind and sincere. I nod, even though she may not be able to fully see me. "Thank you," I say, my voice strong like rushing water.

We hug, and I forgive my friend. We walk back to our tents, arms linked. When we get to my tent, Vanessa finds Benny. He shines his flashlight on us as we approach.

"Hey, Benny," she says. Vanessa's voice warbles. "Callie told me that I was wrong to joke about eyes. She's right. I just really wanted to say how sorry I am."

Benny doesn't say anything for a moment. "Our eyes are beautiful," he says simply.

Life force flows through me, like the Heavenly Water that it is. "Like shining half-moons," I say.

The cool air rustles the trees, and the river bubbles with music in the background.

Benny reaches behind his back and holds out a Ziploc bag. Its contents are half gone. "So, do you want some chocolate?

Sometimes You Just Need Your Prima

EMMA OTHEGUY

The school nurse sent us home with a box of samples, but I'm never using brand-name pads and tampons. That's how you catch "gustos latifundistas," which is what my mom calls it when you act like a rich person—like people who get candy at movie theaters or buy their kids toys at museum gift shops. I squish the box into the bottom of my backpack. It's not like I'm going to need it anytime soon. I'm the shortest girl in the fifth grade, so I don't think my body is getting grown-up stuff like periods yet.

My best friend, Leila, stacks her sample box on top of her binder and pulls her backpack zipper tight. The loose-leaf in her binder is always perfectly straight, even though it's jammed with notes, since she's the head of the Student

Council and a part of Kids Helping Kids. Our teachers say she's ready for middle school. My mom says she's ready for the boardroom. I say she's just plain *ready*. Leila looks like an eighth grader. She's tall and she has to wear a bra. When she started wearing one, I asked my mom to get me one so we could match, but my mom said it was ridiculous to wear a bra with nothing to go in it. Sometimes my mom talks to me like I'm a little kid.

On the walk home from school, Leila asks, "Want to come to youth group tonight?"

I groan. Leila's youth group is too goody-goody for me. "Can you come to my apartment instead?"

"I can't skip. We're making relief kits for the Dominican Republic people, remember?"

I hold back another groan. The way Leila says "the Dominican Republic people" sounds so *weird*. Why doesn't she just say "Dominicans" like everyone else on the planet?

"You know how important this is, Mira."

I do know. There have been two Category 5 hurricanes in the Caribbean this year. My mom is from Cuba, which is in the Caribbean. We've been sending packages to her family there. My mom always used to save my nicest hand-me-downs for Sonia, her cousin Nuria's daughter, but since the hurricanes, we send stuff every month and not just clothing. Now it's everything my mom can think of.

"Yeah, yeah, I know it's important."

Leila keeps talking about the relief kits. Her youth group gets pictures from ministers in different countries in the Caribbean, like Cuba and the Dominican Republic and Haiti, and Leila describes how the people there have to boil water and how they haven't had electricity since the hurricane. When she talks about the Caribbean, it doesn't sound like a real place. It's like the people there are characters in a sad fairy tale Leila is making up. They're not her family.

Sometimes I want to tell Leila off. But sometimes I wonder if she really *does* know more about the Caribbean than I do. My mom only talks about Nuria and Sonia when there's a reason, like if we need to go to the store to buy vitamins for them. Otherwise it's like Nuria and Sonia are top secret, along with everything else that happened to my mom in Cuba. She doesn't like it when I ask questions. Sometimes Cuba feels like a big gap between me and my mom, one I can never fill. At least Leila gets photos of all those people.

Luckily, Leila switches to talking about Tania Goldberg, who got her period last weekend.

"I mean, Tania is like a little *kid*," Leila says. "She drinks *juice boxes* for lunch, and at Student Council meetings she doodles pandas. What's adult about her? How is *she* the first person to get it?"

"Yeah," I echo, trying to be nice. "It's weird."

Leila makes a *humph* noise, so I add, "You'll get yours soon. Really."

I mean it, too. Sometimes I wonder, if I were as grown up as Leila, would my mom trust me with her stories about Cuba? Maybe then I wouldn't be left out, listening to my best friend talk about people in the Caribbean but knowing so little about my own family there.

"¡Edelmira!" my mom calls when she walks in the door that evening. She always calls me by my full name because she's the only one who likes it. My dad thinks Edelmira is an old lady's name, so he and everyone else call me Mira (pronounced *Mee-ra*) for short. The only problem is "Mira" also means "Look!" in Spanish, so it can get confusing.

My mom waves me toward her room. "¡Ven a ayudarme!"

While my dad entertains my three-year-old brother, Diego, I help my mom. She just did a big Discount World shopping trip for supplies to send to Nuria and Sonia. First we dump the bags onto my mom's bed. We don't want to mail all the bulky packaging the stuff comes in, so I grab a box of Ziploc bags.

We pour the contents of Tylenol and vitamin bottles into the bags, then we add individually wrapped beef-flavored bouillon cubes and frutas secas, which you would think means dried fruit but really means mixed nuts. Then we get to the tampons and pads, tossing the folded instructions when we take them out of their boxes.

"The nurse gave us some samples today," I mention casually.

"¿Samples de qué?"

My face feels a little hot. "You know. 'Equipo femenino.' It was the class where we get *the talk*? About periods."

"Equipo femenino" is what my dad calls pads and tampons. This is probably why he doesn't help my mom with packages for Cuba: he would be afraid to even touch the stuff. Sometimes when my mom laughs, it's like a cackle, sort of croaky. This is one of those times. "They sent you to that class?" She flicks her wrist as if she's waving away a bug, but it means, *We're a long way away from that.* "¿Y tú tan pequeñita? Me parece que te falta."

I roll my eyes and try to pretend I don't mind. "Yeah, I *know* I'm not going to get it for a long time because I'm small for my age. I was just telling you."

As my mom zips the brown packing tape across the box, she clears her throat.

"You know what to do when it happens, right?"

"I'm informed." I try to sound like it's no big deal, and my mom looks relieved. I guess it would be pretty unpleasant if she had to explain periods and sex and all that to me.

Leila and her mom have these marathon heart-to-hearts, but my mom and I are mostly business. Then I remember how Leila thought she would be the first in our class to get her period because her mom was the first to get it in *her* fifth-grade class.

"Mami," I ask, "do you know when you got *your* period? Then maybe I'll know when mine is coming."

"I was the last one."

"The last one in your class?"

"Nope. The last one in my family." My mom reaches for a permanent marker and writes the address on top of the box.

My mom's parents weren't exactly around, so she was raised by her grandparents, with Nuria, her cousin in Cuba, and her other cousin, Beatriz, who lives in Boston. They were all less than two years apart.

"Huh," I say. "I guess that's sort of surprising. Aren't you older than Nuria?" I hold my breath while my mom finishes writing the mailing information, wondering if she's about to spill the story of her first period, if she'll let another little tidbit about Nuria and Cuba drop, another drop I can use to try and fill the space between us.

But she just dots the *i*'s, caps the marker, and carries the box to our entry.

★

While my mom goes to the shipping store, I lay on the couch and watch my dad and Diego build with blocks.

"Hey, Pa," I say, propping my head up. "Were Mami and Nuria friends when they were little, or were they always like this?"

"Like what?"

"You know"—I search for the words to describe how my mom works so hard to send Nuria these packages but then sometimes acts like she doesn't exist. "Like so . . . *transactional.*"

That makes my dad laugh. He asks me where I learned such a fancy word, and I joke, "What are you sending me to school for? Vocabulary!"

My dad chuckles again, but then he's quiet for a while, maybe because Diego is bugging him to build a bridge, or maybe because he's thinking. Then he says, "Mami and Nuria were very close when they were kids. They could have been twins."

There's a knot in my stomach. "Then what happened?"

My dad sighs. "I've talked to you about the Revolution, Mira."

Sixty-something years ago, a dictator called Castro took over the Cuban government. People call it "the Revolution" and talk about it all the time, even though it was before my parents were even born. Castro was a communist, which meant he didn't want wealthy people to have their own houses or businesses, and definitely not fancy things like jewels or private schools. He wanted the government to have more control. The Revolution and communism were *supposed* to be these beautiful things that helped poor and sick people in Cuba, but since then, there have been times where it's hard to get food or medicine, and people don't have freedom to say or do stuff that the government doesn't like. Most of my mom's family didn't agree with communism and came to the United States as soon as they could.

"What does the Revolution have to do with Nuria?"

My dad looks up from Diego's blocks and meets my eyes. "It's the reason Nuria stayed in Cuba. Twenty years ago, when Mami and Beatriz came here, Nuria decided that the Revolution was wonderful and she wanted to be a communist."

I imagine Nuria wearing an olive-green uniform, ready to shout orders at people, because my dad says in communism you have to follow rules and you can go to jail just for writing something bad about the government. If Nuria became a communist, I would get why my mom didn't want to hang out with her, except for the single Most Important Thing about my mom: Family is important to her.

She might not be the bake-you-cookies kind of mom, but she makes sure you eat three big meals and do your homework. One night when there were sirens wailing outside the apartment for hours, she told me how she was scared when her family had to leave Cuba, but she knew that her cousins and grandparents would always be with her, and she would always be with me. My mom doesn't say comforting stuff like that a lot, so I always remember that night.

It helped when my mom said that, and I believed her because my mom and her other cousin, Beatriz, are still best friends. They talk every single day, and when my mom is worried, she calls Beatriz and always hangs up smiling. "Sometimes you just need your prima," she'll say with a sigh. My mom survived leaving Cuba because of family, and that means I'll survive whatever happens to us in New York because of family.

I roll the other direction, so I'm facing the back of the couch and stuff a cushion between my knees. Of course my mom loves Nuria. She sends her a big package every month, after all.

But they don't talk, not the way Beatriz and my mom do.

"Papi?" I ask.

"Hmmm?"

"What happened twenty years ago? That made Nuria decide to become a communist?"

Papi shrugs. "People just change."

The thought of changing, of becoming someone my mom wouldn't want to talk to anymore, scares me more than the sirens ever did.

On Tuesday afternoon, I get home from school before anyone else. Nice. I serve myself a chunk of guava paste with a big slather of cream cheese, but before I take a bite, my stomach starts to hurt. I head to the bathroom, and just as I'm sitting down on the toilet, it's like someone popped a Gusher candy. A glug of something sticky drops into the bowl, except it's brown, not red. I stare at it in shock.

It doesn't make sense. There's no way I'm getting my period. I mean, I'm the smallest girl in my grade. For a while I sit on the toilet and wonder if I'm having the world's weirdest poop, but as another dark, jellylike blob oozes out, I know I'm not.

All of a sudden, I'm angry. Of all the stupid information the nurse gave us about the different tubes in your body, she could have told us that your period isn't necessarily red. When she said "blood," I and everyone else thought "red." Instead I've got this sticky rusty-looking stuff. Gross.

I stuff a wad of toilet paper in there and waddle into the living room, hoping no one walks in. This is just too awkward to explain. I grab my backpack off the floor and go back to the bathroom. The box of sample pads is totally smooshed, but I rip it open and grab one. I stuff the wrapper and the box in my backpack when I'm done, then splash some cold water on my face.

When my mom gets home and asks me how school was, I almost tell her about my period. I want to know if they're usually brown or if mine is weird or what. But even just thinking that makes the tips of my ears hot.

"School was good." For a second I have this wild fantasy where my mom guesses that I got my period, and we order takeout and cuddle up and chat about it until past bedtime. Instead, my mom asks if I've finished my homework and starts cooking dinner.

That night I borrow my parents' tablet and settle into bed. The weight of pillows plus the tablet feels good on my stomach. I'm about to call Leila, but then I think about how upset she was when Tania got her period. I open up the camera app just so I can see my own face. I don't *look* like someone who just got her period, but Leila might guess.

I swipe around the tablet. I feel like getting your period is a big-enough deal that you should tell *someone*, but I don't have anyone to tell. I end up clicking on one of my mom's social media accounts.

As I'm scrolling mindlessly through her boring birthday-announcement messages, my eye catches a name I didn't expect to see: Sonia, Nuria's daughter. I tap, and a blue bubble pops up.

Tía, the message begins, and my hand trembles.

The message goes on in Spanish:

> *I know we have never met and that you and my mom aren't close anymore. But my mom says family is important, and I know you must love her because you always send us such nice things.*
>
> *I'm writing because we've had a hard time since the hurricane. My school is closed and we're still patching up our house. Sometimes my mom mopes around all day.*
>
> *I didn't know who to talk to, so I'm telling you. We're so grateful for the ayudita you send us each month, but I think right now my mom needs her prima more than the packages.*
>
> *Sonia*

I read the note one more time, hot and guilty all at once. Then I check when it was sent. Months ago.

My mother got this message from her niece, and I wonder, Did she call Nuria? Sonia's words don't match my idea of Nuria as someone who shouts orders. Sonia makes her mom sound sensitive. My stomach hurts worse than ever.

It's as if my fingers are attached to someone else's hands, and I type, *Hola, Sonia. Did you get my reply?*

Almost immediately, three dots appear. Someone is typing on the other end, someone near and far at the same time, right here in this tablet and also more than a thousand miles away in Cuba.

Tía! No, I didn't know you had answered!

I bite my lip. Then I decide to come clean. My Spanish isn't exactly perfect, but anyway I type: *It's actually Mira, not my mom.*

I imagine Sonia making a face while she types, so when her words appear I'm glad she doesn't sound mad.

Hola, Mira! It's SO cool to hear from you. I can't believe we've never met!

For a long time I stare at the screen. Then I write, *How's your mom now?*

She's okay. She's still sad. The hurricane was hard for her. She loves Cuba so much and works so hard to make people's lives better.

I dig my fingernails into the inside of my palms. Sonia makes it sound like Nuria is some kind of superhero, when I know that Nuria is a communist.

My mom doesn't have any family in Cuba besides me anymore, Sonia types.

Now I imagine being left all alone while my mom and dad and Diego move to another country. The thought makes me shiver, and I wriggle down into the bed, pulling the comforter up high.

My mom told me that she and your mom used to be like twins, Sonia adds. *But I've never heard from your mom, so I don't really believe it. I just thought writing was worth a shot.*

Suddenly my fingers are flying across the glowy tablet keyboard. *Don't feel bad. My mom is really weird sometimes. There are things she doesn't like to say. She's not one of those people you can just talk to. Can you tell your mom stuff?*

I tap the screen impatiently while the three dots blink. Maybe it'll turn out Nuria is like my mom, that this is just something they picked up growing up together, that it's not me or my fault that it's so hard to talk to my mom about some stuff—

Are you kidding me? My mom is my best friend. Every night we cuddle on her bed and tell each other everything that happened during the day.

My mental picture of Nuria is changing so fast that I can't rearrange my brain pixels fast enough. She doesn't sound like a scary communist, that's for sure. She sounds like someone you could talk to about awkward things and not feel embarrassed. Things like periods.

I wish my mom were like that, I write. *Don't get me wrong: she's great. She has a hard job and she still has time to cook for us and all of that. But she's not someone you can talk to about life. I got my period today and I don't even know how to bring it up.*

Sonia's reply comes right away.

You got your period? Congratulations! I got mine a few weeks ago. You should totally tell your mom! When I got mine, my mom let me nap all day and made my favorite foods.

I shake my head, as if Sonia could see me. *My mom might make fun of me. She thinks I'm a little kid because I look so young.*

So she'll be impressed that you have it!

More likely she'll be mad that I'm not more mature now.

Getting your period doesn't mean you have to be mature. And it doesn't even mean you have to look grown up (I'm sure you look great, but you said yourself you look young for your age). It just means your body is ready for your period. That's it. You should tell your mom!

Okay. I'll think about it. Then I add, *Hey, when you got your period, what color was it?*

It was a gross color. Like, sometimes magenta, sometimes brown, always gooey.

EWWW. Mine is gooey, too.

Sonia sends back a puke emoji, and I laugh out loud. Then I type, *Thanks, prima.*

Hey, can you do me a favor? Can you ask your mom to reach out to my mom? I just think it would make my mom less sad.

I take a big shaky breath.

I can try.

After I delete my exchange with Sonia so my mom doesn't see it, I spend the week thinking of ways I could tell my mom about Nuria. I could tell her that I got a letter from a long-lost relative about some treasure buried in the yard of my mom's old house in Cuba so she would have to contact Nuria to dig it up—but that sounds far-fetched, even to me. Sonia's words swirl around my mind as I change pads and clean up my period mess, hiding everything in my backpack. The bleeding has slowed to a trickle by Friday, and I'm about to go to the bathroom to change my pad one last time when my mom walks in. I freeze, my backpack slung over one shoulder.

"Hi, Ma," I say. "I was just, um, going to the bathroom."

"With your backpack on?"

I slap my hand to my forehead. "Right! Forgot I was wearing it."

My mom raises her eyebrows. Before she can ask any questions, I blurt out, "Nuria needs you!" Not the slickest way to bring it up.

My mom looks like she's been slapped.

"What do you mean Nuria needs me? What do you know about Nuria?"

"Not much," I say coolly, "considering you never talk about her."

"Of course I talk about her."

"Not the important things. It's like—you don't even want me to know my aunt!" I clench my fists, angry at my mom for giving up on her own cousin so easily when I know now that Nuria can't be all bad. "You act like she's a monster or something. If I decided to"—I try to think of something bad I might do someday—"if I change, are you going to shut me out, too?"

"What have you done?" my mom asks, as if I'm a toddler who just painted the walls with lipstick.

"Nothing!" I'm angry and my underwear feels full and wet, and I'm sick of the way my mom never trusts me, like even carrying a backpack into a bathroom is suspicious. "People change, Ma, I could be different—I'm going to be a *teenager* in two years—and you're like, you abandoned your cousin just like that."

"I didn't *abandon* her, Mira. Por Dios, where is this coming from—?"

"I read your messages!" I shout. "I read that Sonia sent you a message to say that Nuria was having a hard time, and what did you do? Absolutely nothing!"

My mom has iron in her voice when she asks, "You read my messages?"

I try and look casual. "It's not like you ever check them."

"Edelmira! You know better than to read someone else's messages."

But I'm not apologizing. "If you won't tell me anything, why shouldn't I?"

"Edelmira, ¡Cállate ya! You have no idea what you're saying, and you know nothing about Nuria. I forbid you to contact them again."

"I can talk to whoever I want! They're my family, too, you know."

My mom sets down her shoulder bag, the armpit of her silky work shirt sweaty and stained. "Edelmira, you have no right to touch my messages. If you don't want to apologize, you can go to your room." Then my mom turns her back firmly and goes into the kitchen.

When I see Leila on Monday, she is still obsessed with her youth group project. After school, we sit on a bench while she goes on about it.

"Look at those little faces, Mira," she says, holding up her phone to show me a photo of a kid whose cheeks are streaked with mud, dressed in a tank top full of holes. "They must be so miserable."

"Leila, what do you know about them?" I snap. "People in the Caribbean are more than just sob-story photos."

Leila looks hurt. "Mira, I'm trying to help people who are *suffering.*"

Things are hard, I think, remembering what Sonia said about her school. But Sonia also said her mom needed her prima more than packages.

I roll my eyes at Leila. "Just because someone's going through a hard thing doesn't mean they want you looking at them like a museum exhibit. You don't know those kids. My family was hurt by the hurricanes, Leila—are you going to show me photos of them, too?"

"I—I—" Leila stutters. Then she clams up her mouth, and we sit there on the bench staring at each other.

"I forgot about your family in Cuba," Leila says in a high-pitched voice. Then she adds, "Sorry," and hangs her head.

I know I made Leila feel bad, but I tap my foot

impatiently on the pavement. "It's just I was messaging with my cousin Sonia—"

Leila gasps dramatically. "The *communist's* daughter?"

"Except that's the thing!" I explode. "Everyone thinks they know people in Cuba just because of *one* thing about them. You think the kids in your photos are just poor. My mom thinks her cousin is just a communist. But they're nice and sensitive, too. Sonia is really cool. Like, super cool. If she came here, she would be the most popular kid in our grade."

Leila's back stiffens, and I can tell she's jealous, but instead of saying anything, she swipes through her phone. I think she's ignoring me, but then she holds up the photo of the kid with the tattered clothing. She drags it to the trash icon.

"Maybe," Leila says slowly, "your cousin Sonia could send us some pictures of where she lives? That would be more . . ." She takes a deep breath and starts again. "I bet that would be nice. For both of us."

I swallow hard and my cheeks feel hot, but I'm not angry anymore. Suddenly I think that Leila is more than one thing, too: sure, she's sensitive and she can't stand it when other people are more grown up or cool than she is—but in the end, she takes my side.

★

I'm waiting for my mom in the entry. We don't have long before Diego needs to be picked up, so I am standing up very straight, trying to look like someone who deserves to be spoken to like an adult.

"I have to talk to you," I announce.

My mom sets down her bag on the couch, eyeing me. "Yes?"

"It's not fair that you don't talk to me about Nuria and Sonia. I'm not a little kid anymore, and I should be told what's going on."

My mom laughs. "Mira, you're in the fifth grade."

"But I'm not a baby anymore, and I can understand stuff." I straighten up a little more. "I got my period last week."

"But . . ." My mom looks confused.

"You were at work until dinnertime, anyway. I didn't need you." But my breath catches in my throat as I say that, like I'm about to let out a sob or something, so I add quickly, "I just need to know why you would ignore someone you used to love."

"I still love Nuria," my mom says slowly. "I think about Sonia and not knowing her and being a part of my life, and my heart aches."

"Then why wouldn't you *talk* to them?"

"When Nuria and I talk, it's about politics. We can't

help ourselves. We fight. Nuria thinks Beatriz and I are sell-outs, I know she does—and I think she put pie-in-the-sky wishes above family. It's easier not to talk. It's easier for me to give her the things rather than the words she needs."

Which makes sense, because my mom has always given me everything I need—food and clothing and all the rest—but I have to ask for the words I need.

"But Nuria wasn't like that when you were growing up? She was like you and Beatriz . . ." I search for words to explain it. "She lived under communism but she didn't agree with it?"

"People change," my mom says simply.

It's these words that are eating me most, these words that have made me snap at my mom and my best friend twice in the same week. "What if *I* change? What if I live in a foreign country someday, will you stop talking to me, too? I mean—I'm getting my period now. You think it's never going to happen because I'm so short, but someday I'm going to look different and, who knows, I might *be* different."

My mom has a sad and sort of scared look, but she doesn't snap. "Whoever you are, and wherever you went, I would be your mom. I would make sure you had food and clothing and medicine, no matter how far away you lived. I should think that was obvious from . . . certain things I do."

I nod, gulping.

"I didn't have that. A mom who could take care of me. So I've tried to be the sort of person who is capaz. Who knows how to handle things, for your sake."

After a long while, I say, "Mami, if you won't talk to Nuria, can I talk to Sonia? Like, if she and I were friends, would you be okay with that?"

My mom sighs. "Do you promise not to sneak?"

I grin.

That evening, I log into the messenger app—my own account, with my own name—and write to Sonia.

I finally told my mom about my period. I don't know if she'll write to your mom. But can I write to you sometimes?

Are you kidding me? Of course!

Also, my friend Leila would love to meet you someday. She wants you to send her pictures.

I lean back on the pillows and hit send.

Sometimes you just need your prima.

Cannibal at the Door

ELISE MCMULLEN-CIOTTI

I missed Aunt Callie's house. I don't know why I couldn't just stay there. I was old enough to take care of Aunt Callie. Eleven-year-olds can do all kinds of things. We can go on adventures, solve mysteries, and even win cooking competitions. Why was this lady—*Ms. Avalon*, the paper taped to her desk said—telling me that I had to go back home to my mama?

Didn't Ms. Avalon know what it was like living with my mama? Didn't she know that she'd thrown me and all my clothes out on the porch the last time I was there?

"Twyla, your mom has worked real hard to get better," Ms. Avalon said. "She's healthy. She has a steady job at Chili's as a manager. And the family house has been all cleaned up." Ms. Avalon smiled at me, looking relieved like she was on some kind of victory lap.

I could feel a hot coal burning inside me, ready to shoot flames at the woman, her paper name tag, and the whole darn room. "Does she still have a boyfriend?" I asked, crossing my arms.

"I don't see anything about that in the file, hon. What I do know, though, is that your aunt Callie is still in the hospital, and she's been there twice in the past three months. She's been a good caregiver, but she's getting too old to be taking care of young children."

"I'm in middle school," I said.

"That doesn't make your great-aunt any younger."

You don't know my family, I thought, staring her down, coal flames flying out my eyes. "Doesn't my mama have to pass some kind of test before she can even see me?"

"She's done that, Twyla. And I know she misses you a lot."

Right, I thought, rolling my eyes.

I'd been at the Johnsons' house with some other kids for the past two weeks, and it was *not* okay. Those people lacked any kind of warmth or humor. Aunt Callie was filled with humor. And no one in the Johnson house was Cherokee. Weren't we supposed to be placed with other Cherokee somehow?

"Is Aunt Callie going to be okay?" I asked. This was the longest Aunt Callie had ever been in the hospital, and that was worrying me. In Cherokee, she's not even called my aunt but my grandmother, my taline agilisi. She was the most important person in the world to me, my only real family. What wasn't this lady telling me?

"Yes, hon, she's going to be okay. Don't you worry about that," she said, giving me that reassuring smile all adults think looks convincing.

I had no intention of going back to Mama. I was going home. Real home. "I'll wait for Aunt Callie to get out of the hospital," I said. "I don't want to deal with any boyfriends."

"I just can't do that, Twyla. I'll be at the Johnsons' first thing in the morning, and we'll head over. It's going to be okay."

All day at school, I tried to remember the stories Aunt Callie had told me about being strong in the face of danger, because I was terrified. When the last bell rang, it dawned on me. *I know!* I thought. *The one she told us last Christmas!* I already felt a little better.

Last Christmas break, my best friend, Byrdie, and his little sister, Fiona, had come to Aunt Callie's for a sleepover. We had been friends since forever, and they never made me feel bad about my mama. They were the closest thing I had to a brother and sister. If their family wasn't living in that tiny garage apartment, I know Social Services would have let me stay with them instead of the Johnsons.

We had sat in a circle in Aunt Callie's tiny living room, wrapped in afghans that smelled of the cedar trunks they were kept in and wearing matching bunny slippers she had bought us for Christmas. Byrdie on one side of me and Fiona on the other. Tortilla chips, hot sauce, cheesy sauce, pickles, and sliced apples lay out on paper plates in front of us. We pulled the afghans around our shoulders. The fire sparked and snapped and warmed us all around.

Aunt Callie was sitting in her wingback chair with a bowl of unshelled pecans in her lap. She'd crack them open and then use a little pick to remove the paper from their grooves. "You kids want to hear a Cherokee tale?"

"Is this a sad one or a happy one?" Byrdie asked.

"It's a spooky one," she said, leaning forward with her eyes wide and bulging. Byrdie jumped and then laughed so hard he got the hiccups.

"Are we old enough for this spooky one?" I asked, pointing at Fiona. I loved Aunt Callie, but sometimes Cherokee tales, well . . . they can be darn scary.

"Yes, ma'am, I do believe you are," she said, resituating herself back in her chair.

Aunt Callie began.

"Back in the day, when we lived in our village towns like the one over by the cultural center, hunters would go out in the hills and plains and valleys around us to hunt for deer and other animals for food. Before they had rifles, they had bows and blow guns. A Cherokee hunter could bring down a deer with one shot so as not to cause our deer brothers any pain.

"Sometimes they'd have to travel and hunt for days on end to get what they needed—all while keeping an eye out for attackers.

"One day, a hunter was keeping watch on a nearby ridge as his brothers were tracking a set of deer. When he looked out over the land, he noticed something that looked like stacked rocks moving under some trees in the distance. The rocks stood taller than a man, and in what looked like a set of large stone hands was a long wooden staff. When the rocks moved into the light, they would transform into the appearance of a man, and then turn back into rocks in the shade. Then the top rock turned just right in the light, showing the most terrible of faces. The hunter's eyes widened in horror. It was Stonecoat! Nunyunuwi! The giant cannibal monster that ate hunters for breakfast, lunch, and dinner."

"Aunt Callie, you said that we were old enough for this story," Byrdie said.

"And you are. Now, listen close."

We huddled together in our afghans and leaned in.

"When the hunter realized that the tall rocks were really the monster, he became very still and observant. He watched Stonecoat's movements, how he would point the end of his staff toward the hunters and then sniff the staff. The hunter knew this was how the monster could find them. The more hunters there were, the stronger the smell. The hunter was just about to jump down from his ledge and go warn his brothers when Stonecoat turned and pointed his staff toward the village, toward his home.

"'Oh, no,' whispered the hunter. 'If he makes it to our village, he'll eat them all!'

"The hunter hooted out the terrible sound of the horned owl, the signal that there was great danger.

"The other hunters came quickly. 'What is it?' they asked. 'What danger is in our midst?'

"The hunter told them that Stonecoat was en route to the village, and they must get there before Stonecoat did to warn everyone. They set out at once, as swiftly and quietly as they could."

Aunt Callie paused. She set her pecans down on the table beside her and got up and stretched a little. She then headed to the kitchen.

"Wait!" I said. "Is that all? Stonecoat is just going to go

down to the village and eat everyone? That's not a good story, Aunt Callie."

"Yeah, and what kind of monster is he?" Byrdie asked. "I've never heard of one made of rocks before."

Fiona sat there with her eyes big and wide. "I don't know if I want to know the ending."

"Now, now, hold your horses. I'm just getting some iced tea."

Our eyes rolled. It was such a silly saying, holding horses. Aunt Callie made her way back to her wingback chair. She smoothed down her shoulder-length white hair, which seemed to glow in the firelight.

"Where were we?"

"Stonecoat is on the way to the village, and the hunters are trying to get there first," I said.

"Howa," she said. "The hunters ran faster than they ever had before. Faster than they had when they trained to be hunters and warriors. And even though they ran as fast as they could, Stonecoat seemed to be moving just as fast. They began to doubt that they would get there before he did. They needed at least a half a day's lead on the ugly monster.

"Funny thing is, monsters need rest, too. So at one point, Stonecoat stopped for a while, sitting down on the ground, more like a bag of rocks falling from a hill than one of the deadliest monsters ever seen in all seven directions."

"What are the seven directions again?" Fiona asked.

"North, south, east, west, above, below, and right where we are at the center," Aunt Callie answered.

"Oh, yeah. I remember now. Go on, Aunt Callie."

Aunt Callie chuckled. "Osda. So Stonecoat had sat down like a bag of rocks in a field to take a rest. Thankfully the hunters were able to get a full half-day's lead on the monster, but they didn't know how long he'd sit there.

"When they arrived, they ran in calling for the elders. They called for the War Chief, and the Clan Mothers, and the Seven Men Council. They called for all the clans' Medicine Men and Women. They even called for their honored Beloved Woman, who was a War Woman.

"Then with great urgency, the hunters told them that Stonecoat was on his way.

"'He's the last of his kind,' the oldest Medicine Man said. 'Stonecoat is not from this world, and he roams the land taking only and sharing nothing.'

"A Clan Mother stepped forward. 'This monster owes us a large blood debt. He's been a plague upon our hunters for many generations. We do not want to flee. We want to defeat him.'

"The War Chief stepped forward. 'His name is also Stoneskin. None of our weapons can pierce his body.'

"A Medicine Woman spoke. 'I have heard that this

monster cannot live in the presence of a menstruating woman.'"

"Wait, what? Men-stroo . . . ?" Fiona asked.

"Men-stru-a-ting. Menstruation. It's when a woman has her monthly bleeding."

"Yuck!" Byrdie exclaimed. "Why on earth would I want to hear a story about that?"

I couldn't believe Aunt Callie was going to talk about menstruation. I mean, Byrdie and I had received the "talk" last year in fifth grade. They showed us a silly documentary about it that looked like it had been made a hundred years ago! We'd heard different things, though, since he was taken to a room with all boys, and I was sent to a room with all girls. I wondered where this whole Stonecoat story was going.

"There is power in blood, Michael Byrd. Life is in blood. Men and women both have had their hands in blood. These hunters had to respect the blood of the animals they brought back for food. And our warriors going into battle also had to be willing to shed blood for the good of our nation. Today, our doctors and nurses, who help the injured, they also hold life in their hands. And women have an honored place when it comes to blood, and don't you forget it. Because it is with the shedding of their own blood that they are able to bring life into the world."

When Aunt Callie said this, somewhere in the deep recesses of my heart, I knew it was true. "So, Aunt Callie," Fiona said, "are you saying that Stonecoat was afraid of menstru . . . menstr—"

"Menstruating women. That's right. Shall I keep going?"

"This is getting weirder and weirder," Byrdie said.

"You'll be fine, Byrdie. I'm not scared and I'm eight," Fiona said.

"I didn't say I was scared, Fi, just that it was weird."

"Uh-huh," Fiona said, unbelieving.

Aunt Callie cleared her throat, and we all looked up at her, ready for more.

"Then the old Medicine Man turned to the Beloved Woman, 'If you agree, would you join me in finding seven menstruating women to line up between our village and where Stonecoat now sits? We will place the oldest of these women the farthest out, and a woman in her first year of menstruation at our village gate. As he makes his way near, he will weaken.'

"'I agree with you,' she said. 'Our life-giving women will defeat this creature of death.'

"So they quickly called for seven menstruating women to gather at the entrance to the village. Once gathered, the oldest began walking in the direction Stonecoat sat, the next oldest followed, and then the next, leaving the youngest of the women at the gate.

"Sure enough, back outside the village, Stonecoat felt he had enough rest. He had also grown hungrier than he had felt in a long time. He looked up at the moon rising in the east and saw the light of a star hanging near it. He longed for those stars. He longed to be rid of this earth, where food was plentiful but there were none of his kind to share it. He was a lonely and hungry monster.

"As Stonecoat headed toward the village, he came first to the oldest woman. Pain seared through his stony skin. He looked upon his arms, and they appeared pierced. Blood seeped up from underneath. 'What are you doing here, woman? Why do you vex me?'

"He stumbled farther along, breathing heavily, until he came upon the next woman. This time he cursed her as pain seared in his legs.

"But the monster was too hungry and angry and tired and lonely to stop now. He would find a young hunter if it was the last thing he'd do!

"But he felt no relief, because with each woman he passed, he bled more and weakened more. So weak that his stony heart and mind began to soften. He could feel that this day could be his last.

"When he came upon the last of the women, one of

eleven years in her first bleeding, he fell to his knees in defeat. 'You,' he said. 'Your glow of life is my demise. I have been a selfish creature. I have stolen life from your people.'

"At that, the old Medicine Man stepped forward and, with seven men, drove seven stakes of sourwood through the monster."

"Whoa! That's cool!" said Byrdie.

"It's not cool—it's gross and sad!" Fiona said.

"How is it sad?" I asked her. "He was going to eat people."

"But he is the only one left of his kind and he's lonely."

"He still can't be eating people. Didn't you hear? Cannibalistic monster?" I said.

"So did he die, Aunt Callie?" Byrdie asked.

Aunt Callie smiled. "Yes, he died, but not before atoning for his wrongs. After many generations listening to hunters in the fields, he knew all their songs, so to atone, he taught us the songs we had forgotten, songs for good hunting."

"Was he just lying there with stakes in him singing?" Byrdie asked.

"Something like that, yes. But then they set him on fire."

"EEEEkkk! Aunt Callie, that's terrible!" Fiona cried.

Byrdie and I tried to suppress our laughter. "It's a story, Fi. Let's hear the rest."

Fiona looked at us as if we'd lost all reason. "Fine," she said.

Aunt Callie had a glint in her eye, like she was saving the best for last. "Setting fire to him was exactly what they needed to do. Fire purifies. So they set fire to Stonecoat. But remember, he wasn't like us. He was from another world. The monster looked up at the stars as his stone skin fell away, and he left the world singing. In his place remained a pool of red paint, filled with healing properties.

"The seven women who had lined up for the good of the village were honored that night. And the village was grateful."

Silence filled the living room.

"It looks like we need to put another log on that fire. Would you take care of it for us, Michael Byrd?"

"Yes, ma'am," Byrdie said, heading to the fireplace.

"Aunt Callie, do you think that when girls begin their menstruation, they become more powerful?" I asked.

"Well, they do take on a newer understanding of things. And with newer understanding comes wisdom. And with wisdom comes many ways to help our family, our clan, and our people."

*

When I snapped back from my daydream, I was already standing in front of the Johnsons' house. I stared at the bumpy sidewalk under my feet. The roots of nearby trees had crawled their way under the concrete slabs, causing them to rise and shift all kinds of ways. The trees rustled their leaves, just barely, as if they were waking from a nap. I wondered why Mama seemed so unwise. She had been menstruating forever. I decided I'd never be like her. Someday I'd be the right kind of strong. Someday soon, because I was eleven now. My time couldn't be that far away.

Ms. Avalon didn't say much on our drive over to Mama's. As we pulled into our old driveway, my heart began to pound. This was it.

I was barely out of the car before Mama was in front of me. At least I thought it was Mama. This woman was smiling—and she was normal sized. Gone was the bony frame and baggy clothes. She wore a brightly colored T-shirt that was tucked into a nice pair of jeans.

"Twyla, you're . . . you're so beautiful," she said, reaching her arms out to hug me. I flinched, stepping back. She quickly stopped and took my hands instead. I didn't remember when the last time was that she touched me. "It's good to see you." She smiled. I snatched my hands back.

Everything moved forward in a blur. I was upstairs in

my old house but standing in my new room. Ms. Avalon and Mama were speaking, but I wasn't listening. The room had freshly painted pale-blue walls, a desk by the window, a new, fluffy white rug on the floor by the bed.

I wish I could like it, I thought.

Because, I mean, it was nice. And Mama seemed nice, or nicer. But part of me wanted to scream and throw all this newness into a bonfire and set it ablaze. I set my backpack on the floor and looked out the window. The pecan tree blew its leafy fingers ever so slightly in my direction. I took a breath.

Mama's phone rang. She stepped out into the hall to take the call.

Ms. Avalon turned to me staring out the window. "Twyla? You okay?" she asked, but didn't let me answer. "What a beautiful room, right? Your mama has done a lot of work."

I turned around and met her gaze. "Does Aunt Callie know I'm here?"

Ms. Avalon sat down on the end of the bed. "Twyla, I know this is a lot for you to take in right now. But the truth is you're one of the lucky ones. It doesn't happen very often that I get to bring a foster child home to a parent who's gone above and beyond to make things right and show they really do love their kids."

"How do you know if she's really changed?" *And how do you know she loves me?* I wondered.

"Twyla, it's not easy getting over an addiction. Nor is it easy to face your mistakes. Your mama has done that. She's still doing that. She's been sober for about as long as you've been apart. She nearly died."

"May I come in?" Mama asked, returning from her call.

"This used to be your room," I said, not looking at her.

"Oh, I didn't need that much space, so my room is down the hall. Besides, this one has the bathroom attached to it. You'll be a teenager soon. Wantin' some more privacy."

You don't know me, I said with my eyes, but looking at the floor.

Mama showed us the rest of the house. Her room that smelled like new wood and perfume. The new downstairs guest room with aloe plants sitting on a small desk by a window. The kitchen and its adjoining living room with large windows from one end of the house to the other that looked out onto the porch.

"Everything looks wonderful, Shayla," Ms. Avalon said, pointing at a few pieces of paper and a pen on the table. "Why don't we finish up these papers, and I'll leave you to it?"

Mama read over the documents and signed here and there. Then Ms. Avalon gathered up her purse and the same manila folder she had had on her desk when we met.

"I'll be back Friday to check on you, Twyla, and see how you're doing." With that, she was out the door.

After Ms. Avalon left, Mama and I didn't really know what to do with each other. Finally, Mama said, "How about you go up to your room and get settled? I'll make us some lunch here in a while. Sound good?"

I nodded and escaped up the stairs. It's not like I had anywhere else I could go.

I sat in my room, angry, with a cramp in my belly, its pain radiating around to my back. After a few seconds, it subsided. I closed my eyes and tried to relax, but the anger returned like the snap of a rubber band.

I wished Aunt Callie was there to smile and pull me into one of her projects like scrapbooking or quilting. Doing things together always made the world better. Her stories made things better. I found my bunny slippers and my afghan in a box in the closet and took them over to the bed. I held a bunny slipper in my hands, looked into its stitched eyes. "Can't you send some secret message off to Aunt Callie and tell her I need her?"

Aunt Callie had told me that women are represented by the sun, because we have all that power of life deep inside us. I thought about her Stonecoat story. I could really use some extra courage right about now. Some sun power. Woman's power.

I could have used that power on my last night with Mama. The night I walked in on Tyrel sticking Mama's arm with a needle. The night I ran over to protect her, beating Tyrel with my fists, my little girl fists. The night Mama turned on me, telling me I was disrespectful. Eyes dazed and angry. Face pale and sweaty. The night she threw my clothes and me out on the porch. She'd said . . .

I didn't want to think about what she'd said.

Darkness rolled over my eyelids, and I fell into a fitful sleep. I dreamed of a creature with straight steel wires for hair and flint for hands that was trying to get into our house. I locked the door as he made his way onto the porch, but then I realized that all the windows were left open. I ran from window to window trying to close them. I couldn't move fast enough. The monster pointed a long staff at me as I tried to close the last open window. A smile broke through his face. I tried to scream—

"Twyla," Mama said, touching my shoulder. I jumped awake. Mama's eyes were concerned. "Lunch is ready. Would you like something to eat?"

No, I thought. But my stomach growled, and I grudgingly followed her to the kitchen.

"I know you probably have lots of questions for me," Mama said as we sat across from each other at the table, eating grilled cheese sandwiches and chips. I remained silent, staring at the bite marks in my sandwich. When I didn't say anything, she took a deep breath and continued. "I first want to tell you how very sorry I am for not being the proper mama you've needed these past two years. I became addicted to a terrible drug and didn't know what I was doing. That is no excuse for how I treated you, though."

"Is it true you nearly died?" I asked, giving her no sign of how I was feeling. I ate a potato chip.

"I don't remember everything, but yes. That's when Aunt Callie took you in. But none of that was your fault. Not one bit. I know it may take you a while to trust me, but I hope we can at least try to respect each other while we adjust, okay?"

I half nodded, the bread and cheese sat in my chest, unable to reach my stomach.

"This is also just a trial period. They're going to keep checking on us. And if I can't show them . . . Well, if this doesn't work out—"

"I'll be taken away and put in a foster home," I snapped. "You know, we wouldn't even be in this mess if you had just taken care of me the first time."

"Yes. That's right, Twyla. You're exactly right." Tears formed in her eyes.

✶

The rest of the week, I hung out in my room and worried about things. Was Tyrel really gone? Was Aunt Callie really going to be okay? Almost every night, I had the dream. Stonecoat on the porch. Stonecoat at the window.

Just like she said, Ms. Avalon came by on Friday to check on us. She inspected *everything*. It was so weird. What if I had real private stuff sitting somewhere? Like, I don't know, my underwear?

"Everything looks great," she said, heading to the door. "See you next Friday!"

Really? I thought. *A clean house means I'm okay?*

No information about Aunt Callie, nothing about Tyrel. After fuming in my room a while, I couldn't take it anymore. I stomped down the hall to deal with this once and for all. Mama was on the phone, but I walked in anyway. "Mama," I said, interrupting her. The word *Mama* coming out of my mouth after not saying it for two years felt strange and stiff, like a rusty door.

"I'll have to call you back," she said, hanging up and coming around to the other side of the bed to me. Her eyes were red like she'd been crying. I didn't care. "What can I do for you, baby? Can I get you something?"

"Do you remember the clothes?"

"The clothes?"

"The night you threw all my clothes out on the porch and said . . . said you never wanted to see my face again."

Mama's face turned white. "I said that to you, Twyla?"

"Yes, and you threw my clothes—"

"Oh my god, baby." She was up and had her arms wrapped around me before I could tell her to stop. "Come here. Sit down next to me."

"That's okay," I said, hanging back. "I just want an answer. Do you remember?"

"No, baby, I don't. There's a lot I don't remember. But I don't want you to not call me on it or not tell me what I did, okay?"

I looked down at my feet. "And what about Tyrel? You're not secretly with him, are you?"

"Absolutely not. I kicked his toothless butt to the curb," she said, trying to lighten the room a little.. I didn't feel light.

"Where is he?" I asked.

"Last I heard, he was in Oklahoma City," she said, looking a little nervous. "And I have a restraining order out on him. He's not allowed to come anywhere near me or you or this house or your school or my work. If he does, he'll get picked up by police."

I felt uneasy. This whole thing felt like a bunch of

matchsticks lined up ready to burst into flames. "I don't believe you," I said, turning and running back to my room.

That weekend, Mama and I barely spoke, but on Monday, we got the best news ever. Aunt Callie was finally well and leaving the hospital. She planned to visit us that weekend. Mama even said Byrdie and Fiona could come for a sleepover and to listen to Aunt Callie spin a tale. I couldn't wait to hug them all!

As I was washing the dinner dishes that evening, Mama came to the sink to fill the kettle for tea. "Sorry to get in your way. Gotta stock up. Aunt Callie doesn't know what to do without her iced tea."

"Sure, Mama, go ahead." I couldn't believe my own voice. I actually sounded pleasant. Truth is, nothing could make me feel bad. Aunt Callie was coming.

Suddenly there was a knock on the door, and I jumped clear out of my skin.

I looked out the kitchen window and onto the porch. It was a man. Maybe a delivery person? At seven-thirty p.m.?

I looked at Mama "What if it's . . . ?"

Mama's eyes widened. "You go upstairs," she said, turning off the faucet.

I ran toward the stairs, but when I passed the living room, I noticed the front windows were open. I ran to them and closed them.

Mama yelled through the door. "Who is it?"

"Um . . . hey . . . yeah. I'ma lookin' for Shayla. Is that you?"

My heart started pounding. Tyrel.

"You gonna open the door? I just need to talk to you, Shayla." Tyrel began walking around on the front porch, yelling out. "You know I can just wait out here. I know how to wait for a woman. I know how you like to take your time."

Mama turned to me and said, "Twyla. Go upstairs."

"No," I said, looking Mama square in the eye. What if she backed down? What if Tyrel convinces her to let him in? "Where's your phone?"

"That's right, baby," Mama said. "Go get my phone and call 911. If he knows the cops could haul him off, he'll go on his own."

I looked out the window. Tyrel was pacing now like he owned the place. His baggy shorts barely covered his pasty-white knees. His dirty blond hair was shaved up around the sides, and the top was faded green.

I grabbed Mama's phone out of her purse in the kitchen and dialed 911, but didn't hit send. Mama looked at me. My heart beat a mile a minute in my chest. My hands were sweaty. I could feel every ounce of my skin on fire. It felt like my dream.

Mama opened the door, and Tyrel whipped around with a hopeful expression on his face.

"Hey. HEY, Shayla. I knew you'd open up—"

"Get the hell off my porch, Tyrel," Mama said, her voice low.

"Come on. Don't be like that. I've come to make peace is all."

"I mean it, Tyrel. Leave." Mama tried to shut the door, but Tyrel quickly shoved his foot in the doorway.

"Wait just wait a minute . . ." he said, giving a hard smile. He looked like a fuse about to be lit.

Mama looked at me. I saw the desperation in her eyes. Then something came over me. I hit the send button.

All my anger, all my fire, vaulted me toward the door, toward Mama.

Reaching her, I swung the door open wide and stepped in front of Mama. Tyrel lost his balance and stumbled forward then back, looking up.

"Well, hey, little lady, look at you all grown up," he said, fake grinning.

"Back off, Tyrel," I heard myself say. "Better that you take your stanky self off this porch."

"What? Why all the hate? Come on, now. Thought I'd see how Shayla was gettin' on."

"She's gotten on out of your life, Tyrel. I've called 911," I said, holding up the phone. "The police are about to haul you out of here, if you don't do it yourself first."

"Now, now. No need to get the police all up in our business. I just wanted—"

"That's your cue, Tyrel," Mama said, pulling me back from the door.

"I'll get on goin'. I'm goin'." He shoved his hands into his pockets and lightly jogged to his car.

"Tyrel!" Mama yelled. He turned about. "If I ever see your face on this property again, you'll regret it." We held our ground as he shook his head, got into his car, and drove off down the street.

I smiled. Tyrel didn't scare me anymore.

Mama had stood up to him. Maybe I could trust her. Maybe.

When Saturday arrived, I couldn't stop grinning. Mama and I spent all morning getting the house ready for Aunt Callie. At one point, I ran upstairs to go to the bathroom, and that's when I saw it. I'd started my period. I got a wild feeling inside of me. Something strong, but sad, too. I wasn't little anymore. I was a young woman, powerful enough to stand up to the Tyrels of the world. I looked under the sink and found some panty liners. I followed the instructions and cleaned up.

"Mama?" I called, leaning out of the bathroom door and yelling down the stairs. Mama stuck her head around from the kitchen and looked up at me.

"Whatcha need, baby?"

"Could you come up here a minute?" I asked.

"Sure, give me just a second," she said.

I waited in the bathroom for her. I washed my face and brushed my long hair. I looked into my own eyes in the mirror. The girl looking back was the same, but different.

Mama was at the door. "You okay?"

"Mama," I said. Realizing that I really was glad she was there, right then. She was there for me. "I started my period."

Her eyes lit up. "That's wonderful, Twyla! I was wondering if that would happen soon. Did you find what you needed under the sink?"

"Yes. Thank you, Mama." I then reached for her and hugged her. It was the first time I had hugged her willingly since I moved in.

Later that day, a special taxi service for elders dropped Aunt Callie off at our house. Mama and I showed her the guest room where she would be staying, and after a very slow climb upstairs, we showed her my room. I filled her ears with every bit of news I had, and how we got rid of Tyrel. She listened and took it all in. I couldn't stop hugging her.

Looking around my room, she seemed happy about everything Mama had done.

"I'm going back downstairs to make some iced tea," Mama said, and winked at me, leaving me alone to talk to Aunt Callie.

When we were alone, I told Aunt Callie about how I had started my period. She lifted my chin and looked me in the eyes. "You will be a wise one, my Twyla. I just know it. I am very proud of my grandniece."

I tried not to cry, but I cried a little anyway. For the first time in a long time, I didn't feel angry. I felt safe. No stonecoats here.

Thicker than Water

HILDA EUNICE BURGOS

"¡Ay, Ramona, por Dios!" Mami drapes an itchy sweater over my shoulders. "A señorita must be discreet. You don't want to attract the wrong kind of attention."

"But it's summer." I wiggle until the sweater drops off. "And Marta's wearing the same thing as me!" When Abuela gave me and my sister these matching halter tops, Mami's eyes bugged out, but she didn't say anything.

She shakes her head. "You know that's different. Here, put this on." She hands me a wrinkled T-shirt that looks like it's size triple XL.

I roll my eyes but take the shirt and go back to my room because I can't win this argument. I never do. Marta is three whole years older than I am, but she gets to wear a summery top to the Fourth of July block party, and I have to dress like a nun. It's bad enough that this underwire bra is pinching my skin and smushing my already sore breasts. Now I'm not allowed to feel a cool breeze on my back, either? But Marta can. Of course. She isn't even wearing a bra, and Mami thinks that's fine. I know she's as flat as a piece of casabe, but still, it's the principle of the thing. I mean, shouldn't a fourteen-year-old dress more like a "modest woman" than an eleven-year-old kid like me?

I slide the giant T-shirt over my head and stand on the bed to see in the mirror. Maybe if I tie up the front so it doesn't cover my new white cutoff shorts, I can still move around and feel comfy. I twirl and look at my back in the mirror—oh, crap! "No, no, no!" I punch the air when I see the deep-red stain spreading across my bottom. My period isn't supposed to be here for another two days! Why is this happening to me?

"At least you noticed it now, and not at the party," Marta says when she runs in to ask what I'm screaming about. "Don't worry: I'll help you find something else to wear." She opens my drawers and rummages around, then pulls out some stiff and scratchy jeans.

"Forget it. I'm staying home." I go in the bathroom to change and clean up my mess. *I hate this*, I think as I run water over my underwear and watch the red flow out of them. *I hate this so much.* The familiar dull pain throbs below my belly button. No matter how much I scrub, my white shorts still have a faint pink spot on them.

"Come on, you don't want to miss the party." Marta puts her arm around me and leads me to my shoes. "Those blue jeans look adorable, and we'll have fun."

"No, *you'll* have fun. You're not the one with cramps. You don't even know what cramps are!" I want to jump into bed and stay there all day, but then I might have to wash the sheets. So instead I sit at my desk and put my head down.

"Do you want an aspirin or something?"

I blow out hard through my mouth. "Aspirin doesn't help for cramps. You don't know anything."

When I look at my sister, she has tears in her eyes. "I'm only trying to help," she whispers.

For a second, I feel kind of guilty. I mean, it's not her fault I first got my period the day I turned ten. It's not her fault I wear a C cup, and it's not her fault this stupid period decided to come today of all days. But still, my big sister should do things before me. She should understand about them and help me out. Instead, Marta looks like a clueless little kid, and she acts like one, too.

"Just go. Have fun. Don't worry about me." I drop my head back on the desk.

Marta lets out a whooshing breath. Her flip-flops slap across the floor and out of the room. The door thumps closed but opens again a minute later. *Now* what does she want?

"Young lady, you are not going to sit here feeling sorry for yourself!" Mami slams a cup of water on the desk and pokes two pills into my hand. "I don't want to hear you complain all summer about missing the party." She folds her arms across her chest and watches me swallow the pills. "Good. Now, vámonos." Mami sashays out of the room without looking back.

I sigh and push off the desk onto my feet. Maybe this won't be so bad. My cramps don't hurt that much yet. They'll be worse tomorrow, I know, but today I can still have fun.

I follow Mami down the stairs carrying a pan of quipes.

"Gracias, mi amor." She takes the pan when we're outside. "Now, go play with your friends." She heads to the food table in front of Tía Yaya's building across the street.

"You came!" Marta runs toward me, making water footprints on the sidewalk. She slides her slippery hand in mine and leads me to the open fire hydrant.

I hesitate. I've never gotten wet while wearing a pad before. Will it fall apart and bleed through? Will everyone see it?

"Come on, Ramona!" Joodi and Melina squeeze Marta out of the way and shove me into the water. I shriek when the first cold splash hits my shoulder. We whirl through the spray, holding hands in a circle and giggling like we've done every year since kindergarten. Back then we were all the same size, and people called us the triplets. Now I look like the big sister, but I still feel like a triplet.

"¡Ay, ay, ay!" Mami's voice booms louder than the screaming kids. "Girls, come eat!" She swoops over and smothers me with a giant towel. "Keep that on until you're dry."

"It's a hundred degrees out here!" I say. "The sun will dry me."

Mami argues but I press the towel into her arms and run off to Joodi and Melina's building next door. We sit on the second-floor fire escape and eat quipes and empanadas as we watch the wet kids and dancing grown-ups. Marta walks right up to Mami and has a whole conversation while sopping wet. "My mom isn't making Marta dry herself," I mumble.

Joodi licks her fingers. "Yeah, what's up with that?"

"Hey there, beautiful!" Two teenage boys stare at me from the sidewalk. "You're the winner of the wet T-shirt contest, hands down!" They laugh and pat each other on the backs.

I cross my arms over my chest, breathing like I just ran up the three flights to my apartment. I wish I had that towel now.

Melina stands. "Let's go inside."

My friends and I swing our legs through the window and drop into Melina's kitchen.

"Are you cold?" Joodi asks me.

I wipe the sweat from my upper lip and nod.

"You can wear this." Melina takes a folded shirt out of the laundry basket and hands it to me. "My mom won't mind."

"Thanks." I'm relieved to go back out wearing an ugly gray sack. Now those teenagers won't bother me.

"Por favor, Virgencita, ayude a mi niña." Mami is kneeling in front of the framed picture of the Virgen de la Altagracia. What could she be asking la Virgencita to do for me? Make my periods less painful? Stop my breasts from continuing to grow so I don't end up with back problems like Tía Yaya? Mami worries about my "developing body." She was nine the first time she menstruated, so she sat me down and explained it all to me when I was eight, just in case. "It's a beautiful, natural process," she said. "But I was terrified because I didn't know what it was. My heart almost beat out of my chest that day. I was sure I was dying, and I don't want you to be scared like that." Mami's words didn't make sense to eight-year-old me. And the book she pulled out with pictures of people's insides was kind of gross and confusing. Less than two years later, though, I had to admit she was right. I would have fainted if I had found blood in my undies without already knowing what to expect.

Now Mami's praying because she knows it's hard to live with this body that feels too old for me.

"Gracias, Mami." I bend over and hug her.

She unclasps her hands and tilts her head. "Why are you thanking me?"

"For your prayers."

Mami smiles and stands. "You're a good sister, mija."

"Huh?"

"I'm glad you understand my concern for Marta. She's not lucky like you."

"Huh?"

"The poor thing." Mami takes my hand and leads me to the kitchen. "To be fourteen and still not developed . . ." She does the sign of the cross and shakes her head. "Do you want a meriendita?" She opens the refrigerator.

"You were praying for Marta?" I put my hands on my hips.

"Of course! Didn't you know?"

I sigh and turn around. "No, but I should have." I go to my room without having that snack.

"Hey, Ramonita." Marta is sitting on her bed, her back against the frame, surrounded by clinking bottles of nail polish. "I have this great idea: I'll match my right foot with my left hand, and the other way around. What do you think?" She wiggles her eyebrows and smiles.

I shrug. "Whatever." Marta is always looking for ways to stand out. Fancy hairdos. Rhinestone-studded blouses. Makeup and nail polish. Why does she want to be noticed so much? I just want to look like everyone else.

"Come on, I'll paint your toenails! You can have any color." She sweeps her hand over the bottles like a game-show model. "You'll look so cute for the beach tomorrow."

I shake my head, put in my earbuds, and turn my back to my sister.

We meet Tía Yaya, her two daughters, son-in-law, and grandson outside at the crack of dawn and decide who's carrying what to the subway. My cousin Sandi already has her hands full with the baby, but her husband grabs the giant lemonade thermos and two chairs. "Fela, take some of the other chairs," Sandi bosses her younger sister. But

Fela doesn't want to chip her freshly polished nails. She picks up the towels. Marta lunges for the sandwich coolers, so Mami and I end up hauling the chairs.

"Vamos, vamos." Tía Yaya holds the umbrella up like a flag as she leads us to the number one subway entrance. When we get to the platform, she wags a finger at us. "Don't fall asleep. We have to get out at Times Square and walk to the Q."

An hour and a half later, the Q train pulls into our stop, and we trudge down the steps and across the street toward the beach entrance. Tía Yaya rips off her sandals and races in, elbowing people out of the way until she finds the perfect spot. "There." She spears the umbrella into the sand and opens it, then stands back and dusts off her hands as we pile our stuff in its shade. "Ay, mira," she says when I peel off my T-shirt. "This one's going to be like us!" She tries to claw at my breasts, but I duck away fast.

"Leave her alone, Mamá," Fela says. "Can't you see she's embarrassed?" My cousin puts her arm around me and holds me against her giant boobs. "You might not like them now, Ramonita, but in high school these will get you lots of dates and the other girls will be jealous."

As if we're in a movie, two guys walk by at that very moment and wink and whistle at Fela. One of them looks me up and down, his eyes slowing down at my chest as he shows off his crooked teeth. "Hola, mamacita."

I lean in closer to Fela.

"Váyanse de aquí." Tía Yaya shoos the creeps away, muttering about all the tígueres ruining a fun family day at the beach.

Mami chuckles and Marta looks away, unsmiling. What's *she* sad about? Icky guys aren't staring at *her*. When Sandi starts to nurse Luisito, Marta jumps up and goes for a swim. She doesn't wrap her arms across her bust to keep it from jiggling as she runs into the water, and she doesn't worry about anyone staring at her butt in her tiny bikini bottom. She doesn't have to because she has no bust and no butt. I sigh.

"I used to be like you," Sandi says. She pries Luisito off her breast and switches him to the other side. "Fela loves being gawked at, but I hated it, and I always tried to hide my body."

Sandi isn't hiding her breasts now. Which is good because it's hot and Luisito couldn't enjoy his meal—or breathe—if he had a beach towel over his face.

"It's not about attracting boys or making anyone jealous," she says. "Your body is yours and it's beautiful. Stand up tall and be proud!"

I un-slouch my back and watch Luis Andrés lift a full

and sleepy Luisito out of Sandi's arms. He holds him over his shoulder and pats his back until the baby lets out a super-loud belch. Tía Yaya laughs and points at Sandi. "The first time you burped like that, your father was so proud! 'She got that from me!' he said."

We've heard that story before, but still we laugh. Tío Felo always cracked us up, even after he got sick. He might not be around anymore, but he still brings a smile to our faces. Not like my dad, whose name makes Mami and Tía Yaya scowl. I wonder if he ever burped me or even held me. I was a baby when my parents split up. Marta and I are supposed to spend every other weekend with our dad, but he stopped showing up a long time ago. Marta remembers being disappointed by him. I don't remember him at all.

"What are you going to do?" Tía Yaya whispers to Mami.

"I'm taking her to the doctor tomorrow," Mami says.

"Who?" I ask.

"Ay, Ramona, why are you sticking yourself into our private conversation?"

"It's not private," I say. "You're talking all loud out here on a public beach!"

Tía Yaya chuckles.

Mami rolls her eyes. "Your sister, that's who, okay? Now, go join her in the water and stop being so nosy."

*

The next day, Mami and Marta come home from the doctor looking all sad and worried. Mami dials Tía Yaya's number and locks herself in the bathroom. I follow Marta to our room. "What's wrong?"

My sister shrugs and sinks into her bed. "They're running some blood tests. Tomorrow I go in for an ultrasound."

"What's that?"

"It's a picture of my insides." Marta hugs her knees and keeps her eyes closed. "Down there."

My mouth drops open. "Why? Do you feel sick?"

Marta shakes her head. "It's because I haven't gotten my period yet. Mami's freaking out. She's been expecting it 'any day' for a few years now. Since you got yours last year, she's convinced there's something seriously wrong with me."

"But . . ." I sit next to Marta. "What does she think is wrong? What did the doctor say?"

"That most girls get it by fourteen. Sometimes as old as sixteen, but only if late periods run in the family, and that's definitely not the case for me."

"Oh." I blink and crack my knuckles. What if Marta never gets her period? What if she never has a cramp or ruins a favorite pair of shorts? That sounds pretty sweet, actually. "It's good you don't have to deal with this stuff, right? I mean, what's a period good for, anyway?"

"What's it good for?!" My sister jumps up and glares at me. "Didn't Mami explain it to you? I thought you were the mature one who knew all about periods! And you don't know that women need them to lead healthy lives? You don't know how lucky you are to be normal!" She storms out of the room.

Marta's footsteps get farther away, and the car horns and shouting voices outside the window sound extra loud. I never said I was mature, did I? I definitely never asked for this dumb period. Would I be worried if I were fourteen and still didn't have it? Probably. But still, that doesn't mean I like having it now.

The downstairs buzzer blares in the hallway. I open the bedroom door just as Mami yells, "Come on up!" into the intercom. "Ramona, come out here!" she calls.

I guess Tía Yaya is joining us for dinner again, but I don't smell anything cooking yet. I plop onto my bed and examine the cracks on the ceiling. Mami always sends Marta to get me when I take too long. I look at the door and wait a few minutes, but Marta doesn't come. I stand and tiptoe down the hallway into the living room. La Virgencita's picture sits on the coffee table, and Mami is on the couch with her eyes closed, one hand clutching Marta's and the other holding a rosary. Tía Yaya is at Marta's other side, mirroring Mami. Fela and Sandi are in the two rocking chairs that face the couch. Fela sees me first. "Ramona's here now," she says. Mami opens her eyes and nods as I sit cross-legged next to the floor fan on the shaggy carpet. We say our Hail Marys and Our Fathers, Mami and Tía Yaya in Spanish, Marta, my cousins, and me in English, but all at the same time without missing a beat. Then Mami asks God to bring forth Marta's period by summer's end, and Tía Yaya prays for my sister's health and strength. We stand, and Fela and Sandi lift Marta into a loving sandwich of a hug.

"Thank you for coming." Mami blows her nose. "Will you stay for dinner?"

"No, gracias, mi amor," Tía Yaya says. "We need to get going."

"Yeah." Sandi holds up her phone. "Luis Andrés is freaking out because Luisito finished the last of the milk I left for him."

Poor Luis Andrés. He loves his baby so much, but he's always nervous about being alone with him. That's because when he runs out of food, he can't make more like Sandi does. Still, that doesn't stop him from spending time with Luisito.

We hug goodbye, and I turn to Mami after she locks

the door behind them. "Did my dad ever hang out with us when you went out?"

"Ay, no me hables de ese hombre." Mami holds up her hand as she walks to the bathroom. She doesn't even look at me.

I roll my eyes. I know any mention of my father puts Mami in a bad mood, but still, can't I ask one little question?

I shuffle into the kitchen and take the orange juice out of the fridge. Marta follows me. She looks me in the eye. "I don't recall ever being alone with him."

I pull a glass out of the cupboard. "At least you remember for yourself. Why won't Mami answer my questions?" My hand trembles and some juice splatters as I pour it. "And why does she have to call him *that man*, like he's a stranger?"

"Believe me, there are no good memories of those days." Marta rips off a paper towel and wipes the counter. "It was always a lot of yelling and crying. We're better off without him."

The day after Marta's ultrasound, Mami wakes us up before leaving for work. "Here's a list and some money," she says. "You can get everything at the bodega, so don't go any farther than that. Come lock this door."

Marta gets up to put the chains on the door after Mami leaves. I doze off again and wake up to the smell of scrambled eggs and toast.

"Hurry up and eat." Marta hands me a plate when I come into the kitchen. "I have to shower."

By the time we leave the apartment, it's after noon. As Marta clicks all the locks shut, I wonder about her ultrasound. She told me yesterday that the results should be in soon. But what are they looking for? She shrugged when I asked her. She doesn't look sick or anything. I don't understand.

It's a good thing the library is on the way to the bodega. "Can I check out some books?" I ask my sister.

"Sure."

We've barely stepped inside when Marta runs into two of her friends, and they get all excited comparing nail polish and sparkly flip-flops. I slip past them and snag the one free computer to search medical websites about what's wrong with a fourteen-year-old who doesn't get her period. There are a bunch of possible reasons. But Marta isn't super skinny or muscular. I'm 99 percent sure she's not pregnant. She doesn't have an eating disorder. The websites say there could be something wrong with her ovaries or her hormones. They say it could be cancer!

According to Mami, I'm lucky to have a "normally

developing" body. I never thought being the first girl in my class to need a bra was "normal." It definitely never felt lucky. But these websites seem to agree with Mami. Maybe they're right. I mean, my body is working the way it should, which is good. If my period ever stopped coming, that would be a big problem. And if Marta never gets hers—

"Did you find your books?"

I click out of the screen and turn to my sister, my heart pounding.

"What's wrong?" Marta takes my hand and looks at me with worried eyes.

I shake my head. "Nothing, I just didn't realize how late it is." I stand and shove my hands into my pockets. "I'll get books another day. Let's buy the groceries before Mami gets home."

Marta looks at me funny but doesn't argue. "Bye, Mrs. G.," we say to the librarian as we head to the door.

I follow my sister outside and squint when I step onto the sunny sidewalk. The loud raps and merengues pulsing out of the cars on the street hurt my ears. We jump out of the way of some little kids playing tag and shrieking with laughter. Why is everyone so happy?

Marta pulls out the shopping list as we walk. "Mami wants six plátanos, a pack of chicken, two aguacates, and some eggs and milk."

"Okay." Should I tell my sister what I read in the library? The doctor probably already explained all that stuff to her, so she already knows, right? Maybe she's trying to ignore her problems.

We step into the bodega and I decide I'm going to ignore them, too. If that's what makes her happy . . . "Should we get green or ripe plátanos?" I ask.

"Whatever you want," she says.

I love crispy tostones covered in salt, but Marta has a sweet tooth. I rummage through the pile of plátanos and pick out six big ones that are so ripe they're almost black. "Let's have maduros tonight."

She smiles.

What if my sister really has cancer? She's too young to die. There are so many things she wants to do. Like wear a fancy gown to her quinceañera and go to college and fly a rocket into space. And what about everything we need to do together? Like visit the Dominican Republic to see the towns where our parents were born. And—

"Mami gave us extra money for a snack," Marta says. "Do you want chips?"

My mouth waters at the thought of crunchy, salty chips. "Nah, let's get those cookies you like."

"Cool!" Marta grabs the cookies and takes everything to the cashier.

"I'll carry this." I scoop the two bags from the counter as she pockets the change.

"I can take one of them," she says.

"It's okay, I need the exercise."

"Why are you being so weird?"

I walk ahead, making sure she doesn't see me blinking back my tears.

Mami has just put the rice on the stove when the phone rings. She looks at the caller ID and rolls her eyes. "Will you get that, please?"

Mami's always liked my father's mother, but lately Abuela has been nonstop telling old stories about her family, and Mami doesn't want to hear how cute and funny my sinvergüenza father was as a child. So she's avoiding my grandmother's calls. "Hola, Abuela."

"Ay, Ramonita," Abuela says, all dramatic-like. "I had a presentimiento that something's not right with one of my granddaughters, and I had to check."

"Oh." Is Abuela psychic? Does she know about Marta's cancer?

"Well? Is there anything wrong?"

"Um." I step away from Mami and stroll down the hall toward the bedrooms. "It's Marta," I whisper. "She's fourteen and still hasn't, um, developed."

"Fourteen? That's all?" Abuela laughs and laughs. "I was sixteen when I started to bleed, and your tía Gabi was fifteen. Martita is the spitting image of my Gabi!"

My shoulders loosen like a noodle in a pot of boiling water. "I never knew that," I say. "I thought all the women in the family developed young."

"Ay, no, no, no. That's your mami's family. Remember, you have a papi, too."

My father is pretty easy to forget, but of course he's a part of Marta and me. My sister doesn't want to be anything like him, and maybe I don't, either. But what if we can't help it? His blood runs through our veins, too thick to get rid of, no matter how much of it I lose each month.

"Let me talk to Martita," Abuela says. "I'll tell her not to worry."

I run to my sister. "Abuela wants to talk to you."

Marta blows her hair off her face and plucks the phone from my hand. I back away while she says, "Uh-huh, uh-huh," over and over.

"What's up with your abuela?" Mami asks when I come into the kitchen.

"Um . . . she had a presentimiento about Marta."

"Oh?" Mami lifts her eyebrows.

"Did you know Abuela was sixteen the first time she got her period?"

Mami stops stirring the beans. "I did not."

Marta walks in biting back a smile. "Abuela sends you saludos," she tells Mami as she hangs up the phone.

Marta's test results come back negative. No cancer. No hormone problem. She's probably a late bloomer, like the women on our dad's side of the family. Marta phones Abuela to let her know. When Abuela calls again the following week, Mami glances at the caller ID and picks up the phone right away. She invites Abuela to come shopping for school clothes with us. At the store, Abuela scowls at the blouses Mami picks out for me, which look like the ones Sandi wore when she was pregnant. "Ramona has a lovely cuerpecito!" Abuela says. "She should show it off." She reaches for a purple tube top about the size of a hair scrunchy.

"Of course her body is beautiful," Mami says. "But walking around naked is illegal!"

Abuela shakes her head and turns to me. "What do you want, Ramonita? You're proud of your figure, aren't you?"

I look at my curves in the dressing room mirrors and nod. "Yes," I say honestly. "But it's *my* body, and I decide how much of it I want people to see. And I need to be comfy so I can play with my friends."

Mami and Abuela smile. They both approve of the

flowered short-sleeved poplin blouse I try on. It covers my collarbone and fits snug around my chest and waist. Most important, it's stretchy and easy to move around in. Marta gives it two thumbs up.

When we get back home, Abuela pulls a photo album out of her bag. Marta looks exactly like Tía Gabi at fourteen. "And you have your father's eyebrows." Abuela hands me a picture of a teenager with bushy eyebrows and unruly curls on his head. I always wondered where I got my wild hair. "You can keep that if you want."

I glance at Mami and she nods. She leans forward and presses her palm on Abuela's arm. "Tell them about the time he ran away from home."

Abuela opens her eyes wide and smiles. "You want to hear that story? Vengan, niñas, sit." She tells us how our dad got mad because she wouldn't let him eat dessert without first finishing his vegetables.

"I ran away for that same reason!" Marta throws her head back and laughs. "But I only went across the street to Tía Yaya's house."

"You got farther than your papi did," Abuela says. "He climbed into the cherry tree in front of our house and said he would live there forever."

"Cherries do taste good," I say with a nod.

"Well, he didn't stay long. Turns out he forgot to use

the facilities before he left." Abuela shakes her head and we all laugh.

I'm curious about what my father is like now, but I don't ask because that might spoil the mood. I'm sure Mami doesn't want to hear any news about him, and neither does Marta. Abuela reaches for my hand and squeezes. "He only calls me to borrow money," she says. "I'll always love him, but I wonder where I went wrong raising him." Mami wraps her arms around Abuela and holds her while she cries.

The night before the first day of school, Marta and I lay out our new outfits. "High school will be so much fun!" Marta says as she pins her hair up in a doobie wrap. I keep her up half the night asking questions about middle school. Still, we're not tired at all in the morning.

When I get up from the breakfast table, Mami lets out a yelp. "¡Ay, mira!" She points to my butt.

I turn and see a bright-red stain on my new pale-pink capris. My shoulders slump and I throw back my head, preparing to scream in frustration.

My sister jumps out of her seat and takes my hand. "Don't worry, Ramonita. I'll help you find another pair of pants."

I sigh and drop my head. Out of the corner of my eye, I see a red spot on Marta's chair. "Look!" I point.

Marta twists her head to see her bottom. "Yes!" She lifts her arms like a triumphant athlete.

I shake my head at her new beige pants, which have the same stain as my capris. She'll never get that out. But when I look at her face, I see she doesn't care about the pants. Not one bit. Her huge smile is like a contagious yawn that spreads to Mami and me. There's more than happiness in her eyes, and in Mami's, too. They're both relieved. Even though the doctors and Abuela told us not to worry, we were all a little nervous, because you never know, right? But now we do. Now we have something to be happy about. And not just for Marta. My cycle is right on time, as it should be, and that's worth celebrating.

The three of us hug and laugh together.

Shakthi Means Strength

PADMA VENKATRAMAN

HALF LIVES

I am Shakthi

Indian   American

Listening to

Sanskrit Prayers   English Rap

Wearing

Colorful Salwar Kameez   Faded Jeans and T-shirts

Best friend

Maya's   Catalina's

Tall   Short

Pretty, round, and healthy   Plump and not athletic

Acting so American   Never American enough

Writing Poems

Wanting to Belong

Longing to be one

FROM FAR AWAY

Fridays might be date nights
for non-desi parents,
but for ours, it's always been
for family.

Family might be blood relatives
for non-immigrant parents,
but for ours, it also means
treasured friends.

Fridays are fragrant:
soft gray curls of sandalwood smoke
unfurling from a long incense stick,
a tiny white piece of a carefully crushed camphor cube
flaring in a handheld brass lamp.

Fridays are to taste tradition,
sharing dishes from family recipes,
hot, spicy, sweet-sour and sweet-sweet
food, entwined with memories:
long-ago laughter, sun-splashed kitchens,
          mothers' hands guiding daughters
learning to grind sun-dried chilies in granite mortars
          with gigantic pestles.

Fridays are riots of color
combinations swirling together in swishing saris,
        unbounded by rules, working
joyfully, forbidden color pairings: green and orange,
        crisp as garden-fresh carrots;
purple and red, luscious as a bowl filled with plump
        grapes and apples;
pink swirling into orange as if inspired by a twilight sky;
golden brown and black, like our sun-bronzed skin
        and night-bright hair.

Fridays are for rejoicing
in newfound old-strong friendships, for celebrating
faith carried carefully across seas to a new home.

A SIMPLE QUESTION

Today, it's the twins' parents' turn to host.
Between the beeps of their video game
behind Maya's giggles about Ricardo
(the definitely-not-South-Asian boy she likes)
the sound of chanting floats up
from the floor beneath,
where my "aunties" and "uncles"
sit comfortably cross-legged
for over an hour.

Maya means illusion
but Maya's been my most solid
non-school friend
since we were seven and she found
a poem I'd scribbled on the back cover
of a book I'd lent her.
I was scared she'd laugh but instead
she said,
"It's the best poem I ever read!"

The only secret I keep from Maya:
I LOVE
hearing
resonant, deep,
sonorous voices, rising in unison:
repeating four-thousand-year-old prayers in Sanskrit,
          a language
I don't fully understand but which sounds
richer than any other to my ears.

Our faith makes me feel
connected to a country and a culture
that's equally mine and Maya's
except she's always managed to switch easily
between burgers and biriyani,

English and Telugu,
Hollywood and Bollywood.

Maya feels twice as tall as me
though she's at least a head shorter.
She feels older, too,
as she sweeps through her life, so together,
            so confident,
though I've got my period and she hasn't yet,
though my breasts bulge and her chest is still flat.

She has the sort of voice
everyone listens to when she strides into a room.

I don't.

SHUNNED

Prayer completed, Jayanthi Aunty calls.
Come, children.
Time for prasadam.

I race downstairs
with the others.

Amma's eyes,
fixed on Jayanthi Aunty as she raises the brass lamp
            with one hand,
don't meet mine.

The peal of the handheld bell
fades.

Kamala begins offering everyone the plate, piled high
with the blessed food: perfectly spherical
golden laddus.

My period's so light, so easy, so painless,
I don't think of it, don't remember the ridiculous
rules Amma told me about,
until I pick up a laddu and Amma
sucks in her breath and cries, *No!*

In two strides, Amma crosses the room and swats my hand.

Oh! Jayanthi Aunty's eyes widen with understanding.

Why can't Shakthi have a laddu, Mom? Kamala asks.

The antique grandfather clock ticks off time
second by slow second.

Aruna Aunty opens her mouth.
I wait for her to defend me.
She's a scientist and proud she was the only
BIPOC female in freshman physics class.
I'm sure she's about to say,
We're American!
We should do away with superstition!
or
We need to throw out
this rude, ridiculous custom!
or
something, anything to
support me.
But she just shuts her mouth again
before any words spill out.

Aunties and uncles all stare
at the sprinkles of light cut and tossed by the
                crystal chandelier
onto the soft Kashmiri carpet
at anything, everything
except me.

Jayanthi Aunty breaks the silence
with a frozen smile and a lie.
Shakthi's . . . unwell—sweets aren't good for her right now.

You have diabetes? Concern fills
Karthik's voice.
Daddy can help! He's the world's best doctor!

My face burns with indignation.
And embarrassment, which is worse.
And which I hate.

Because I should *not* be embarrassed.
Because I'm on my period and that's *good.*
Not shameful.

My fault. Amma laughs softly, apologetically. *Sorry.*
I forgot to remind her.

Don't worry, no problem, I made too much, as usual,
         Jayanthi Aunty babbles.
Go on, Shakthi, sweetie, you may as well eat the laddu.
You already touched it.

Jayanthi Aunty smiles at me, but

she snatches the plate with the remaining laddus out
　　　of Kamala's hands
and bustles off to the kitchen.

I hear Jayanthi Aunty tossing the perfectly clean
delicious laddus into the trash. I didn't even touch them.
All I did was touch the one I'm still holding.
But just my hand hovering
above the plate
is too polluting for her taste.

I hear her scrub the empty plate.
Water runs and runs and runs as she rinses and rinses
　　　and rinses her hands.

Anger flares inside me like a cube of camphor on fire.
Words rush into my mouth. I want
to spit them out but I hold them back

only because my hands are shaking and I'm scared my
　　　voice will shake, too,
if I speak and tears might pour down my cheeks and the
　　　aunties will fuss
assuming I'm sad. I'm not. I'm angry.

The last thing I want is their womanly sympathy.
I crush the laddu in my hands, let the crumbs fall on
     the floor,
turn on my heel, and stomp

up the stairs, enter Kamala and Karthik's bedroom,
     slam the door
though it's Jayanthi Aunty's house, not ours, but before
     I can lock myself in,
Maya races up, flops on the bed, though it isn't her house,
     either, and lies
gulping like a fish out of water.

Sorry, she says when she catches her breath again.
Scowling, I turn away.
But she stays.

BROKEN CIRCLE

Prayer felt
magical
until just now
     until Amma
     and everyone else
          forced me out of the

circle
            as if my touch polluted

food
                    as if my presence is unholy

            as if suddenly I'm unclean

just because I'm

female
            and all the others
            every male and even worse
            every female
    watched wordlessly
                        failing

        to
STAND UP.

HUNGRY

Come downstairs. Now.
I hear Amma's annoyance
in how she speaks
through her gritted teeth
through the door

we've locked, Maya and I.
Can't believe how badly you're behaving.
You're disappointing me.

Can't believe how badly YOU'RE behaving.
You're disappointing me, too.
Anger and hurt—no, actually
rage and pain
crisscross in a sticky web
constricting my throat
strangling the words
I want to say.

She sighs.
I'm silent.
Another sigh from her.
More silence from me.
She mumbles
words I can't quite catch.
Waiting games are my strength,
her weakness.

Shakthi, please.
You, too, Maya. Come, eat.
You're overreacting!

These days,
here in America,
you can do anything
except pray in the circle.
You can eat everything
except the blessed food!
You have it so much better
than we did.

Better?
All these years, I always heard
we came to America because they wanted the
best
for us.

A SMALL VICTORY

At last

    Amma's

        defeated footsteps

            tramp down the wooden stairs.

Despite the shut door,
dinner scents waft up and creep into my nose,
delicious.

Maya's stomach growls.
I giggle.

Should we skip dinner?
Maya asks.

I love that she says *we.*

Footsteps stampede upstairs.
Knocks rain on the door.
It's us! Kamala cries.
Thank you! We unlock the door.
Sorry we took over your room.

That's okay!
Kamala and Karthik enter, carrying
plates piled high with food.
You're only mad at Mom, right?
Not me? Kamala asks.

Not you, I say.

Why didn't they give you prasadam?
Karthik asks. *They never stop me!*

Not you, Maya says.
But they'll shun me, too,
and Kamala,
and my little sisters,
when they get older.

The twins' identical eyebrows go up the exact same
        amount,
in their confusion. But they're
not identical.
One's a girl; one's a boy.
The boy will never be treated
as if he had a catching disease.
His body will always be clean enough to enter a temple
no matter what he says or thinks.
He won't ever be cast out.

Only Kamala will.
She'll be banished from the home altar when she bleeds.

TRUCE

I've never felt
as close
to the twins or even to Maya
as when we four, oldest "children"

troop downstairs together
stomachs full
          hearts sharing the same hurt.

It's easier to face the aunties and uncles,
who smile and pretend nothing happened
except for when it's time to leave
and Jayanthi Aunty
          carefully

offers
Amma a pinch of holy vermilion powder
bright as life-blood

(and ignores me
like I'm invisible)

                    APPA'S SILENCE

Petals of snow
float in the cone of light
cast by our car as
Appa drives home
saying nothing.
Amma says a lot,
So embarrassed!

Can't believe you
threw a temper tantrum!
Twelve years old!

Maybe I should have thrown a few earlier.

All this American nonsense about teenagers . . .
My parents would never let me say a peep!
So obedient we were!
What did we do wrong
raising you?

Raising? You let me down!

How could you forget
your Indian manners?
When did you become
so American?

You're forgetting
I've been American
since I was born.

POEMS

I write
I write
Into the night

Words bleed
Out of me
Wrong and right

No net of feeling's
Too tough for my
Fingers to pull apart

Into the night
I write
I write

MY IDEA

You okay?
Maya's message interrupts
my poetry
but makes me smile.
Me: *Wrote lots of poems, but still no peace.*
I wish I could DO something.

Maya: *What?*

Me: *Make them stop.*

Maya: *How?*

Me: *Maybe . . .*

Maya: *Yeah?*

Me: *Maybe we should—never mind—*

Maya: *Tell me!*

Me: *We could have a protest.*

Maya: *YES! Next Friday?*

Me: *When your parents host?*

Maya: *Sure! You can speak.*

Me: *NO, I'm not speaking.*

Maya: *You should.*

YOUR idea.

Me: *I'm Not a Speaker.*

Maya: *Just read your poems.*

We'll stand behind you.

Me, Kamala, and Karthik.

Me: *The protest was MY idea! So do it MY way.*

I'll give you my poems, but

YOU have to read them aloud.

Maya: *Sorry. Not doing that.*

Me:

Maya: *Shakthi?*

Me:

Maya: *You still there?*

Me:

Maya: *OK. How about if*
we read some poems and then
you do, too?

WHILE I TRY TO SLEEP

Maya bombards me with texts:
The twins agreed to read!
They're two whole years
younger than us.
Me: *Stop trying to shame me into it.*
Had enough shaming today.
Maya: *This isn't about us. We're*
fighting for Mina and Mira's future.
It's a while since I heard Maya
refer to her little sisters by name,
instead of calling them the Pests.
Maya: *I'm not giving up*
Until you give in.
Me: *Okay. Maybe.*
Maya: *YAY!!!!!!!*
Me: *I said MAYbe . . .*
Maya: *YAY!!!!*

NUMBER ONE FEAR

Appa once tried excusing my shyness, saying,
I read somewhere,
lots of people prefer dying to public speaking.

First-world people only,
Amma said.

I'm a
first-world girl.

Now that Maya's set on me reading aloud
my poetry, I wish I'd never said the word
protest.

My brain and heart and stomach
churn too much to think. My hands
tremble too much to type.

EMPTY

What's up?
My best school friend,
Catalina, asks
two minutes after I get on the bus.
Nothing, I mumble

What kind of nothing? Catalina wiggles her ears,
which always get me laughing,
which always helps
when something's bothering me.
I got my period, I tell her. *Three months back.*
Why'd you
keep that secret? she
asks, but she waits
patiently, until

I tell why. *I didn't tell . . . because . . . because*
your moms had a party for you—
you're all
so cool,
your family, your moms' friends,
but my parents and "aunties" and "uncles"
shun me
for it.
What? Catalina's eyes grow round.
I explain some more.
Wow! That's so . . . Her voice trails off.

I hate it. I tell her. *Not sure I*
even
want to be Hindu anymore.

Catalina shrugs. *Hey . . .* she says.
Everyone's religion
has stuff like that.
At least that's what Mama says.
Sometimes church
makes me really angry.

I told Maya we should protest.

Cool! Catalina smiles.

I want Maya to read my poems aloud.
But she says I should.
"You go, Shakthi!"
I want to go to the other end of the earth.

Catalina gives me no sympathy. She says, *Protest. Wow.*
Way cooler than my celebration!

It's not. I'm stuck!
Can't get a single word out.

Catalina laughs.
I can't see what's funny.
I wrote lots last night

but this morning I looked at it
and it's terrible.

At last Catalina's sympathy surfaces. *Feeling pressured,*
        huh?
Ask Mrs. Williams for help.
She'd love your poems. You should show her.

DEAR MRS. WILLIAMS

In class, I write
my teacher a note
explaining everything and asking
for help.

It's a weird thing to do but
my voice works best when I write.

A QUIET CHAT IN THE LIBRARY

Want some sweet iced tea, Shakthi?

No, thanks, Mrs. Williams.
I like spicy
masala ginger tea
steaming hot,
however hot the day may be.

Thanks for sharing your poetry with me, she says.
It's some of the strongest work
I've ever seen.

Thanks, Mrs. Williams.

Thought I'd share
some poems with you, too.
She shows me poetry
her sister wrote and recited
at Black Lives Matter protests;
songs her parents sang as they marched
for Civil Rights for all Americans.
I'm honored you trusted me
enough to tell me about this protest
you're organizing. I'm so proud of you!

Thanks, Mrs. Williams.

I'm a reader, not a poet, but if I were you, I'd try
beginning with what you love
about your religion and culture. Allow
your angry words to root themselves in love
so they can burst into flowers of flame,
powerful but productive.

But, I confess . . . I have writer's block.
I didn't show you the poems
I wrote when I was mad at how
they shunned me when I had my period.
Those are really bad.

My sister always
says her work is bad, too, at first, Mrs. Williams continues.
Then she looks at it again and likes it.
Sounds like something all poets go through.

But I have to write something good! Real soon!
By Friday!

Ever heard of Found Poetry?
Start with research.
Find others' words that resonate.
Then reshape, reclaim, reinvent,
re-envision, rearrange, rebirth them.
Or . . . just . . .
allow them to inspire you . . .

I'm scared, Mrs. Williams.

She nods. *I'd be a bit scared, too, if I were you.*

But I'd be proud, too. Truly proud.
Poets are the first people
Fascists send to prison.
You know why?
Because
POEMS
HAVE
POWER!

DELVING DEEP

Catalina helps
Me discover

Hindu women saints
Hindu social reformers
Hindu freedom fighters

I never heard of before.

The more
Deeply we dig
The prouder of my
Roots
I grow.

So many Indians
So many South Asians
So many South Asian Indian Americans
Inspire me:
Mirabai, Andal, Tilak, Shankaracharya, Avvaiyar . . .

Why did no aunty or uncle ever mention them?

Buddha was the first
To accept women as nuns, I discover.
He didn't shun menstruating women.

Buddhists believe
Menses are a natural phenomenon that women
         go through on a monthly basis.
No more, no less.

Hindus believe
Buddha is an incarnation of God Vishnu, Amma said.
Yet neither Amma nor Appa told me how accepting
         He was.

DAY BY DAY

As Catalina and I
accumulate evidence,

poems pour out onto my pages again.

I shiver shake echo
No! I'm not reading them myself!

Catalina coaches listens corrects
                    repeats repeats repeats
You rock, Shakthi!

She's my rock.

EVERY EVENING

Every now and then I see I
can be Captain.

Maya's a great first mate.
We choose poems for her and Kamala to read.

Karthik says he's writing his own speech.
If they don't listen to us after this, Maya declares,
        we'll refuse to eat on Fridays.
I love food, Kamala says. *We better not fail.*

They were always my American family.
Now we're becoming an unbreakable foursome of friends.

FINALLY

When Amma announces it's time for prayer,
I say, *Actually, aunties and uncles,*
we've prepared a program for you.
A surprise.

Maya reads:
And before you dismiss us, telling us we've become too
    Americanized,
let me just say we're fighting only because we love you and
    we believe
in what you taught us.
You've taught us to respect both cultures.
You've told us to be proud of India and America.

If we didn't care, about the younger ones,
if we didn't know that unless we stop, this custom
    will continue,
shaming our little sisters,
if we didn't hold our sisters and brothers in our hearts,
we might not have had the strength to speak up.

Saint Vivekananda once said Hinduism had

shrunk into a meaningless set of rituals about
        "pots and pans"
but he believed, as we do, that at its core, Hinduism is
about equality and embracing everyone.

Protesting "the myth of menstrual pollution" isn't
        American.
It isn't Indian.
It's just human.

Indians have fought battles against this ugly oppression.
Rajan Gurukkal, Hindu, Indian, historian, says,
        "There's neither
ritual sanctity nor scientific justification for this sinful
        shunning."

Challenged by women's rights activists, the Indian Supreme
        Court said,
"We have no hesitation . . . such an exclusionary practice
violates the right of women to visit and enter a temple
to freely to practice Hindu religion. . . .
Denial . . . significantly denudes them of their right to
        worship."

You've taught us

Sanskrit prayers that speak of "spiritual cleanliness"
of our bodies as temples.
You've taught us the Holy Upanishads say,
"God is genderless and formless.
God is oneness within everyone."
By turning against women
you're turning against all we've learned.
All you've taught us.

Kamala unfurls a poster
of three Indian women who fought for gender equality:
Mira, Andal, Avvaiyar.
These women are my inspiration.
Were there some days on which they were unholy?
She unfurls another poster,
of Saraswathi, Goddess of Learning.
Saraswathi lives in truth, in books, in music, in speech,
*   in knowledge.*
Aren't those things "eternally sacred"?
Don't we worship a goddess, not god, of learning?

Karthik just says,
Kamala is my twin.
If you ban her from something,
you better ban me, too.

I begin to read.
My hands shake, but my voice doesn't.

Amma, you've told me,
when you were a girl, growing up in India, you had to
        stay outside the house
when you had your period. Three days or more, alone,
        in a tiny room,
right near the reeking toilet. No air-conditioning. No fans.
Not even large windows—just tiny ones set up high—
        so you wouldn't
be seen. Just seeing a menstruating woman was
considered unclean.
Even in the height of summer, you weren't allowed
        to shower.
You were bathed in sweat.
Your meals were left
on a specially marked plate on the ground near the
        outhouse door.
You couldn't even come in the house to get water.

I listened and it broke my heart.

Amma, you've told me,
when you moved to Delhi, your apartment was too small
        for you to go elsewhere,

SHAKTHI MEANS STRENGTH   277

but your mother wouldn't let you sleep on the bed or sit
      on a chair.
When you bled, you'd be forced to lie on a straw mat on
      the floor. No pillow.
Not allowed to touch anyone else.
Not allowed to touch books, either.
That was hardest for you, you said, being kept away
not just from school but also from books.
Each day felt long as a year, you said, because you loved
      reading so much.

I felt your pain, Amma.
Reading to me in your soft voice, you gave me my love
      of books.
Patiently your guiding hand helped mine shape my
      first words.

All you have to do is keep in mind a few small rules,
you said, the first day of my first period.
When tears dotted my eyes, you asked,
Can't you see we've come a long, long way?

I see.
But can't you agree, we've got much further to travel?

FOUND

As the four of us come together
to read aloud my final poem,

our voices curl together and spread through the room
powerful as incense.

I feel more than strong.
I feel whole.

Shakthi
means Strength.

And I am Shakthi
every single day of every single month.

God's light burns so strong in me
no one and no custom can ever dim my shine.

I am Shakthi.
I am Shakthi.
I am Shakthi.

Part of the Team

YAMILE SAIED MÉNDEZ

"You play like a girl!" an angry voice shouted.

Angela shot.

The silence that followed made her ears rumble. Like the rest of the people crowding the Titan Middle School's gym, she stared at the ball and counted under her breath.

Her team's future depended on this shot. Her future on the team depended on this shot.

Un Mississippi.

Dos, Mississippi.

Tres, Mississippi.

The ball circled the rim of the basket, teasing.

She willed the ball to tip a millimeter off its orbit and make it into the basket.

In the silence before, she counted to four long years of practice, a constellation of hopes and dreams, until finally . . .

ROAR!

A triple to take her team to the top of the scoreboard just as the clock ticked down to zero and the final horn blared.

The scene that followed belonged in a movie.

Pandemonium exploded in the gym.

The cheer squad did a victory routine and threw confetti on the players while the whole school chanted the Titans' battle song. Angela's best friend, Mariela, winked at her and waved the blue-and-yellow pom-poms in her direction.

Angela waved back. Part of her wished to turn back time.

Last year, Mariela and several of the cheerleaders were on the girls' basketball team. The one that had set euphoria-inducing records, the kind that made dreams bubble.

But in spite of all their success, the girls had dropped off of the roster one by one, until they didn't have enough players for a team.

The team got disbanded, and the principal suggested Angela join the boys' team.

Coach Hendrick had promised that if she played half as

well as her brothers, she'd get her fair share of playing time. He loved the spark that the Argentine Silverio boys had brought to the team year after year. Everything was going well until a few parents complained she'd stolen a spot that belonged to a boy. Her parents told her not to worry about the haters, to do her magic on the court, but it was hard not to feel discouraged when her minutes decreased just as she scored consistently. Still, she never missed a practice and cheered for boys with not even half her skills.

The announcer's voice brought her back to the present. "The Titans score and are off to the Utah Junior High Championship game!"

No mention of her name.

It was as if no one even wanted to say aloud that Angela was part of the boys' team because then it would be true. Even her jersey read Silverio, her last name, instead of her first name. She'd inherited it from her brother Javier, who was four years older than her and was so good, he played on the varsity team although he was a high school junior.

She shook off the dark thoughts. In the end, no one but Angela would remember who'd scored the final winning shot. All that mattered was that the Titans had won.

She ran to hug her teammates and tried not to gag at how bad they smelled, any deodorant they'd been wearing had most likely been sweated out ages ago. They ran all over the basketball court, trying their best to make Coach Kendrick proud. But she was fresh as a rose, sharp thorns and all. She'd gone in just the last three minutes of the last quarter, but she'd done her job.

If she only had the chance, she could do so much more.

She hadn't signed up for this, to be a benchwarmer, but having grown up watching movies and reading underdog inspirational stories, she trusted Coach Hendrick's integrity.

She had faith in her dad's saying, that "if you work hard enough, the results will follow." After years working in the landscaping company, he'd finally risen to the manager position, and although he didn't make more money, the fact that his boss trusted him enough to supervise the fancy jobs at the rich houses in Suncrest was enough.

Angela's teammates patted her hard on her back and shoulders. They gave her high fives that she returned with all the strength she could muster.

"Chest bump!" Nico challenged her.

She pretended she hadn't heard and gave him a high five instead. Her breasts, or the tiny points that passed as breasts, had been hurting these last few weeks. Under any other circumstances, she'd have chest-bumped him easily. She was tall for her age, taller than all the other seventh graders after her growth spurt last year, when she turned twelve. She'd towered over the boys.

Now they were catching up to her. Soon, they'd outgrow her. But she was still the fastest, most agile one on the roster. Anguila Eléctrica, her father called her. She wished he'd chosen an animal that was a little prettier than an electric eel, though. She tried to smile as her teammates planned a celebration party at the bowling alley, even though none of them came over to invite her. True, she could take the first step and get the details and ask her mom to drive her there. The thought made her shrivel, though. Why couldn't she be as bold off the court as she was on it?

She gathered her things, trying not to glance at Coach Hendrick, who was taking a long time to put the equipment and his notes away, as if he wanted to tell her something.

And finally, he looked in her direction, his bright, striking blue eyes boring into her. "Not bad, Angela," he said. He pronounced her name in English, even though she'd specified on the tryout form that the *g* sounded like an *h*.

Then he added, "Next time stick to the play."

"But the shot was perfect." She wished she could take the words back as soon as they left her lips.

Coach didn't tolerate any back talk.

A flash of annoyance crossed his blue eyes. Immediately, her mouth went dry, but her eyes prickled. She couldn't swallow the treacherous tears making her throat hurt, but she had to.

Growing up with four brothers, she'd learned her tears could disarm the hardest of souls, including Javier. With Coach, though, she didn't even want to see what would happen if she did cry. None of the boys would cry if they were unjustly told off, would they?

Coach raked a hand over his blond hair and said, "You were lucky this time, but imagine if you'd missed. I don't think my heart can take that kind of drama." He repeated, "What if you'd missed?"

"But she didn't miss, Coach," Mami said.

Angela wanted to shrug off her mom's words just as she shrugged her mom's hand off her shoulder. Didn't Mami realize she was making things worse? How couldn't she see the flashes in Coach's eyes that meant he was holding back words that couldn't mean good news for Angela?

"Ready to go, Coach?" Nico, one of the boys, asked.

Coach didn't reply to Angela's mom. Instead, he ruffled Nico's hair, and when he looked at Angela, he said, "Next time stick to the play. Okay?"

He left with Nico and the rest of the team before she could even say okay back. Mami muttered forbidden words under her breath, which made Angela wish she could teleport to next week's game already.

Coach's words hurt, but he was right. What if she'd missed? Mami shouldn't have meddled. When the adults got involved, things snowballed really fast. Angela was a tall girl, a strong girl, but not tall and strong enough to stop a snowball going full speed down a mountain.

The gym was already empty except for Mr. Jensen, the janitor, who swiped the confetti and streamers aside. When he felt her eyes on him, he smiled briefly and said, "Great shot."

Mami pressed her shoulder again and pulled her closer in an embrace, and this time, Angela didn't have the strength to shake it off. Her stomach hurt so much, she was afraid she'd throw up and make matters worse for Mr. Jensen.

"Yes, mi amor," Mami said. "Great shot."

The sun was setting. The snowcapped Wasatch Mountains behind the school were the perfect backdrop for the celebration party in the parking lot.

But Angela didn't feel like celebrating. Even if she'd scored the winning shot, after Coach's reaction, she felt like the loneliest person in the world, even among all the people.

What if she'd missed the shot? She shivered.

Mariela ran to her as she was putting her things in the trunk of the car and hugged her, making her lose her balance.

"Hey!" Angela complained.

Mariela playfully pushed her with her bum again and said, "Great shot, Anguila Eléctrica! Are you coming to the party?"

Angela's face lit up for a second. "The team invited the cheerleaders?"

The look on Mariela's face said more than words, but Mariela still clarified, "No. Of course they didn't. We're meeting at Saylor's for pizza and pedis. You used to love pizza and pedi night."

Mami turned on the car's engine, and Angela quickly got in the passenger seat.

Angela had loved pizza and pedi night when they were all on the girls' basketball team. Now that Mariela and the others had turned into cheerleaders, she didn't fit in with the girls, just as she didn't fit in with the boys on the team.

"I need to go home," she said, her heart tugging at how Mariela's smile slid off her pretty face. Angela clicked her seat belt on. "Besides, my stomach's killing. I need to rest for a while."

Mariela didn't argue. Mami drove away. In the mirror, Angela saw her friend standing in the middle of the parking lot until Saylor grabbed her by the arm and pulled her toward the cheerleaders' van.

Mami didn't say anything for a long time, although Angela knew her mom was bursting to say something.

Finally, when the silence was suffocating and she was afraid she'd get carsick, Angela said, "What, Mami? Are you disappointed, too?"

Mami sighed but kept her eyes on the winding mountain road ahead. "Por supuesto I'm not disappointed. I'm proud of you. Never forget that." She didn't sound disappointed—she sounded upset—but stretched a hand back and pressed Angela's knee briefly.

Angela wiped the tears she couldn't swallow anymore. "I'm sorry," she whispered, not knowing what she was apologizing for.

Making the winning shot? Being the only girl on the team? Stealing a spot that belonged to a boy?

Maybe she was just angry that she had to choose between the boys and the girls, playing or cheering. Why couldn't she choose both? Be girlie like she'd always been and still play basketball?

Why was life so complicated now that she was growing up?

Her head pounded, so she pressed her forehead on the cold window. The glass went foggy when she took a deep breath to calm herself. She didn't know why she was crying. The emotion had come suddenly, without a particular reason. But she couldn't help the tears this time, and her stomach grumbled with a hunger not even her mom's empanadas argentinas or tres leches cake could satisfy.

A week later, the morning of the championship game, Angela woke up with an upset stomach. Again. She hoped her mom wouldn't notice she spent more than an hour in the bathroom. What if Mami didn't let her play? Angela hadn't practiced more than the boys or sacrificed her spa nights with the girls for nothing.

When her brother Javier knocked on the door for the third time, Angela gave a last look at the mirror and pinched her cheeks so she wouldn't look so pale, so greenish. She didn't know how to fix the excruciating pain in her back, though. It felt like two giants were pulling at her from opposite directions.

She opened the door.

"Why are you so pale?" Javier asked.

It was so easy to hide her fear and anger at the world, but she couldn't fake it in front of her brother. She scoffed without saying a word.

"Pregame jitters? You never used to get them when you played for the girls," he jabbed. "Now that you play the real game with boys, you understand how intense it really is, right?"

Angela didn't even bother to reply.

"Javier!" their dad bellowed from the end of the hall-way, and Javier ducked.

"Oops," he said.

Papi gave him an earful, and when Angela was about to go back to her room, he called to her, "Angela, wait, please." His voice was so soft, she couldn't ignore him.

"What, Papi?" she asked when he just stared at her.

"I only want you to remember that basketball is beau-tiful, and you're a strong, young woman . . ."

Something inside her squirmed when he called her young woman. She didn't feel like a woman, not even a young one. She wasn't ready to be one yet. She didn't know how.

"But?" she said, motioning with her hand for him to continue.

"No *buts*. Just remember to have fun. You got this." He hugged her and she hid her face against her dad's chest, hoping he couldn't tell how fast her heart was beating or feel the nerves twisting in her stomach.

Her stomach kept clenching all the way to the school, and she tried to take deep breaths to calm her anxiety. They didn't work.

If anything, her nerves got worse when Coach Hendrick walked up to her during warm-ups and placed a hand on her shoulder, saying, "You're starting, Silverio. Ready to work your magic?"

She wanted to scream with joy, but she only nodded, and by the time she smiled, he'd already moved on to the bench.

The rest of the warm-up went by in a blur. Before she realized she'd been running on adrenaline, the game had started and she'd scored the first double, which was just what Coach had told her to do.

The look of pride and confidence on his face had been worth the nerves and the last whole season when she'd watched with longing from the bench.

The cheerleaders chanted her name, "Give me an A-N-G-E-L-A, ANGELA!"

They sang her name, Angela. Not Silverio, the last name that carried her brothers' reputation. She could hear her four brothers and her parents cheering for her somewhere in the crowd.

Angela zigzagged among the rival team's boys, stealing, defending, passing like she'd never done before, just like she did in her fantasies at night, when she saw herself in the WNBA, even though Javier teased her that no one ever watched the women because no one cared about their games.

After the first shot, she passed the ball to her teammates, and they all scored, possessed by the same urge to win for their coach, their school, and their families. By the third quarter, no one had scored more than Nico, though, and he returned the favor, assisting Angela in two more doubles and a triple that made the gym quake with excitement.

Angela didn't see the rival team's number twenty-four barreling in her direction until she was already flying in the air.

She landed with a dry thump that echoed on the walls, followed by the sound of agony from the audience. She swallowed her gasp when she tasted blood in her mouth. She couldn't show weakness. Not now.

The ref marked the foul, and after checking that Coach gave the okay, Angela got back on her feet to take the free throws.

She stooped to bounce the ball and take the time to slow her breaths. Right when she was about to shoot, a boy from the other team exclaimed, "Look! She's bleeding!"

Angela's first reaction was to touch her mouth, see if the cut in her lip was worse than she'd imagined.

But when the whole gym went silent, and then the boys on the other team started laughing and pointing at her, a horrible realization fell on her like the anvils in the old cartoons Papi liked to watch.

They were pointing at her lower body. At her shorts. Her white shorts.

¡Ay!

In the interminable second that followed, Angela didn't want to look. Mariela, on her feet with the other cheerleaders, had a hand over her mouth. Behind the cheerleaders and the fans wanting to take a closer look at what was happening, Mami was elbowing her way through the crowd blocking the stairs.

Even in the distance, Angela saw the tears on her mom's cheeks. Was it that bad, then?

She took a deep breath and looked down. A trickle of blood ran down the dark skin of her leg. It was a brownish red. Her stomach clenched again, as if an iron vise were pressing her lower body. She bit her lip to silence her moan of pain. More blood trickled down.

Someone placed a towel over Angela's shoulders, and when she looked up, surprised, she saw Coach's concerned face. The boys were making a barrier between Angela and the other team, protecting her? Hiding her?

"Go to the lockers, sweetheart," he said in the kindest voice Angela had ever heard him use.

He never called any of the boys *sweetheart*.

It would've been better if he'd been angry. If he had reminded her she didn't belong in the team, she would've understood. Coach was sending the sub in, but Angela was rooted in place. Mami took her gently by the arm and led her toward the lockers. In her walk of shame, Angela tried to avoid making eye contact with the people staring at her, but she couldn't ignore the looks of support and understanding from the cheerleaders, especially Mariela.

She sat in the bathroom stall, not knowing what to do. Someone opened the door, and the sounds of the crowd cheering and celebrating slithered in along with Mami's floral perfume.

"How are they doing?" Angela asked, staring at her mom's shoes.

From the other side of the metal stall door, her mom laughed.

"What's so funny?" Angela asked, and her voice sounded like it came from the depths of her belly, which quaked and spasmed painfully. She stared at her distorted reflection on the metal door.

"I'm not laughing at you, mi amor," Mami said. "I would never."

"Then what were you laughing at?" Angela said, aware she'd raised her voice at Mami, who had done nothing but stay by her side the whole time.

"When Javier broke his arm, and they had to put him to sleep to fix it, the first thing he asked when he woke up was how his team had done. I'll never share your passion for basketball, but I sure admire you kids. I sure admire you, Angela."

When Javier had broken his arm, he'd returned to the team as a hero. He'd been injured for fighting for a crucial ball. How was Angela going to go back and face the team? She'd have to move to another country. Another world where girls didn't get their periods in front of the whole school. Had this been her punishment for trying to play against the odds? For being in love with the game?

"They're winning," Mami said. "And all because of you. The game's almost over. Congratulations, campeona!"

But all Angela heard was that the game was ending. She had to leave the school before people started coming out of the gym. She couldn't let anyone see her like this.

"Mami," she said, "please take me home."

"But—"

"Please, Mami. I can't do this."

Mami didn't say anything else but passed her a baggie under the door. It was the emergency kit Angela had packed in her bag since fourth grade, for just in case. She opened it and took out the flower-print panties and the black yoga pants, and a small white square. A pad. She knew how to apply it. In fifth grade, the school nurse had showed her and the other girls what to do. Her mom had encouraged her to wear dailies to get used to having a pad on her panties, and Angela was quietly grateful that for once she'd obeyed her mom. Mariela had told her that when she first got *it*, she'd applied the pad upside down. It wasn't fun when the pad stuck to your skin and little hairs instead of the panties.

Angela threw away the plastic wrapper in the little container she'd been so curious about when she was younger.

When she came out of the stall, Mami watched her in expectation, and another cheer exploded in the gym.

Angela said, "Let's go, Mami."

And without a word, Mami followed her to the parking lot and the car, and they were silent all the way home.

Now that she wanted to cry, the tears wouldn't come. She didn't know how to feel. She'd arrived as a star athlete and was leaving as if she'd done something wrong.

But what had she done? She couldn't control her body. She knew her menstruation would start one day, in the future, when it was convenient, perhaps. But why today and, even more, during the game?

"One day—"

"No, Mami," Angela said. "I won't laugh about today. I promise I won't."

Angela's mom didn't argue. When they arrived home, Angela took a Midol her mom offered for the pain, and a shorter shower than what she craved. Even if a tiny pill could take some of the pain in her body, no shower could wash away the feelings roiling over her. Besides, she had to run to her room if she wanted to avoid seeing her dad and her brothers, especially Javier. Whatever he said, he'd be right. Angela hated it.

How did women go about their daily lives knowing they couldn't control even their own bodies?

Angela put on her earphones and played the loudest, angriest songs she could find in her old iPod. She didn't understand all the words Bebe sang in her Spanish from Spain, but the meaning of the lyrics washed over her, as she closed her eyes and imagined what could've been if today she hadn't gotten her period in front of the school, during the most important game of her life.

She'd done all she could, but still she didn't get the results she'd worked for. She'd been having fun, and then it had happened . . .

A soft hand shook her out of her sorrow. When she opened her eyes, the first thing she saw was Javier's bright smile in spite of the semidarkness of her room. He said something Angela couldn't hear, and she took off her earphones.

"How are you feeling?" he asked, taking her hand.

She didn't snatch her hand away. When they were little, they'd been the best of friends, partners in mischief.

Los hermanos Macana, Mami called them. But as the years passed, they'd grown apart. She had missed him, this tenderness in him that he tried to hide to impress his friends, the whole world.

"I'm okay," she said. Her belly didn't hurt as much anymore. The Midol must have worked its magic.

"I could've never done what you did. You're amazing, Anguila Eléctrica." Javi's smile wavered. "You left before you could get your medal. Do you want us to go get it for you?"

The realization that she'd left her medal behind hit her like an anvil on the head. Yes, getting her period in front of everyone had been nightmarish.

She'd been in pain, but she kept playing. She was a strong young person. The word "woman" still didn't fit her, but she was a girl who played like a girl: giving her all.

She deserved her medal, and she was going to be the one to go and get what was hers.

"Are they still at the party?" she asked.

"The team and the cheer squad." Javi nodded. "Papi said he'd drive you anywhere. He and Mami are ready if you are."

Was she ready to face everyone after running away?

Angela took a deep breath and turned to look at the mirror on top of her dresser. She brushed her hair with her hand and tied it in a high ponytail. She looked the same as she had this morning, except she wasn't as pale anymore. She hadn't expected the pain she felt with her period. She'd have to ask Mami if it was normal. But with pain and all, her period meant she was growing up; she was healthy.

Before he walked out of the room, Javi said, "When you're in the WNBA, you'll tell the story of today, and some kid will be inspired to keep fighting. I know I am."

She didn't know if one day she'd make it to the big leagues, but she wanted to. She'd work hard for it.

Her parents were waiting for her in the kitchen, and together they headed to Coach's house. The music played softly, and Angela looked out the window, wondering if she'd made the right call, coming over like this.

When they arrived, she took a deep breath. Mami looked at her as if asking if she was sure, if she really wanted to face the team and the squad. But the truth was that Angela had never been surer of anything in her life. She was part of the team, and she was friends with everyone on the squad, after all. They were here celebrating because of the collective effort, but also because of her hard work and determination.

In the backyard of the brick rambler house, there were her friends. She couldn't imagine her life without these boys just as she couldn't imagine it without the girls she'd grown up with.

The boys were lined up, taking photos with the trophy. Quietly, she stood last in line. Nico lifted the trophy, posing for his mother, when he finally saw her. His eyes went wide with shock. And happiness.

Everyone else turned to look at her and, without hesitation, the whole team cheered, chanting her name, including the parents and Coach Kendrick.

Mariela ran up to her, and Angela hugged her. Mariela smelled of sweat. Cheering up a whole team took a lot of work, but it was worth it.

Coach waited for his turn to shake Angela's hand. His striking blue eyes were soft, and when she held his gaze, he was the first one to lower his eyes. "I'm proud of you, Angela. I'm honored to have you on my team!"

"Honored to be on it," she said. "Now, how about a little more playtime in Regionals?"

Behind Coach, Mami and Papi nodded in approval.

Coach chuckled. "You've earned it!"

Angela took the team's trophy from Nico's hands and lifted it up to the sky and celebrated with her friends. The boys and the girls. The team and the squad.

Bloodline

IBI ZOBOI

Today is not my birthday, but it feels like it. Grandma says that this will be unlike any other birthday because today, according to my mother and grandmother, I am being born again. So I'm calling it Birthday 2.0. Grandma and Mama call it my New Moon Rebirth because today I just got my very first period. It's as if I am born a whole new person because of it. I was Adjoa before, but now I guess I'm Adjoa 2.0, an upgraded, better version of myself.

Mama walks into the kitchen carrying bags of groceries for my New Moon Rebirth ceremony tonight. I have so many questions. What kind of ceremony will it be? Why can't I just have a celebration with red velvet cake? The word *ceremony* makes it sound so serious, and it makes my belly stir a little bit. Or is it *cramps*?

Grandma has been giving me clues and riddles for a while. "You are coming out of yourself, Adjoa. You will no longer be a little girl. You will become the woman that is waiting for you."

Grandma's riddles always make me scratch my head. I learned when I was little not to ask her more questions because her answers just make me more confused. I just listen to her riddles as she folds laundry, or as she crushes dried herbs in a mortar for her teas, or as she stirs a pot of stew for dinner. I don't ask her to explain. I just let her words dance around the room like butterflies. I can't catch them because they are too fast and too beautiful to hold in my hands or in my head.

Grandma has been boiling a big pot of tea since this morning. I sit on a stool as she stands in front of the stove, stirring and humming and smiling back at me. The thick pad feels like a diaper, and I can't help but feel a little more special with it on—as if I'm holding a secret that no one else knows. I sit up taller on the stool, making sure that I start holding myself up like the lady I am now, as Mama would say.

Mama comes into the kitchen, bringing more groceries and other stuff for the ceremony. This is my favorite place in the world—Grandma's kitchen. Except it's Mama's kitchen. Grandma just takes over.

Usually, I'm supposed to help wash dishes, chop vegetables, and clean. But today, I can do whatever I want, and sitting in this kitchen watching Mama and Grandma is like a warm hug and a kiss on the forehead when I'm scared or too nervous about something. And that something is the ceremony tonight. I'm not even scared of having my period now that it's here and it wasn't as big of a deal as I thought it would be.

The smell from Grandma's pot fills the whole house— a mix of bright springtime flowers and colorful fall leaves on the ground.

"Sip, child. Your womb renews itself every month, and each time, it gets stronger and stronger," Grandma says.

I sniff the warmth before taking a sip. "What's in it, Grandma?" I ask.

Grandma names all the herbs in the tea and asks me to repeat them: red raspberry leaf, black cohosh, nettles, oat straw, and red clover.

"It's like a potion," I say, smiling only a little bit because I know it will taste terrible, just like Grandma's other teas.

"Are you calling me a witch?" Grandma asks without smiling. She turns to me with one hand on her hip, looking down over the rim of her glasses. Her short Afro is so white that it's like fluffy snow. Her skin is a deep brown with soft ripples along her cheeks and forehead. I know there's a laugh hidden behind that fake serious face of hers. She doesn't mind being called a witch.

"You're a good witch, Grandma," I say, smiling wide.

"If she's the good witch, then what does that make me?" Mama says as she pulls stuff out of the bags and places them on the counter. Her long locks are tucked under a colorful scarf. Her forehead is glistening with sweat, and I know she's already tired from cleaning and shopping early this morning.

"You're a good witch, too!" I tell her. Then I ask, "Mama, are you sure I can't help you?"

"Adjoa, stay your little narrow, eager behind on that stool. You're gonna need all your energy for tonight."

I sigh and drop my shoulders. It's not about helping Mama; it's about all these strange clues they've been giving me about tonight. My older cousins have had New Moon Rebirth ceremonies, but I don't remember them very well because I was too busy playing games on Mama's phone. Deidre, my cousin who is four years older than me, won't tell me anything about what's going to happen tonight, even though she'll be here to see it all go down.

But what I do know: I'll be wearing all white as if I'm about to get married or something. And Mama had this celebration when she was my age and so did her big sister, Carol, and so did their mother, my grandma. Her mama and her mama, too, going all the way back to Africa, where our people are really from.

I sit up on the stool when I finally think of a question to ask. "If this family tradition is from Africa, how come none of the other girls I know have to do this? Madison's people are from Africa. So are Taylor's, Keturah's, and Jasmine's. They all got family from Africa, and they never told me about no ceremony for their New Moon Rebirth."

"Well, Adjoa, the thing about traditions is that some people keep them and most people lose them. Like keys or one sock from a pair. Sometimes you lose them forever, and other times, you have to look hard to find them again," Grandma says.

If I scratch my head any more, I'll be bald! Sometimes I think I need a cheat sheet for Grandma's sayings—like the ones my big brother uses for his video games. None of what Grandma says makes sense.

"Don't you worry your little head about what I'm trying to tell you, Adjoa. One day, it'll all make sense," Mama says.

I think both my mama and grandma can read my mind. So I leave the kitchen and return to my bedroom, where my outfit is laid out on the bed. It's a long white dress with embroidery and ruffles, and I hate it. It looks like a wedding dress, except one that a farmer's daughter from long ago would wear. That's because this dress is the one Grandma wore during her New Moon Rebirth when she was my age. So Grandma passed it on to Aunt Carol, who passed it on to Mama. Then Mama passed it on to her nieces, Denise and Deidre, and now it's my turn. These are all the girls and women in my family, and they all went through what I'm about to go through.

I move the dress aside and plop down on my bed. I hold my chin in my hands. And that's when my stomach starts to hurt again. I check the spot I'm sitting on to make sure it's still clean. Yesterday, my cramps were so bad that I climbed into Mama's bed and cried into her arms. I felt silly, but it really hurt. I've been trying so hard not to do babyish things.

I've been helping out around the house more. I've been making sure my room is neat, and I sit up straight at the dinner table, using a knife with my fork and everything. I never used to like carrying around a bag if I wasn't going to school, but Grandma said now that I was becoming a young lady, I should carry around a pocketbook.

But I didn't know which pocketbook she was talking about since Grandma calls my private part down there a "pocketbook."

Then Mama said, "It's not a pocketbook, Adjoa. It's a vagina. A womb. A uterus with ovaries. And you've got labia and a clitoris, too."

Then Grandma scrunched up her face and said, "Hush, now. You don't have to be so *technical*, Rhonda. Makes it sound like a science project. Adjoa, a *pocketbook* is your own special thing, and you've got stuff inside of it that belongs to only you."

So Mama said, "Aw, Mama. Come on, now."

Grandma won that argument because she pulled me in, kissed my forehead, and whispered into my ear, "It's your pocketbook. You hear me? And when your big day comes, we're gonna give you some special things just for your pocketbook."

I've looked all around the apartment for the special things they got for me. When both Mama and Grandma were out doing their hair and Ngozi was playing video games, I searched Mama's closet and Grandma's room for my gifts—just like I do every year before Kwanzaa. But I didn't find anything.

Time stretches like a long piece of slime sticking to my hands and fingers, like how the yesterdays stick to my memory. And whatever is going to happen tonight is a song I let play over and over again trying to hear every instrument and every word in the lyrics. I keep imagining what it will be like because I want to understand everything.

Someone comes into the bedroom, and before I turn around, I notice that it's getting darker outside. The sun is setting, and soon the moon will be high in the sky.

"Adjoa," Mama says softly, "it's time for you to get ready now."

I don't like how I look in the white dress. The top of the sleeves puff up and out, and there's a collar with frilly lace at the edges. The dress reaches down to my ankles, and it's loose around my chest. I wonder if both Grandma and Mama *blossomed* by the time they were my age. My chest is the same way it was when I was nine, which was the same way it was when I was five. Flat. There's a long piece of white fabric that comes with the dress, and I don't know where it goes, but in no time, Mama comes in, takes one look at me, and smiles big and bright.

"You look beautiful, Adjoa!" she sings.

"I thought I'm not supposed to wear white when I get my period," I say.

"But this is special. You'll be okay," Mama says. "It represents new beginnings."

"I look like Harriet Tubman," I whine.

"And why is that such a bad thing?"

"'Cause she was from the eighteen hundreds," I say.

"She was a hero," Mama says. "And besides, what's old is not ugly. What's old is sacred."

I know Mama doesn't understand what I mean, and if I try to explain, I'll hear more riddles.

Mama takes the long fabric and starts to wrap it around my Afro, pulling up my thick hair into a cloud above my head. She wraps the white fabric and tucks and tightens it until I look like a ghost from the past. A holy ghost.

There are voices outside the room, and more people are coming into our apartment. I hear my aunts, uncles, cousins, friends, and neighbors. And I don't want any of them to see me like this.

Grandma comes in holding a white sheet in her hands, and I wonder what in the world it's for. She hands the sheet to Mama, and from a pocket of her dress, she pulls out a small, clear bottle of Florida water. This is what both Grandma and Mama use to call "down spirits." It smells like flowers and memory, if memory had a scent. Grandma starts to hum one of her many, many songs, and I know that she's getting into her mood again—the one where she becomes more than my grandma. She becomes magic, as if she's from another time and place. It doesn't scare me—it just makes me feel safe and warm. Mama starts to hum, too, and their singing is a hug from an old, old thing I can't name.

"Adjoa, do not be afraid of yourself. You are with family, and the ancestors are watching over you," Grandma whispers. "Close your eyes and be still."

I do what they say. A chill runs down my spine, and I get goose bumps. My belly is still hurting. It's like my private part—my pocketbook, my womb—is curling in on itself, tightening into a fist.

Grandma slowly places the sheet over my head, and my heart starts to race. Mama hums louder now, and then she starts to sing the words. It's not in English, but it's a song I've heard since I was little. She doesn't sing it often, but when she does, it's like honey for my ears. Her sweet voice dances around me like sparkling dust, and it touches my soul.

Mama takes my hand from beneath the sheet, and Grandma takes the other.

"Are you ready, Adjoa?" Mama whispers.

I nod, and I hope she sees my head move under the sheet. Slowly, they walk me to the door and open it. Everyone is as quiet as air. I keep my eyes closed, even though I wouldn't be able to see through the sheet. I can feel my aunts and cousins in here, watching and smiling and knowing exactly what's about to happen.

Suddenly, I start to remember Deidre's New Moon Rebirth and how she came out with a sheet over her head and I didn't think anything of it. She had disappeared into another room for a long while, and when she came out, she really did look like a woman. I mean, she didn't grow taller or anything or suddenly have grown-woman curves, as Mama would say. After her New Moon Rebirth celebration, my cousin Deidre looked as if she held a secret in her heart and in her soul, and she was proud to have it. As if Grandma had given her something very special for her pocketbook. My heart starts to beat even faster and louder just thinking about what's waiting for me on the other side of this celebration.

"Family, we are celebrating my first and only daughter, Adjoa Nubia Freeman Lawson, during her New Moon Rebirth," Mama says to everyone.

And they clap. My heart swells.

"This is a tradition that has been in our family going far back to our people in the Carolinas, the Sea Islands, and maybe off the shores of what is now Senegal," Grandma says with her deep but sweet voice like thick molasses. "What we are celebrating here is memory. This tradition was handed down to me by my mother and her mother before her."

Grandma goes on and on about our people coming up

north from down south and the Gullah islands, and somewhere in Africa way before that. I start to get hot, and my
belly hurts again. Mama said it'll feel like a bellyache, but
it won't be coming from my belly. So I should call it what
it is—cramps. I have cramps.

Mama walks me to Grandma's room. She closes the
door behind her and removes the sheet from over my
head. It's dark in there except for a bunch of candles sitting on Grandma's altar. It's the most candles I've ever seen
in her room, and the whole table is so white that it lights
up the room.

"Adjoa," Mama whispers, "I know this is Grandma's
room, but for now, this is your sacred space."

She walks me to the altar, and there's a package in the
middle of it—something wrapped in cloth and string, and
I'm hoping that none of the candles fall and burn it. It must
be a gift from Grandma for my pocketbook. There's also
a few incense sticks and sage burning on top of a small
wooden bowl. I'm used to seeing these things in Mama's
and Grandma's rooms. If my friends saw this, they'd definitely think that I was from a family of witches.

"May I open it now?" I ask.

"Not yet," Mama says. Then she motions for me to sit
on Grandma's old wooden and wicker chair, something
she's had since she was a little girl. "I want you to sit with

what you are about to open. You'll be here alone, and I want you to read every word. Take in everything, Adjoa."

More riddles. So I do as Mama says when she walks out of the bedroom and leaves me here in front of Grandma's altar with all these candles, incense, sage, and a mysterious package. I take in a long, deep breath and place my hand on the package. The cloth is thin with tiny flowers that are faded. I look closer to see that the fabric used to be white but maybe it's dirty. Why would Grandma and Mama wrap my gift in something so dingy? Why wouldn't they use brown wrapping paper like they usually do?

Slowly, I put the package on my lap and start to unwrap it. It's a thick rectangle, and I know it's a big book that I'll be forced to read. When I finally open it, the first thing I can't stop staring at is the brown leather cover. Not only is it a book—it's a fancy, old book. It's a Bible. Why would Grandma and Mama give me a Bible when they have so many around the house? The leather is faded and the pages are so thin that I'm afraid to touch them. So I have to be very careful when I open the first page, and then the next few pages. And then I see it.

There's a long list of marks and names and scribbles and small drawings and dates. My heart races as if I just found a treasure. I did!

I turn the page and then the other to see what's at the

bottom of the last list. *Deidre Shanae Freeman McKinney, age eleven, daughter of Carol*, and then the date. Denise is before her and Mama . . . I see Mama's handwriting—*Rhonda Lisa Freeman, age twelve, daughter of Annette*. Before her is Aunt Carol and she was thirteen, and before her is a woman named Bernadette. I remember her story. She was Grandma's little sister who passed away before I was born.

Then I see Grandma's handwriting. *Annette Lucinda Freeman Charles, age fourteen, daughter of Tabitha*, and then the date. I look up and over at the candles. That's when I notice the photos, as if they've been there all along, invisible, and my eyes have become magic. There are a bunch of photos on the altar behind the candles, color and black-and-white pictures. Some are in frames; others are in a small pile.

I don't know what to do next: go through the list of names or go through the old pics. So I grab as many photos as I can and put them in the fold of my long dress. There are so many pictures of girls who look like me and women who look like Mama and Grandma and Aunt Carol. I don't even know if I can match the name with the pictures, because that doesn't even matter.

So I read them out loud. One by one. Going back from Great-Grandma Tabitha to the very first X on the Bible. I stare at the faded X for what seems like hours. This X is my ancestor. This *X* was the first owner of this Bible, and she is my mother's, mother's, mother's mother, and beyond.

I wonder if she was a little girl. I wonder if she was a grown woman. I wonder how all her daughters after her kept this Bible.

There were five *X*s before the first person wrote only their first name: *Beth. 1893.*

It was 1914 when the first person wrote her age: *Fifteen.*

It was 1930 when the first person wrote her entire name, her age, the year, and the name of her mother: *Carol Freeman James, age eleven, daughter of Bessie.*

I stare at the photos. There are little girls in fancy dresses, bows, and socks that reach up to their knees. They are leaning on porches and old cars. They are in front of churches and tall buildings. Some are sad and others are smiling, and I wish so bad that I knew their stories. I turn one of the photos around to see a name and a date: *Little Tabitha. Sunday school. Raleigh, North Carolina. 1949.*

That's my great-grandma.

In that same moment, my cramps make me double over and clench my teeth. I take in a deep breath and then another. Tears well up in my eyes, it hurts so bad. My head starts to spin, but before I get up to use the bathroom and drink some water, I look around for a pen or pencil to make my mark in this Bible.

There's one at the edge of the altar, and I carefully flip to the page where I saw my cousins' names. Right below Deidre's, I write: *Adjoa Nubia Freeman Lawson, age twelve, daughter of Rhonda.* And then the date.

All these women are daughters of that very first *X* in this Bible. All these women before me gave birth to me. I am connected to all of them.

These are all the women in my family, and they all went through what I'm about to go through.

I wrap the Bible exactly the way it was and place it back on the altar. Slowly, I make my way out of Grandma's room. I open the door and there they are—Grandma, Mama, Aunt Carol, Denise, and Deidre waiting for me with big bright smiles.

I can't help but cry, not from my cramps, but from this new person I feel I'm becoming. It's like I'm not the same anymore. Just by seeing those names in the Bible and just staring at all those old pictures for so long, I know something so old, and so precious, that I can't even make words out of it. It's a secret. And they know this secret, too. I run into Mama's arms and everyone comes to hug me. Here we are, all of us, daughters of daughters of daughters.

I am born again. I am new like the moon.

The Hadiyyeh

SUSAN MUADDI DARRAJ

Tuesday morning is the only time our apartment is ever quiet.

Every other morning, there's chaos. My older sister, Hanine, gabs loudly with her friends on the phone, and Baba and Mama yell at her to stop because *Yallah! Ya bint, it's only eight a.m.* Meanwhile, my sitti relaxes before work by watching the Arabic soap operas she missed the day before—on volume ten because she can't hear above the chaos that is our home.

But Tuesday mornings are different. On Tuesday mornings, the only other person home with me is Baba. Hanine leaves at 6:45 a.m. for her art club meeting at the high school, and Sitti starts her shift, working the cash register for Antonio's grocery store, by seven a.m. Mama works at the hospital cafeteria, so she starts earlier than us all—at five a.m. Baba works at the hospital, too, cleaning the wing where the kids are, but his shift begins after I leave for school.

That's why when I wake up, I call out for him. He enters my room, drinking his coffee, reading the *Jerusalem Post* in Arabic on his cell phone. It's how he starts every day. "Sabah al kheir, Rana," he says in his deep voice.

"My stomach hurts," I moan. It's more like monsters have turned my stomach into a wad of Silly Putty. *They* stretch it *out, out, out,* and then—just to mess with me— jam it back into a tight ball.

Setting his coffee down, he hoists himself up the ladder to my top bunk. I lean over so he can press his lips to my forehead, his mustache tickling my skin. This is seriously how the adults in my family take your temperature. Hanine calls it the Palestinian thermometer, but they insist that it's accurate.

"No fever. I make you food . . . maybe you hungry."

But the thought of eating anything grosses me out. I want to ask if I can stay home, but then he'd have to skip work, which he can't. Or I'll have to stay at Antonio's store, with Sitti, and watch her click the register and help her stock the shelves.

Plus, I don't want to miss science. Today is the fourth grade's turn to use the microscopes again, and Anna, my best friend, would be upset if I wasn't there because we're lab partners.

So when Baba leaves my room, I climb down and trudge to the bathroom. There are always newspapers on the back of the toilet, but I never read them. Instead, I pull up my nightgown, sit, and wake up my cell phone to check Instagram.

I glance down at my panties—and that's when I drop my phone, right on the linoleum floor. Gasping, I snatch it up, examining it closely for cracks. None.

Then just as carefully, I study my panties.

Right there, in the center, sits a big splotchy brown stain, like the cells we've been looking at under the microscopes.

I bunch some toilet paper—I don't care how wasteful it is—and I wipe, then study the tissue. It's streaked with a jagged bolt of red lightning.

Have I cut myself somehow? When? Yesterday, in gym, during the mile run? To save money, I've been wearing the same uniform gym shorts (they'd been Hanine's) for over a year, and they've been getting tight, but . . . did they scrape me while I was running?

Down there?

I bend my head, trying to think like a scientist, looking for the wound. Maybe it's like a nosebleed, where you apply pressure to make it stop. I jam more toilet paper between my legs, then pull up my panties.

Outside the door, in the hallway, Baba hums one of his Arabic songs. "Your breakfast is ready, habibti," he calls, knocking lightly on the door.

"Baba!" I call out. "I need your help!"

"Rana?" he asks nervously. "Iftahi al baab."

I open the door as he requests and blurt out, "I'm bleeding!"

He scans me up and down, his eyes wide and worried. "Where, habibti?"

Well. This is embarrassing.

"From . . . my private area."

His eyes grow rounder, his pupils like planets floating in white galaxies. "One second." I follow him to the balcony and hear him talking to Mama on the phone. As he hangs up, he pats my hair and smiles his big sad-mustache smile at me. "Mama too busy now. Is breakfast time there, so I be back soon." He goes to the front door and puts his shoes on.

"Wait! Where are you going?"

"I need to get you something."

✶

An hour later, I close the apartment's door behind me, climb the eighteen steps down to the main entrance, and step over the forty-two sidewalk cracks on my walk to school. Mama called me before I left and explained some of it.

Here's what she said, quickly, because she had the morning eggs cooking in the big oven at work: this thing is called *my period*.

It's funny, right? If they wanted to name it after a punctuation mark, it should have been called an *exclamation point*.

Because! It! Is! Wild!

"I'll explain it more after school, okay? Is okay, my love! Is all okay!" She laughed as she hung up, like I'd just told her a big joke.

As I walk, I text Anna that I have big news, so she's waiting for me when I find her at our lockers.

"I got my period," I tell her, feeling suddenly like I'm older, especially when she looks confused.

"Your what?"

"I'm bleeding . . . *down there*."

"Right now?" she asks, looking me up and down the way Baba did earlier. "Are you okay?"

"I guess?" I reply. "My mom said it's something we'll learn about next year, anyway. When we take that health class."

Everyone in our school knows that, at the end of fifth grade, they make your parents sign a paper so you can take a class where they show you the human body. The *whole* body. The private parts and everything.

"My mom said she's not letting me take it," Anna says as we walk to our first class. "She says she'll talk to me about that stuff when it's time."

In science, Ms. Sims says that before we use the microscopes, we have to complete a lab unit on the computers. She hands out the iPads she keeps on her cart. Anna and I finish before everyone else, as usual, and that's when she whispers, "Let's google it."

"What?"

"OMG, Rana. Your period!" she hisses.

When she types *period* into the browser, we get a bunch of grammar sites, so I say, "Type 'blood.'"

She adds it to the search, and bingo.

"This. Is. Wow," she says, as we skim over a teen health site, "A Teen Girl's Guide to Her Period." As we read, we keep glancing at Ms. Sims, but she's helping the other kids catch up. "Rana," Anna hisses, "this says it's going to happen every month."

"Every month?" I gasp. So far today, I've only been confused. But the thought of bleeding, of having that Silly Putty feeling in my belly, *every month* suddenly scares me.

On the way home, I step over those forty-two cracks in the sidewalk, planning out what I'm going to ask Mama. The every-month thing is number one on my list. When I enter the front door, the giggling in the kitchen tells me:

1. She's waiting for me.
2. So are Sitti and Hanine.
3. Mama has already told them.

They clap and hug me when I walk in, like they did when I won first place at the science fair last month. They ask me for all the details, cracking up when I explain how Baba bought me pads.

"Worst timing ever!" Hanine screeches.

"Why?" Did I do something embarrassing by asking Baba for help? I think back to the morning when Baba returned, huffing, from the corner store and handed me a paper bag.

Inside was a box with small squares wrapped in pink plastic. "How do I use it?" I asked.

"Put it . . . put it down there. And take one to school."

"Okay." My voice shook as I closed the bathroom door.

"Rana, don't be afraid, *habibti*," he called softly through the door in Arabic. "It's . . . it's something special."

He'd been totally cool about it. And super nice. So why do I suddenly feel bad?

Hanine shrugs now, still giggling. "It's just funny that

we didn't have any left in the apartment. And it's kinda
cute, that's all . . . imagining Baba running down the block
to buy pads." She laughs. "Rana's lucky—he bought her the
fancy ones."

They explain that they usually buy the plain unwrapped
ones. "That's why I keep old newspaper in the bathroom,"
Mama says, pouring hot water over the maryamiyyeh
leaves in her metal teapot. "Too expensive to wrap them
up in toilet paper." She sets out four cups. "Now you get to
drink this with us."

Sitti reaches over and takes my face between her
papery palms. "I'm glad we can finally talk to you about it.
You're only ten! We thought we had another year."

It turns out that Mama got hers when she was fourteen.
Hanine was twelve.

"So, basically, I beat you all," I say, and they laugh.

"I should have known," Mama says, looking thoughtful, as her cell phone rings. "Be right back." She steps out
of the kitchen.

I know what she meant.

Over the last year . . . my body has changed. A lot.
There's hair under my arms, between my legs. Lately, I've
been borrowing Mama's T-shirts because my chest is bigger
and softer. And at night, sometimes, I lie in bed and run my
hands over my hips. Where there'd been only bone, lately

I feel curves, layered around me like a soft blanket. At my thighs and my waist, I can pinch the skin like soft bread.

While Mama is talking on the phone, we let the tea cool and Sitti lets me in on another secret.

So, it turns out that my family thinks they're super-spies or something, because this whole time, when they've talked about a period, they've been using a code word—a word I'd been hearing my whole life.

Hadiyyeh.

Like last month, when Hanine was napping on the couch and Sitti asked her what's wrong? "Nothing," she replied. "I got my hadiyyeh."

Or whenever Mama would ask Sitti to brew hot tea, she'd say, "Ah, you got your hadiyyeh?"

A hadiyyeh is a gift.

Now I know why they always laughed when I asked, "How come Hanine gets a gift and I don't?" or "Who gave you a gift, Mama?"

Now I'm allowed in on the big secret. I'm the last member to join their club.

"You all are *wrong*," I mutter, wrapping my arms around my stomach. "This doesn't feel like a hadiyyeh."

"The maryamiyyeh helps with the cramps," Hanine says, giving a name—*cramps*—to my agony.

Just then, Mama reenters the kitchen, holding her phone.

"That was Anna's mom." She looks at me. "And she's furious."

I lie in bed that night, wondering how something can feel bad, then good, and then bad again.

It doesn't feel like a hadiyyeh when your best friend's mom is super annoyed with you.

Anna's mom didn't want to tell her—at least not yet— about periods and menstrual cycles and blood. How was I supposed to know that?

I climb down from my bunk, get my phone off the charger, and text Anna. *Sorry if you got in trouble for anything.*

She doesn't text me back.

I stare at my screen for twenty minutes, but I get nothing. I try to sleep again, but I stare at the ceiling instead.

Sitti thinks Anna's mom is being ridiculous. "As if it's something shameful," she huffed earlier, then patted my head. "Don't you worry. Drink your tea."

At least the cramps feel better. The maryamiyyeh did help, after all.

"Let's tell Rana why we call it maryamiyyeh?" Mama had said. They all talked over each other, trying to explain the legend: The Virgin Maryam, two thousand years ago, boiled it with hot water to ease her pain after delivering Jesus in the manger.

But Sitti insisted there was a different story. "When the soldiers came looking for the baby Jesus, Maryam tried to hide them both in a sage bush—the plant grew around her and covered them both, so the soldiers rode right past them. That's why we call it maryamiyyeh."

Here's a fact about the women in my family: arguing is their favorite sport. But tonight I think they were trying to entertain me, to make me feel better about Anna's mom.

The Virgin Maryam's image fills every inch of our small apartment: everywhere you look, Mama and Sitti have statues, candles, even refrigerator magnets.

I look across my room now, at a small plaque on the wall, near the window, where the light from the streetlamp outside shines in, and I see her face, with her tiny, secret smile.

The next morning, I wake up to find tiny spots, like bright ladybugs, on my white sheets.

"What do I do?" I call down to Hanine, who sleeps on the bottom bunk.

"Next time, don't sleep on the good sheets," she mumbles sleepily.

"Okay, but what do I do *now*?"

"Wash them out. And be quiet."

I strip the sheets off the mattress, ball them up, and climb carefully down. "Quieeeeeet," Hanine mutters. As I leave, I flick the switch, flooding the room with light. As she gasps in shock, I snicker and rush to the bathroom.

While I scrub my sheets in the tub, Baba walks by in his work uniform. Baba's name is Yacoub, but on his lapel, his American name is embroidered in black thread: Jacob.

"All okay, ya Rana?"

"Yes, Baba." I turn off the water. "Thanks for . . . you know. Yesterday."

He blushes. "Mama has a surprise for you tonight." Before I can ask, he blows me a kiss and leaves.

At school, Anna tells me that her mom is not really *that* mad. "She's okay."

"Sure?"

"She just said that you shouldn't be telling everyone."

"I'm . . . sorry. I only told you."

"I know. It's because it's private stuff. It's fine."

But, of course, everything is *not* fine. Yes, it's private, but it's something that will happen to half the people on the planet.

Nothing seems logical, though. Everything is complicated. And weird.

I want to tell Anna that I'm sorry her mom is so secretive about it. That my family kept it from me for a while, but they'd been planning to tell me soon. I want to tell her that tonight they have a surprise, and I wish I could invite her over to share it.

As I count the cracks in the sidewalk on the way home, I wonder why some people make it sound like a period is something to hide or something you shouldn't talk about. This feels like the first secret Anna and I have ever kept from each other.

When I get home, I change my pad. After finishing my homework, I change it again. Hanine says I'm being obsessive, but I already like the routine: rolling the old pad tightly, like a snowball, in the newspaper and stretching a clean one, like a canvas, over my panties.

Mama and Sitti whisper in the kitchen. "Rana, come in here," they call.

"I think I need more maryamiyyeh," I say, rubbing my palm over my lower stomach. Sitti starts to boil the water, while Mama asks if I said anything to Anna in school today.

"No. We just didn't talk about . . . you know."

Suddenly I don't want to use either word.

My stomach suddenly hurts, and it's not cramps.

And even though I'm officially older now, I act like a little kid and walk right into Mama's arms.

She hugs me tightly. Behind me, I feel Sitti's hands in my hair, soothing me.

"People have different ways of talking about changes," Mama whispers in my ear. "But . . . changes are good. Aren't you happy?"

"I was," I say. "But now I don't know."

"This is a special time, Rana. Tonight we're going to celebrate *you*, okay?"

And that's what we do.

Hanine and even Baba join us at the kitchen table, as Mama settles a big pot of burbarra in the center.

Mama and Sitti only ever make burbarra on special occasions, like when I lost my first tooth or when Hanine aced the SAT. It's a wheat pudding, cooked with sugar and cinnamon. It's named after Saint Barbara, who did something really magical centuries ago—I'm sure everyone will start fighting over exactly *what*—but all I want to do is to eat it. Mama always tosses in extra goodies: pomegranate, shredded coconut, raisins, and almonds. As we each are handed a small bowl, Sitti leans forward to sprinkle white powdered sugar on everyone's burbarra.

When she comes to me, she winks and drops extra sugar like a snowfall, like a hadiyyeh, on mine.

FROM THE EDITORS

Dear Readers,

Menstruation—menses, menarche, moon cycle, luna—has been called as many names as there are people and cultures. As a young girl, I was taught by my family, friends, community, and society at large that menstruation was dirty, a curse, to be feared, silenced, and shamed. I was so scared to get it because of the many terrible names it had been called. However, I knew deep inside that there was something special about what happened to my body. My bleeding was something magical, and it needed to be called something that reflected that. Though I did not have a name for it at the time, the power and beauty of my period revealed itself to me slowly, as I learned from other menstruators and as I blossomed, like the phases of the moon. I waxed into a full understanding of how those of us who menstruate are in sync with the natural rhythms of humanity and with the luminescent orb floating through space on a monthly cycle just outside our stratosphere. It took many years, but I eventually called my menstruation luna—a name that fits me, my cultural heritage, and all that I have learned.

The idea for this anthology came to me after I had published my debut novel, about menstruation, *The Moon Within*. To my dismay, my book was the first middle-grade novel in nearly fifty years to center the topic of menstruation. The one that preceded it was the iconic book by Judy Blume *Are You There, God? It's Me, Margaret*, published in 1970. Also, *The Moon Within* was the first middle-grade novel about menstruation by a BIPOC author. I was shocked because menstruation happens to half of the world's population and every single human being on the planet came from a menstruator. This lack of middle-grade fiction really spoke to how strongly the negative ideas about menstruation are upheld across ethnicities, cultures, and races. And right now, when you might be straddling childhood and adolescence, it is the most important time for stories like these. Menstruation is something *every* person, regardless of gender, should not only know about but cherish because *this* is our source of life.

Though there are quite a few nonfiction books about menstruation that give many essential facts about the process, most of them are written by white authors. So not only did we have few fictional stories about menstruation, but we also had not heard from Black people, Indigenous people, and people of color on this topic almost at all. This inspired me to create a space for some of the most powerful and beloved middle-grade authors writing today to share some previously untold stories from our diverse communities. Breaking the silence in middle-grade fiction is the first step in changing attitudes about menstruation. I reached out to my dear friend and colleague Yamile Saied Méndez, who had written her master's thesis about the lack of periods in children's literature, as she was the perfect partner to help me build this collection.

The book you hold in your hands is ultimately an invitation to reimagine menstruation, dear readers. I hope that you are called into each and every gorgeous story. You are reading the first voices on the topic from many communities represented here. This is special, too. May the wide array of realities, experiences, and feelings about menstruation shared within these stories, as different as the phases of the moon, become part of your blossoming—as a person, as a menstruator, as someone who descends from menstruators. May you receive the calling of our many moon stories and learn to call the moon a special name just for you.

With luna love,
Aida Salazar

✷

When I was halfway through my master's program at the Vermont College of Fine Arts (VCFA), the story of an athletic, competitive girl, the only girl on an all-boys team, came to me in the way stories sometimes do, like someone opening a door and saying, "Here I am. Listen to me. What should I do? Tell me how it ends." It was an early iteration of "Part of the Team."

Now, I know a lot about sports. I'm a soccer and basketball fanatic, but I was unsure of how to tackle this story in which the character's life changes when she gets her first period. I didn't know how to approach this topic in an authentic way.

As always, my first inclination was to turn to books for inspiration and guidance. As a child, the only times I had read about menstruation were either in a romance for adults or in nonfictional accounts that were full of medical terms that were helpful but didn't reflect the internal and emotional changes a person goes through during puberty. I asked other writers for recommendations, including my mentor, Jane Kurtz (who was a contributor to the short-story collection *Period Pieces*). Time after time, the one and only book everyone recommended was Judy Blume's *Are You There, God? It's Me, Margaret.* I loved it immediately, and I looked for more books like it. Unfortunately, very soon I found out that the depiction of puberty in middle-grade fiction is severely lacking, especially when it comes to representing traditionally marginalized communities.

That semester I declared my thesis, and for the remainder of my time at VCFA, I studied all the materials that even tangentially touched on the topic of menstruation and how different cultures weave this exciting and powerful time in a person's life into their storytelling. I delivered a lecture about how we as a society portray growing up in fiction, and the reaction from the audience was overwhelming: people wanted to tell their experiences, whether their experience had been positive or negative. For too long, they hadn't found a space to share them with others. Soon, it was very clear that among those who had a more positive experience coming to terms with growing up and the changes in their bodies were those who had information. As I studied menstruation and the changes that occur in a person's body, the more in awe I was of the process, healing in part the trauma of having developed earlier than most of my young peers.

When my dear friend Aida Salazar invited me to be part of this project, the opportunity to collect stories by BIPOC communities, I saw it as a gift to share the reverence and gratitude I now have for the process of growing up.

I hope this collection of stories will soon become one of

many and that it will open the doors to allow for more information so that as a society, we can normalize this cycle in life that is natural and sacred. It can also be a challenging time in life, but if we have the tools to understand what is happening not only in our bodies but also in our minds and emotions we may have the opportunity to connect with others going through the same experiences.

There is no greater gift than our connection to others, and the moon in all its changes is a perfect metaphor to understand one another with love and compassion. It's about time menstruators reclaim all the ways in which we call our own moon.

With love,
Yamile Saied Méndez

RESOURCES

NONFICTION

Bloom, Naama. *HelloFlo: The Guide, Period.* New York: Dutton, 2017.

Lucy, Janet, and Terri Allison. *Moon Mother, Moon Daughter: Myths and Rituals that Celebrate a Girl's Coming of Age.* 2nd ed. Santa Barbara: Publishing by the Seas, 2011.

Medina, Lara, and Martha R. Gonzalez, eds. *Voices from Our Ancestors: Xicanx and Latinx Spiritual Expressions and Healing Practices.* Tucson: University of Arizona Press, 2019.

Okamoto, Nadya. *Period Power: A Manifesto for the Menstrual Movement.* New York: Simon and Schuster, 2017.

Pearce, Lucy H. *Reaching for the Moon.* 2nd ed. Cork, Ireland: Womancraft, 2015.

Steward, Robyn. *The Autism-Friendly Guide to Periods.* Philadelphia: Jessica Kingsley, 2019.

Stynes, Yumi, and Dr. Melissa Kang. *Welcome to Your Period!* Somerville, MA: Walker Books US, 2021.

FILMS

Snow, Rebecca, dir. *Pandora's Box: Lifting the Lid on Menstruation*. IR Films, 2020.

Zehtabchi, Rayka, dir. *Period. End of Sentence*. Netflix, 2018.

PODCASTS

Feeling My Flo. Lantigua Williams & Co. www.feelingmyflo.com.

Period Is Power. Apple Podcasts. https://podcasts.apple.com/us/podcast/period-is-power/id1474149538.

Period Podcast. https://periodpodcast2.libsyn.com/.

The Sacred Womb. www.thesacredwomb.com/category/podcast/.

SUPPORT ORGANIZATIONS AND WEBSITES

California Latinas for Reproductive Justice: https://californialatinas.org

Days for Girls: www.daysforgirls.org

First Period Stories: https://firstperiodstories.com

The Flow: www.theflow.world

Girly Things (Pakistan): www.girlythings.pk/blog/

I Support the Girls Manila (Philippines): on Instagram
        @isupportthegirlsmnl

Latinx Luna: on Instagram @latinxluna

The Paddling Foundation (India): https://
        paddlingfoundation.org

PERIOD: The Menstrual Movement: www.period.org

SisterSong: Women of Color Reproductive Justice Collective:
        www.sistersong.net

URGE: Unite for Reproductive & Gender Equity: https://
        urge.org

DAYS OF ACTION AND AWARENESS

Menstrual Hygiene Day: May 28

National Period Day: October 10

ABOUT THE CONTRIBUTORS

HILDA EUNICE BURGOS is the author of the middle-grade novels *Ana María Reyes Does Not Live in a Castle* and *Miosotis Flores Never Forgets*, as well as the picture book *The Cot in the Living Room*, illustrated by Gaby D'Alessandro. The daughter of immigrants from the Dominican Republic, she grew up in New York City as one of four sisters. She now lives near Philadelphia, where she and her husband raised their two children and where she works as a lawyer.

VEEDA BYBEE is the author of the middle-grade novels *Lily and the Great Quake: A San Francisco Earthquake Survival Story* and *Li on Angel Island* and contributed a story to the anthology *Rural Voices: 15 Authors Challenge Assumptions About Small-Town America*. Having worked previously as a journalist, she received an MFA from the Vermont College of Fine Arts. She lives with her family in the West and can often be found baking.

SUSAN MUADDI DARRAJ is the author of the Farah Rocks book series, the first chapter-book series to feature a Palestinian American protagonist, and *A Curious Land: Stories from Home*, a linked story collection set in historic

Palestine, which won an American Book Award and an Arab American Book Award. In 2018, she was awarded a United States Artists fellowship for her fiction. She teaches creative writing at Johns Hopkins University and lives in Baltimore with her three children.

SAADIA FARUQI is a Pakistani American author and interfaith activist. She is the author of the popular early reader series Yasmin, as well as other books for children, including middle-grade novels, biographies, picture books, and graphic novels. She is editor in chief of *Blue Minaret*, a magazine for Muslim art, poetry, and prose, and was featured in *O, The Oprah Magazine* as a woman making a difference in her community. She lives in Houston with her husband and children.

A *New York Times* best-selling poet and author, **NIKKI GRIMES** is the recipient of an ALAN Award for significant contributions to young adult literature, a Children's Literature Legacy Award for substantial and lasting contributions to literature for children, a Virginia Hamilton Literary Award, and a National Council of Teachers of English Award for Excellence in Poetry for Children. Her books include the Coretta Scott King Author Award winner *Bronx Masquerade* and five Coretta Scott King Author Honor Books, as well as *Between the Lines*, a YALSA Best Fiction for Young Adults selection; *Words with Wings*, a National Council of Teachers of English Notable Children's Book in the Language Arts; *Garvey's Choice*, a Lee Bennett Hopkins Poetry Award Honor Book; *One Last Word: Wisdom from the Harlem Renaissance*, a *Boston Globe–Horn Book* Honor Book; *Ordinary Hazards: A Memoir*, a Michael L. Printz Honor Book and Robert F. Sibert Honor Book; *Legacy: Women Poets of the Harlem Renaissance*; *Southwest Sunrise*, an American Library Association Notable Children's Book; *Bedtime for Sweet Creatures*, a *Kirkus Reviews* Best Picture Book of the Year; and *Kamala Harris: Rooted in Justice*, an NAACP Image Award nominee. Nikki Grimes lives in Corona, California.

LEAH HENDERSON is the author of the middle-grade novels *The Magic in Changing Your Stars*, an SCBWI Golden Kite Award Finalist, and *One Shadow on the Wall*, a Bank Street College Best Children's Book of the Year. Her picture books include *Together We March*, *A Day for Rememberin'*, *Daddy Speaks Love*, and *Your Voice, Your Vote*. She holds an MFA in writing and is on the faculty of Spalding University's School of Creative and Professional Writing.

ERIN ENTRADA KELLY is the author of the Newbery Medal–winning novel *Hello, Universe*, the Newbery Honor Book *We Dream of Space*, and *The Land of Forgotten Girls*, which received an APALA Children's Literature Award, among other honors. She is also the author and illustrator of *Maybe Maybe Marisol Rainey*. She teaches in Hamline University's MFA program and lives in Delaware.

MASON J. is a Black and Indigenous artist, public speaker, performer, history lover, and youth and elder worker who was raised gender creative by their family in the San Francisco Bay Area. They are a coeditor of the anthology *Still Here San Francisco* and the author of a poetry chapbook, *Crossbones on My Life*. They take great pride in their biracial, music nerd, Two-Spirit, punk, and writer identities.

GUADALUPE GARCÍA MCCALL is the award-winning author of four young adult novels, as well as stories and poems for young readers. Her debut novel, *Under the Mesquite*, won a Pura Belpré Author Award, among many other accolades. Although she calls Texas home and spends summers there with family and friends, she lives with her husband in the Pacific Northwest, where she is an assistant professor of English at George Fox University.

ELISE MCMULLEN-CIOTTI works as a children's book editor. Originally from Texas, she is a proud member of the Cherokee Nation and spent large amounts of her childhood in Oklahoma with her Cherokee grandmother. She is also a food scholar at NYU's Steinhardt's Food Studies master's program and has written numerous essays and blog posts about food and travel. She lives in New York City with her husband, lots of books, and an open kitchen.

YAMILE SAIED MÉNDEZ is the author of the picture book *Where Are You From?*, the middle-grade novel *On These Magic Shores*, and the young adult novel *Furia*, which won a Pura Belpré Author Award and was a Reese's Book Club YA selection, among other titles. She has also contributed to many anthologies. She was an inaugural Walter Dean Myers Grant recipient and received an MFA from the Vermont College of Fine Arts. Born and raised in Argentina, she now lives in a lovely valley surrounded by mountains in Utah.

EMMA OTHEGUY is the author of numerous books for young readers that focus on Latin American history and contemporary Latine families. Her titles include the award-winning bilingual picture book *Martí's Song for Freedom*, the middle-grade novel *Silver Meadows Summer*, and the picture book *A Sled for Gabo*, available in both English and Spanish. She is also the author of *Secrets of the Silver Lion: A Carmen Sandiego Story* and coauthor, with Adam Gidwitz, of *The Unicorn Rescue Society: The Madre de Aguas of Cuba*. She holds a PhD in history from New York University, where she studied colonial Latin America.

AIDA SALAZAR is an award-winning author, translator, and arts activist. Much of her work explores themes of identity and social justice. She is the author of the middle-grade verse novels *The Moon Within*, which was named a National Council of Teachers of English Notable Verse Novel and received an International Latino Book Award, an Américas Award Honorable Mention, and a Golden Poppy Award, and *Land of the Cranes*, which was named a Charlotte Huck Honor Book and received an Américas Award, a California Library Association John and Patricia Beatty Award, and a Jane Addams Children's Book Award Honor. Her other books include *In the Spirit of a Dream: 13 Stories of American Immigrants of Color*, *Jovita Wore Pants: The Story of a Mexican Freedom Fighter*, and *A Seed in the Sun*. She is a founding member of Las Musas, a Latinx kidlit author collective, and of Latinx Luna, a collective working to challenge period stigma in Latinx communities. She lives with her family in Oakland, California.

CHRISTINA SOONTORNVAT is an award-winning author, as well as an engineer and STEM educator. Two of her books, the middle-grade fantasy *A Wish in the Dark* and the nonfiction title *All Thirteen: The Incredible Cave Rescue of the Thai Boys' Soccer Team*, were selected as 2021 Newbery Honor Books. *A Wish in the Dark* was also named a *Washington Post* Best Children's Book of the Year and a *School Library Journal* Best Book of the Year; *All Thirteen* was also named a Robert F. Sibert Honor Book and was a YALSA Award for Excellence in Nonfiction for Young Adults Finalist. Her other titles include several picture books and the Diary of an Ice Princess chapter-book series.

PADMA VENKATRAMAN holds a PhD in marine science; she has explored coral reefs and rain forests, served as chief scientist on oceanographic vessels where she was the only female and only BIPOC person, and worked as a diversity director. She is the author of four award-winning novels for young readers: *The Bridge Home, A Time to Dance, Island's End,* and *Climbing the Stairs. The Bridge Home* won a Walter Dean Myers Award and a Golden Kite Award and was a Global Read Aloud selection. Her latest novel is *Born Behind Bars.*

IBI ZOBOI is the author of National Book Award Finalist *American Street*; the *New York Times* best-selling middle-grade novel *My Life as an Ice Cream Sandwich*; and *Pride*, a contemporary young adult remix of Jane Austen's *Pride and Prejudice*. She is also the editor of the anthology *Black*

Enough: Stories of Being Young & Black in America and the coauthor, with Yusef Salaam of the Exonerated Five, of *Punching the Air*, a young adult novel in verse, which won a Walter Dean Myers Award and a *Los Angeles Times* Book Prize. Born in Haiti and raised in New York City, she now lives in New Jersey with her husband and their three children.

ACKNOWLEDGMENTS

We owe a tremendous debt of gratitude to a beautiful circle of support and love that has made this anthology possible despite an extremely difficult few years for the world.

First and foremost, I offer my profound gratitude to my ancestors, my mother, and my elders, especially those who have bled and given birth. Thank you for guiding me to discover the legacies of resistance, power, and celebration of my luna and our collective cycles. Gracias, querida Yamile; I truly can't imagine anyone more perfect in friendship, heart, craft, courage, and light to have joined me in creating this unprecedented anthology. Gracias hasta la luna to our talented editor, Melanie Cordova, who, though pregnant with her own son during the editorial process, was a patient midwife for this book, breathing with us, correcting our positions, holding our hands, and encouraging us as we grew, shaped, and brought this anthology to life. Melanie, it feels divinely ordered that this book was born alongside your sweet baby boy, Orson—a beautiful culmination to menstruation.

To the extraordinary wordsmiths in this anthology, Christina, Elise, Emma, Erin, Hilda, Guadalupe, Ibi, Leah, Nikki, Mason, Padma, Saadia, Susan, Veeda, and Yamile: What a force! Thank you for giving young readers your unique period stories as rich, as moving, as funny, as illuminating, and as beautiful as you. In calling our moon, in speaking up and out through these stories, you are rewriting damaging narratives, shattering silences in your communities and beyond, and bringing long-overdue dignity to menstruation in children's literature. Biggest love and appreciation!

Thank you to my fierce and loving friend and agent, Marietta Zacker, who holds my work and my heart with such care and integrity. Special thanks to the wonderful home we've found at Candlewick and the dedicated team who dared to take on this controversial subject without shame but with pride. To our surrogate editor, Sarah Ketchersid, who helped us so much while Melanie was on maternity leave, thank you, thank you! To Fahmida Azim, our cover illustrator, much gratitude for your patience and for your brilliant vision and grace in creating this luminous cover!

Besitos y abrazos to my circle of amigas, to my sisters and nieces both by blood and chosen, to my colleagues in struggle and in writing—we will forge on. Special thanks to all period activists, bloggers, podcasters, artists, writers, educators, organizations, and clubs who work so hard to challenge the taboo and who seek health, access, and equity for all menstruators. Shout-out to @latinxluna for striving to decolonize menstruation for Latinx communities!

Finally, thank you to my greatest gifts, Avelina, Amaly, Joao, and John. Your love is sacred nourishment.

Aida Salazar

Working on this project of love during a worldwide pandemic kept the light of hope shining even in the deepest darkness. I wish I had a book like this growing up, and every second I was immersed in this anthology was a refuge and joy. My sincerest gratitude to Aida Salazar, friend and inspiration, for inviting me to jump on board this book of her heart. We became friends because of our common desire to destigmatize menstruation, especially in children's literature. I'm in awe of all you do, amiga.

Thanks to my agent, Linda Camacho, and all the Gallt & Zacker team. Thank you, Melanie Cordova, for believing in this anthology from the beginning and for all the attention and love you poured into it. Also, to Sarah Ketchersid and all the wonderful team at Candlewick, including Matt Roeser, Nathan Pyritz, Jamie Tan, Hannah Mahoney, Erin DeWitt, Kate Hurley, and Juan Botero.

Thank you, Fahmida Azim, for the beautiful cover, and to each of our contributors for the gift of your powerful words.

It was an honor to work on the stories of people I profoundly admire. This lineup is like the moon, each story different but breathtaking in its own way, and I'm so proud of all of you!

My eternal gratitude goes to Jane Kurtz, Cynthia Leitich-Smith, and An Na for being my literary godmothers and helping me develop as a storyteller.

Nothing would be possible without the support and love of my family, my foundation and the reason for everything: Jeffrey, Julián, Magalí, Joaquín, Areli, and Valentino, and also our pets, Cora, Nova, and Rosi. Thanks to my heart sisters Amparo Ortíz and Veeda Bybee. I adore you, chicas!

And most of all, thank you to the readers for being part of this magical process in the life of a story. Please accept this gift from my inner child to you.

Yamile Saied Méndez